A HOUSE IN EARNEST

There is a house that is no more a house
Upon a farm that is no more a farm
And in a town that is no more a town.

This was no playhouse, but a house in
earnest.

ROBERT FROST, "DIRECTIVE"

To my family, and to yours,
however circumstance has
shaped it.

PART I

He looked, I noticed, regarding him with awe — for at that time I had seen very few men back from the front — "not unnerved or even painfully ill — but very, very sad."

VERA BRITTAIN

1. The Fall of Saigon

CHRISTY made love to her the first time on a breakwater rock on North Beach at Hampton. His wadded coat, smelling of wood smoke and apples, was under her shoulders, and he called the rock Redemption and he gave Deborah his philosophy on the teaching of history. He said history is an objective world you and your students immerse yourselves in and when you come out the other end, you find yourselves larger. He sought to do this with his students at Franconia College.

Deborah considered this. Her father had been a teacher of history and had not found the loss of himself into history transforming. He had found it to be the stage for the family's hostilities. She found Christy's dictum on teaching in some ways too subtle for human beings, not knowing then that the hope for this subtlety was what his life depended upon. Christy's voice was deep, gravelly, satiating — his telling wry and at one remove — and he did something to her with his voice. He talked and she took in his grief like the waves disappearing into

3

the cold ocean. She pulled his hand away from the stone seawall and took his fingers into her mouth while he talked, his lips against her ear, and it was from the beginning they made the pact between sex and grief.

They had met in a Portsmouth cemetery where Deborah had been drawn to watch the sunrise. She sat with her back perfectly straight against a thin stone whose inscription was obliterated. Christy had a fondness for cemeteries and women. He stopped a few stones away and they remarked on the pink sun rising over the water and over the bridge that crossed to a school run by the Sisters of Providence. He told her about nuns who ran leprosariums on pristine South China Sea beaches. He said today Saigon was falling. It was April 30, 1975.

The cemetery was that instant new green that comes after weeks of rain. The grass ran along the borders of water that sliced into the land. Christy told her that New Hampshire had been an addiction to him after the war but he had avoided the seacoast. Emil Tero, his friend who had been killed in Vietnam, had talked and talked about it — the bars, the streets, the bridges — so that when Christy got here it was déjà vu. Tero's people were from here. Christy had asked him if they came to fish, but no, his friend had said, they were cooks.

Christy was near enough to see there were small designs on the print of Deborah's dress, it wasn't solid black as it would have appeared from a distance. He was quite near her and her back was to him. Two straps crossed over her back and the curve of her shoulder blade. Beyond her were headstones that sloped low to the green ground and beyond them dogwood trees with new uncurled leaves and beyond them the blue, blue water. Christy was twenty-nine, he said, but he couldn't smell the green grass. He thought he should have been able to smell it. It was as if he had no senses and he thought that was pathetic, that he didn't even feel sad and he couldn't smell the new grass.

They began to walk and Christy seemed drawn to talking. Deborah listened a little but not too much. She walked because she liked to walk. She liked to walk out New Castle Avenue all the way to the New Castle town beach and swim even in May, or down Little Harbor Road to the Lady Isle School. He walked because she did. It was okay with her that he did. She was curious about the war. Nobody she knew had gone. Her friends' lives had been committed to not going. He told quirky stories about GIs and about teaching at Franconia, and she began to listen.

Later they went to a bar called the Rusty Hammer, and watched on the wall TV what would become classic film footage of children and women and men reaching with all their bodies up to a Huey chopper, begging to be reprieved from whatever the Vietcong would do. Mothers pushed infants into the arms of soldiers who leaned out from the choppers to receive them.

They stopped watching and Christy drank whiskey and water, like Christy said he'd have done with Emil Tero. He said she could be a stand-in for Emil. The Hammer reeked of pot at the doorway. A kid she knew from the year she was at the university was playing an old Gibson guitar and singing his version of Cat Stevens's songs about wanting to live in a wigwam and making wild love to the moon. He took his voice deep down and Deborah imagined an orange balloon moon, coming down low to the ocean. Christy talked about Bethlehem where he lived in a cabin. Deborah told him she lived with a guy named Jake in Barrington where they were putting up post-and-beams. At the bar were airmen and sailors, distinctive with their short haircuts and for being without women. Portsmouth was a military town.

Deborah got up to go to the bathroom. She could feel Christy's gaze. Her outfit was loose but he was seeing the shape of her body just the same. The dress was ankle length with a useless and ratty sash at her hips like a girl might wear playing dress-up. She wore earrings with black stones and her hair pulled back and pinned with a barrette at the nape of her neck. When she came back, he was very formal. He said while Deborah had been gone he could hear his own sentences play back in his head and his desire to talk was disquieting.

"So you don't talk to people?" she said.

"Oh, yeah, I talk. I just don't say anything."

To Deborah he said that Emil Tero had a way with women. He had seen it with the nurses in the base camp. He explained that he and Emil weren't in intentional combat, they'd been combat engineers.

Christy's eyes grew brighter when he talked about teaching. She felt them take in her mouth and her neck. He didn't know what it was that had drawn him to Portsmouth, he told her, but he had come, so now it was done and he'd go back to the mountains with those kids in the commune where they kept glass jars of herbs, the way the Teros would have done in the restaurant down on Ceres Street.

He must have come in order to have the fall of Saigon with Emil, Deborah said.

She got up. She said, "So drink to him, drink to me."

"I don't want you to go."

"What happened to him?"

"A mine."

She nodded, but she had no idea what this meant.

"Sweeping for mines," Christy said, "which means you're listening for mines, you're listening for sounds and everything sounds the same. I never could distinguish. Everything was a mine."

She laid the rope strap of her small bag over her shoulder. "Yeah, and so how did it happen to your friend?"

"Sit down," he said, ignoring her question.

She did not sit down. Nevertheless when he took her hand,

her body responded and she knew he knew it. It was in her face. She said, "I need to go."

He said, "Why don't we walk."

He pulled some bills out of his pocket and dropped them on the table and they left the bar. Deborah was wearing brown sandals with wide straps over the tops of her feet and they could hear their footsteps on the pavement and when they crossed over fallen pine needles or decayed leaves, both of their footsteps were silent. She found their silence made her fantasize places she could suggest to him where they could go briefly. She was young and she thought later in her life she would laugh, remembering she had done this with a man.

They walked across the old lift bridge to the navy yard where ten thousand sailors were stationed. Christy said FB111s had flown from Pease Air Force Base across the highway, bound for Vietnam. Now the Cold War was thriving. The area had been built for the Cold War, since the shipyard maintained nuclear subs and the air force base was a Strategic Air Command operation. If you asked an Air Force official if there were nuclear weapons at Pease, Christy said, he'd deny it, even though they could see barricaded sites where wives could not get in to see their husbands.

Christy told her he had grown up in Lowell, but in the summers he used to go to a little town called Bethlehem where there was a place called the Milk and Honey Restaurant and the nearby Ammonoosuc River where he liked to camp and where a waterfall cascaded into a ravine. Sometimes he'd go up alone — he did a few times before he went to Vietnam, and almost every weekend after when he was in grad school in Boston. He camped along Lonesome Lake in a pine bed by the roots of a towering long-needle pine and he would never forget the smell of the pine needles heated by the sun.

They paused on a side street, really a service alley behind a block of restaurants and bars. A woman was on a porch that faced the alley. Sheets hung out to dry slit the porch in half and they could only see the woman when she danced out from behind the sheet-curtain, which she did now and then while she talked to someone they couldn't see. Led Zeppelin blasted from her radio. Christy told Deborah, "I've been home four years from the war and looking at you is the first time I've seen something in these four years and wanted it."

The sheet billowed in the warm breeze. "What have you been doing all those years?" she said.

"The dissertation," he said.

"The dissertation," she repeated, making fun.

"I got hooked on mines," he said.

"A dissertation on mines," she said.

"I find myself still checking out a road," he said, " or any-place where there's a distance in front of me."

"What for?"

"For mines," he said and he had stopped and looked at her, thoughtfully, like the professor he was.

"What do you do when you find them," she said, still lightly, because he was seducing her.

"Blow them." He made a loud exploding sound that was violent on the dear and small street. But he still held her eyes and he became charming and his eyes were piercing and earnest and hungry and almost funny in their exaggeration of how a man could die in a particular moment for a woman. He said, "My insides are a knot of lust and nausea," and Deborah sat down cross-legged in the alley laughing and brought the woman out from behind the sheet and she laughed too.

They stopped at a place for coffee.

Christy said he had burrowed away and buried himself in the extraordinary statistics of war so that by the time he came to prostheses and the hard clomp clomp of a temporary peg leg of a Vietnamese child, he had been overpowered by the numbers. He was a recorder of the numbers and the view of the world that they painted was the world he now lived in. Deborah listened to his intensity more than to his words.

He glanced up at her. He looked at her cheeks, her lips, her eyebrows with that same look in his eyes. Some of her hair had fallen down from the knot she had made of it at her neck and he brushed his hand across it. And she was tempted either to leave finally, or lean across the table and slide her tongue into his mouth. This was only pure sex. It was only his physical manner that was affecting her in this way. She disliked him doing this to her.

"You live in Barrington?" he asked.

"Sort of," she said. "I can't tell you all the places."

She was aware of large hands that seemed too large for scholarship. They could have built one of the grand hotels that had once been on the mountaintops above the town where his college had grown.

"I might go back to the flats," she said.

"What are the flats?"

"Apartments in Durham. It was a barracks for returning soldiers a long time ago. It has a squared-off back corner that is the bathroom, and you can talk to anybody in the flats if you stand in the bathroom and holler."

"What's your name?"

"Deborah."

"Deborah what?"

"Beebe."

"Christy Mahan."

"So we might not stay in this place in Barrington," she said.

"What happened?"

He was very intense, even then. She told him, "I don't know. It's probably just not going to work out with Jake."

"I don't think so either," he said, his wry smile giving over to a laugh. "Okay." He took the waitress's pad from the counter. He ripped several strips of paper lengthwise, scribbled some words, folded them, and dropped them into his coat pocket. "Okay," he said, "Have no fear, put your hand right in here. Choose your particular sin for the day."

"Come on, what do you want me to do?" she said, but she was laughing and he pulled her hand over and held his pocket open and she reached in slowly, feeling the warm, furred lining, and balled up one of the papers.

"And the winner . . ." he said.

She held up her palm, and showed it, a communion wafer. She spread it out on the counter. "Hampton," she said.

"Hampton," he said. "We're off. Like a prom dress."

She laughed. Where did he get these things? "I bet they all say Hampton."

"Well, they do." He had her hand.

They went to Hampton Beach where it was windy and they took off their shoes and socks to begin with and a reggae band was playing. Christy took off his jacket and gave it to her. They sat on the stone seawall and smoked.

They ate huge plates of spaghetti on the deck of a restaurant, where the sun beat down and a cold wind blew. Deborah ate wrapped in Christy's coat and another couple sat by the railing, the woman was in white, and the gulls swooped overhead. Deborah wore bands of friendship bracelets on her wrists, and Christy held them to her skin.

In the dark, she and Christy walked by a breakwater. Christy didn't say anything. He was a muscular man but in sex he was pure emotion. Sex with Christy was lit, animal eyes. Deborah reached her hand up to where he had climbed on the rocks. It was her initiation. It was like reaching up to the next branches of a tree when she was climbing, her arms, one foot, then the next, all her body climbed into him as he pulled her up to the long flat rock he was on. He was made of earth and rock.

◆ ◆ ◆

SHE imagined him spending a lot of time getting out his topo-graphical map and plotting the route, looking for Bow Lake and the backroads she told him the names of when she gave him directions to where she lived. He would feel every bump of the land between Bethlehem and Barrington. He would have spread the map on the car and traced the spidery roads with his fingers. She knew he was coming.

She could imagine his broad hands holding her cup that said NOT EVERYONE WHO WANDERS IS LOST, and his boots on her stone step next to her painted lady beans that wouldn't flower until June when she would be twenty-one. But he didn't come.

When Deborah was downtown again, walking the streets in work boots and a thin, sheath coat, she stopped at a pay phone to call Helen, her mother, on the Cape. She had thought often about dialing this number. She had imagined telling Helen she was in love and somehow this confession would soften her mother, like the hard knot of a peony bud being softened, like Helen had softened sometimes for Deborah's father. When her mother answered, Deborah said, "Dad said I could take the old Mercury."

"That's when he thought you were in school," Helen said. "My daughter the goatherd."

"He said I could take it," Deborah said.

"So why are you talking to me?"

Deborah imagined her mother's hair, which had been dra-matically white since her late twenties, swept up in a coil and the perfect moons on her fingernails. She had wanted to tell her about Christy, but Helen would agree with Jake that her daughter was an awkward, odd girl, maybe because she had loved horses to the exclusion of other things in her girlhood. Her parents summered on the Cape and had two or three cars there, her father's passion. The wide, low, white Mercury she had driven in high school had been languishing.

"Well, I'll use it for a while," Deborah said.

"You always do as you like."

She went to the Dunkin Donuts and sat at the counter and thought about spaghetti on the deck and the cold wind with the sun and Christy's eyes which were blue and composed and she couldn't go back to Jake.

Jake had said she drank too much coffee and ate too many Dunkin Donuts for a girl who was as good a plasterer and framer as she was, which was certainly true. He also said there was something awkward about her, something out of balance. He found her awkward, later, when it was raining, when she put on her yellow slicker and got on her bike and rode away, her left side lower than her right, out of balance.

She followed Christy to his Bethlehem, still reaching up. She was drawn to the reaching up, feeling his legs and arms come tight around her, and then to sit in the hollow of his joints and bones. She loved him in that animal way. Every time she imagined his hand reaching out to her, she felt her body respond, this image mixing with the image of the soldiers reaching out to the women and children from the Huey helicopters as the helicopters rose.

2. The Baker

IT was four days until Christmas, and Deborah was drawn back to the mountains. She had been drawn back every Christmas since she was in her twenties, when she had stayed on and lived in the woods above Franconia Notch and married Christy Mahan and had a child. Actually they'd done it twice, getting married. They always got married in Bethlehem. Once Christy came back to Portsmouth and they walked the streets in the dawn, amazed at the openness and light after their dark place in the woods. Christy stayed in the city as long as he could and then went back to the cabin where he had been for all his winters since '72 when he got out of the army and built the original room which that first year had nothing but a woodstove and a sleeping bag and the wind beating down from Mount Agassiz into his long bones.

Deborah was at the café on Portsmouth's Penhallow Street after hours, baking for the morning regulars and the shoppers. She was waiting for Phuong, the aged Vietnamese man who was the regular night baker and whose teeth were gold. She'd have to remember to give him his present before they left in the dawn. Then she would leave for the mountains.

Deborah was wearing her black sweatpants and a hooded sweat jacket that read EXPLOSION down the front, and her hair — shoulder length and black, streaked with gray — was shoved back with a purple headband. As she worked, an image of Ian, the baby she and Christy had had, flickered through her mind. He had slept at the foot of their bed in the mountains in a box Christy had hammered together.

Phuong came in. "Thank you you come," he exclaimed.

"Thank you *you* come," she said, in the same tone of voice she used when she stood at the counter, hands on her hips, shaking her head, saying, about a lot of things, That was fucking great, as her lazy smile brought out a pronounced dimple almost in the middle of her right cheek.

"Don't worry," Phuong continued to exclaim, rolling up the sleeves of his shirt, a striped one he got at the Goodwill with "Andy" stitched over the pocket. "I'll make the cakes."

Deborah laughed. "I'm not worried. I'll make the curtains." They were kids in a playhouse.

They always leaped into their task, though never quite understanding each other. They tied long cotton aprons around their necks and waists, the small man with the white hair and the glittering teeth and the tall woman in a running suit.

Phuong laid a hardback book, with a spine relaxed into flatness, on the wooden table where they worked. Phuong referred to the book as English lesson, and while they baked they also had English lesson, meaning Phuong and Deborah read novels aloud to each other. Phuong had moved from Harriet Vane to Roald Dahl, whom he liked a great deal. He preferred books with pictures and tonight they were reading *The BFG*. In the background the band Fresh Fish played from the boom box over the refrigerator, and sometimes as Phuong read, Fresh Fish's resonant trumpets began to build and Deborah moved to the music while she kneaded bread dough.

Phuong had already translated the first chapter of *The BFG* into Vietnamese, she saw. He did this by drawing the Vietnamese words above the English ones in the small white space between the lines of text. At first she had told him he wasn't supposed to write in the library books, but he never grasped the idea and kept illustrating with his beautiful Vietnamese script until Deborah decided the library was fortunate now to be able to provide bilingual Roald Dahl. They took turns reading. When it was Deborah's turn the second time, she said, "Ian called."

"Ian and Patience." Phuong held up two fingers together, because it was true, they were inseparable. If Ian came home, Patience came. If Patience needed to come to this home, their home, too, Ian came.

"Yes," she said. Ian, the son, and Patience was the other child from the woods, and she and her mother, Sonia, were part of their family from that community. Patience had told him she didn't want to come home and if she did she'd come with a friend who was driving north.

"She boarded away," Deborah said. "A boarding school, do you know? But it is a farm and she was okay. She could spend her time with the pigs and she had learned to weave. But Ian said they hadn't been able to get in touch with her. He wasn't sure what was going on. She's a cat. Sometimes I come home and here she is in my place, asleep under the comforter."

Phuong shook his head. "Bad luck that girl."

"No," Deborah said. But she was. She was a worry to them all, though they ascribed her wildness and mercurial ways to adolescence, and before that to childhood. There was something ethereal about her, not unlike her mother, but without her mother's glaze of resiliency and show of detachment. Even Deborah tried to bestow these qualities on the girl because they were familiar qualities and useful for survival. What keeps a girl connected, Deborah thought? Out loud she said, because it was Phuong there, "While she is on the front porch at night, why wouldn't she roam? Why wouldn't she when the moon is out and while there are conversations happening other places. What would draw that girl to her own small bed in the perfectly known?"

Phuong shook his head. "No," he said, "she have a broken moon."

"Phuong, Patience always shows up. She's a visitor other places. She steps away. I don't know where. What do you mean broken moon?"

"Maybe broke." He touched his brown fist to his chest.

Phuong's gesture lingered in the kitchen. He would be familiar with that quality in girls when they were young and refugees and sometimes abandoned by their mothers and fathers and finally their country.

"You are going to see your husband?" Phuong said.

Deborah tossed her head from side to side. "He is not my husband."

Phuong shrugged. "What can you do?" he said.

"What do you mean, what can I do?"

"Sometimes that way with husband and wife."

"You drive me crazy."

Phuong smiled. Then he took the English lesson off the work counter in order to make room for long sheet pans and in these he spread the dough he had been working, and over that he flung layers of cheeses and marjoram and rosemary. The Ceres Bakery had taught him to be an earthy crunchy cook, leaving the turtle or rabbit or snake or snails for him to peddle along with the gold bracelets and jade, which was in demand when a baby was born, to assure the baby's good fortune. He always had something in his satchel for sale.

What could she tell him about Franconia and Bethlehem and, by this, about Patience? My friends up there, Michael and others, got this doctor in Vermont to attest to their queerness, weirdness, and insanity so they didn't get drafted and go to your country. So it made them queer, weird, and insane.

There was a knock on the door. Deborah's friend Vincent called, "Yo, yo!" and Deborah went to open it, relieved to escape from the mountains. Her hands were raised and covered with flour. The lights were dimmed in the front of the store. Vincent came in on a blast of guitar and saxophone from speakers and then the fiddles began to build.

"Sweetie," she yelled. "Why're you yelling Yo!" This was part of their greeting.

The traffic was rushed and loud, and Deborah was distracted from the babies in the mountains by the rush and Vincent's cold and bristly rugged cheek against hers and then the sturdiness of his arms.

She poured him some coffee and he said, "Not on your life," and he pulled out three bottles of beer from three different pockets and passed them around. Phuong said, "Very good beer. Very good." He opened his satchel and pulled out a tupperware container and inside was soup. "Very good," Phuong said. "Turtle soup."

"Wonderful," Vincent said and they warmed it up in the microwave, so now the place smelled of Vincent's clean and biting aftershave and the garlic sauce for pizza and bread rising and, now, warmed turtle soup.

"'I'm going up to Bethlehem," Deborah said. She had turned her back to pull a tray of eggs out of the refrigerator. She set them on the counter and cracked an egg against the rim of a stainless steel bowl. "For the shopping night they do at the store, and Patience is up to something."

Vincent took a swallow of beer. He looked at Phuong.

"So are ya coming home by Christmas?" Vincent asked. "We going to have Christmas?" He had a way of talking, both drawled and clipped. His eyes were gray and, from the first, she knew he was aware of everything, aware of her body, aware of the change in the shape of her breasts when her period came, aware of her falsities, words less than honest.

He was tall with disheveled black hair and a generous, crooked smile. He had been a fisherman and now he was a builder.

"'Cause if not," he said, "I'm gonna take a little road trip."

"Fifteen minute, everything be done," Phuong said, slamming the pizzas in the long oven shelves. "Fifteen minute," he shouted, as if perhaps they had not heard. He picked up his coat and was gone, pulling a pack of Chinese cigarettes out of his shirt pocket. He sat on the bench on the sidewalk and they could see him hunched over his knees, his greatcoat making a tent to the sidewalk and his hands cupped around his matchbook.

The music was anxious and loud. What Deborah did with Vincent was a reprieve to her. It crossed her mind that she should not sleep with him. She did not understand why the world lay so heavy. Christy said at AA meetings they said, Wear life like a loose overcoat, like Phuong's. It was so sad in the café now with Vincent, but she didn't know what exactly was sad. Maybe only the air.

She bent back to the batter she was mixing at the counter. Maybe it was her lot to move from one lover to the next.

She had almost no family except for Ian and Patience and Sonia. She had friends such as Phuong with whom she went out for pancakes, women from the store, lovers. She was sometimes aware of holidays because she went for groceries and found herself in crowds and realized people were cooking for Thanksgiving or Fourth of July picnics and families were gathering. Helen and Deborah were curious about families. Deborah had called Helen before she came to work tonight. She left a message on her mother's machine at the Cape house. "I'm off to Bethlehem. We're doing the Gentlemen's Shopping Night again. Have fun on your trip to New York."

"What's the matter?" she said to Vincent. "Sometimes I go home. Sometimes I have to go home."

"To the women," he said. Deborah and Sonia had run a store and he knew about this. But he had not meant the women at all, he had meant, to the man. It wasn't that Christy and Deborah were anything at all. They went months without talking. It was only that a part of her loitered in the cabin.

"It's funny how a man can get obsessed with a person."

"Are you obsessed with me?"

"No, I could leave. I sure could. I'm talking about him."

Deborah imagined her son and his father. She imagined them together on the porch of Mackie's antique store. Christy was about six foot, his hair pulled back in a ponytail, broad shouldered, all long thigh bones, shinbones, and her son carried his body the same way his father did. They both smelled like cut lumber. "What a funny thing to say," Deborah finally said to Vincent. "He has not left one woman above the Notch unfamiliar with him."

Vincent knew about Deborah's life in the woods. He knew she had studied art and poetry someplace in the mountains where they smoked pot every way a person could think of, including in an apple using the core as a filtering chamber and a carrot for a pipe and when it was smoked, they passed the apple around for everyone to take a bite. She explained she had never been as close to someone as she felt like she'd been when they were sharing an apple pipe and then the apple.

"Did you know there were forty-three hotels in Bethlehem once?" Deborah asked him. Vincent bent over his beer.

"You know what your problem is? You're overeducated and you haven't set on a job yet. You know that? You've been waiting tables for twelve years."

"That's not true. One job I got dressed up."

"What do you want? You went to college up there, didn't you? What was it called, Vershire something?"

"Franconia College."

"One of them schools that folded."

"The Vershire School was in Vermont."

"Didn't it fold? Too much sex and drugs and Greenwich kids."

"It wasn't just sex. It wasn't a college."

"You walk in those circles. You need to go. Men are dogs," Vincent said. "Men are steady as they go. Men are dogs. They just want to go along steady. Put a man in a situation and you know basically what he's going to do. Put a woman in a situation, she could do anything."

"Men are dogs," she repeated.

"Yes, exactly. If a man went up to that town where that college was, and he's trying to get his life on track, what would he do?"

She went back to the counter. She picked up the bowl of batter and poured the smooth, white lightning batter down the stainless steel drain since she could not remember what ingredients had already gone in. "I don't know, Vincent. I don't know anything. I don't know why I do anything. I don't know why you do anything. I'm tired of fighting with you."

"A man," Vincent said, "is a ship."

"Oh, Christ."

"He would hang out alone for a while. He might talk to one buddy. If he had a close buddy. Or maybe he'd hang out alone."

"All right, yeah, so what about the woman?"

"Anything," Vincent said, emptying the beer. "She could do anything. Let's work this out, Deborah. I have to go to Montreal. I have to go sit on a balcony and drink French wine."

"I can just see you." Deborah didn't laugh. She squatted down in front of him and put her hands on his thighs.

"So, go," he said. "Figure out what you want. What's it take, three hours?"

"Four, maybe, in the snow through Crawford Notch."

"So tell me about the commune," he said.

She stood up. She felt like talking about the woods. She didn't know what she wanted Vincent to know. Maybe if he could hold some of the emotion of it.

She said, "I wondered if the way we lived up there was something like what war was like. No room for error. It was survival living. The mountains and the rivers are unforgiving."

He stood up too and held the back of her neck in his large warm hand and she could almost stop shivering. She felt suddenly very afraid. She put her arms around him under his sweater. He sighed a great sigh. She pressed him into the wall and, for a little while, time stopped and nobody was going anywhere and it was just the fine and minute details of their bodies, the soft strokes of their tongues in slow motion, the habit of their breath that was instantly erotic, the knowledge of where to place their hands to ease each other, this was what mattered and life was short and they could do this for each other. Deborah always seemed to sleep with men at the end, when they could already taste the loss, and she was resisting it. Not anymore. No more loss.

She was stepping into the never-never land of having to live in a space that you can just possibly conceive, the end of something. You can conceive of it but you can't live in it, not *now*. Not *this* physical pain, not *this* bare bed, not *this* lack of words. Not the lack of this bend of his head over the book, his muscular forearm across the baby's naked shoulder. That was the place she lived in in the woods.

Vincent pulled away from her, got himself some coffee, and sat down at the round table by the window so that Deborah could see both Vincent and beyond him, Phuong.

"Hey, Vincent," she said. She pushed back her headband, which made her hair hug her scalp and exposed her face. "I don't want to go."

"I guess you have to."

"I'm scraping my house. When it thaws."

"More power to ya. If ever a house needed scraping yours does."

"Thanks, Vincent."

"So get in your Saab since that's the only car you got, but I wouldn't trust a Saab down to Peavey's."

"We used to smoke pot on the back porch of the Frost farm up there. We wanted to be poets and thought that would help."

Vincent said, "No doubt it did," and she felt a strong affection for him and his roughness and at the instinctive understanding she often saw in him, in the way he held his hands one inside the other on the table and his observant gray eyes that carried more weight than the snideness of his smile.

The smell of Phuong's pizza filled the café, and the new loaves she now took out of the oven, the wood burning in the fireplace, the sharp soap Vincent used, the faint smell of rose powder from the dried bouquet on the mantel, the busyness of rushed steps on the sidewalk outside. The mountain lacked all this busyness. She felt like she was letting this rhythm go.

Phuong came in. He said nothing but went to work cleaning up so he could begin the croissants. They would be perfect and light. His sheets of pizza lay golden and steaming.

Vincent stood to go and let in the bite of the December air. The street corner then was empty, and a blues trumpet carried to them from a bar on Daniel Street. Deborah touched Vincent's hand and kissed him and he left to go home to his place on the back channel, his yard strewn with nautical gear, lobster traps, buoys on the steps, a dory in a wooden, unattached, and leaning garage, his bed in the room with steam radiators so loud it seemed like they had always made love in a train station.

The door shut. Deborah looked at Phuong and felt like he was holding the odd parts of her life together.

She gave him a small wrapped box that he opened, grinning and glittering. Inside was a wooden bird she had whittled.

3. Into the Notch

THE presence of the mountains was something Deborah felt before she was among them. She anticipated them. From the time she left the seacoast, driving north and west, she prepared for them. From Conway on, the eastern slopes of Mount Washington and the Presidentials were invisible in the fog but she felt their enclosure around her, not just around her car, but around her entire life in all the ages of her life. She drove through Crawford Notch. She came upon the Mount Washington Hotel where Sonia had worked, where many of them had worked at one time or another.

The towns above Franconia Notch were quiet towns with sprawling, abandoned wood-frame hotels left over from the grand hotel era when the steam trains traversed the notches, up past the Old Man or through Crawford Notch where the railroad families lived, and the farm families who had supplied the hotel kitchens with white butter and eggs still warm.

When Deborah drove through the Notch she could feel that edginess she had lived in. Where everything carried weight. It had been that way with her mother. The color of her clothes had carried weight. She had watched signs with Christy, too.

She took the turn south at Twin Mountain so she could drive through Franconia Notch. It was already dark. The road was very narrow at that point and she wondered, Could it have been more open in the days of the college or did she only imagine that? The road curved and it was a single lane. No headlights of oncoming cars blinded her. In the darkness she looked up at the granite wall that rose beside her where the Old Man would be.

In Bethlehem, she drove up the main street where a barren tree gave its look to the whole town. In this small town there had been forty-three hotels and now the main street held the Arlington, the kosher hotel, and the ruins of others with shattered windows and abandoned porches.

On Main Street, before one came to the Alpine Hotel, was the store: once the Milk and Honey Restaurant, and now the Three Eves, of which Deborah had been one. It was a vintage clothing store featuring clothes of the eras of the grand hotels. The Three Eves had begun the tradition in Bethlehem of catering to the men of the town one night of the year, Christmas Eve. They brought in beer and the clerks dressed up as the models and helped men pick out presents for the women in their lives.

When she thought of the Three Eves, she thought of a small room at the bottom of the stairs. The room was by the furnace, where they used to eat grapefruit for lunch and planned who would get the hand plow that weekend. Customers used it to try on the clothes, tossing their own over the couch with the batik cover where she and Christy had once made love. This was in the early days of the store after the Milk and Honey closed.

In that small downstairs room by the furnace, they debated about von Clausewitz's ideas about war, they read the political philosophers. They dressed up in the clothes on the racks, things like white ankle-length dresses with net fabric straps. They were barefoot and wore cloche hats or berets or scarves wrapped around their necks or waists. Sonia and Deborah had no idea where Val dug up some of the stuff. And they had no idea of war except as it came home to them. The feeling of being twenty was taking her over as she drove nearer to the store. She would rather not go there and pulled herself back to the consciousness of now having some cash in her pocket, warm boots, her own car.

The main street was small, really a single block of shops, but with hotels up and down it. They weren't working hotels except for the Arlington, they were hotels in various stages of dissolution, from abandoned buildings to a shell of a burned-out hotel. The same hotels had been there in the 1970s. When Deborah thought about this town, she wondered how the hotels were doing and hoped no more had burned down, which they did now and then mysteriously in the night.

A sign on a sawhorse outside the Three Eves read, GENTLE-MEN'S SHOPPING NIGHT. CHRISTMAS EVE. MODELS WELCOME. She backed up to the closed market where there was a pay phone.

A woman was on the phone but moved as if she were about to get off. The woman was angry. She told whomever she was talking to that she wasn't coming home. "I'll come home when you promise me," she yelled into the phone. The person did not promise her because the woman yelled again and then she slammed the phone down. Pay phones looked like crisis to Deborah. The blue-lit letters signaled trouble. The woman left and the phone was free now and she could call. But she was having trouble stepping up to the blue box. It was about twenty degrees in town. She was safe. Patience might already be home. She went to the phone. She tried to push the silver buttons for her old number but was too clumsy. She took off her right glove.

She was forty-three years old. At this point of her life,

definitely unlike some others, she had a job, she had a place to live. She had paid her rent. She wore a brown-belted city coat, a print scarf tied over her hair. She retied the scarf against the wind, shoved her hands in her pockets, holding the phone with the receiver between her ear and her shoulder. She wondered if Mercury was in retrograde. She should have checked. Shit, Christy. Oh, well, she liked him. Who could help but like him. She liked to hear his voice. He made her laugh. Maybe they would sit down like old-timers. Who else could she be an old-timer with?

She dialed again.

"Hey," she said when he answered.

She could almost hear him readjust the way he was standing.

"What have you heard from Patience?"

"Not too much. Talked to the guy out there," he said. His voice was rumbly and deep and now also thick and she could see how his lips would be taut next to the mouthpiece and his thick shoulders would lean downward against the exposed wall they had never finished. "She told him she was on her way back home. That was this morning."

She could hear Christy inhale, swallow.

"So you came up?" Christy said.

"For Christmas."

She heard a crash on the other end of the line.

"Dennis is about to whelp," he said. "She's nesting."

"Who's Dennis? Do you have a new Dennis?"

"This'll teach her," he said.

She imagined him with this bedraggled dog, a dog struck with adulation for this rugged, deep talking, understated, melancholy master with eyes bright like mica. A man and his dog. A decent man, abandoned, and his pregnant, hyperventilating dog, the two of them against the world. Women brought them food. All kinds of food, Ian said. Put up, steamed, baked, frozen, fresh caught.

"How's my son?" she asked. "I need to see his blue eyes."

"He's around. Haven't seen much of him. You know anything about whelping?"

Deborah tapped her boot on the side of the phone booth to get the snow off. Then she kicked the phone booth. It was as if no time had passed. Or time had. This was their next marriage. He had been between women and she had married him again. Had done the whole thing again and was doomed.

"Where are you staying," he said.

"Sonia's," she said. She heard the new Dennis crying in the background. "I'll stop in to take a look at the dog. Don't you wonder where Patience may be tonight?"

But Christy wouldn't talk about Patience. He just told Deborah, if her car had any weight and was low to the ground, don't even try to get down his road. She knew that.

He hung up. She stood with the phone pressed against her neck as she had begun. He was the man who took care of her body. He was the man who took care of her eyes and showed her his sunsets. Took her deep into a melancholy where they went together, like alcoholics. She would have done anything. To hear him made her want to take his hand and give him whatever would give him a reprieve. Do you want a whore? Let me be this for you. If it would help him to have that instead of a wife.

She hung around by the phone and talked to Vincent in her head. She said, Hello, I'm in Bethlehem. I'm cold. I miss the dead stalks of sunflowers that still stand in your garden and the Seasons Greetings lights on your leaning fence. She hung up the receiver under the blue Bell Atlantic lights. Her cheeks stung with cold. She had lost feeling in her fingers.

Where was Patience in this cold? Patience. Patience was a listener. Christy wasn't a listener. He had a crescendo going on in his head like rivers cascading down the mountains. Ian, from the time he was three, packed his head with data, the height of a river, the ratio of days of rainfall to days fog bound, the probability of avalanche, gear to take winter camping. Ian grew up acquiring gear to keep them all safe. How do these things happen?

Phuong told her that in class, everybody was supposed to speak English. He said the teacher gave students tokens and if they said a word in Khmer or Spanish or Vietnamese, the teacher would take a token away and if anybody still had a token at the end, they got a pass to Canobie Lake or Water Kingdom, both of which have rides like the flume near Lincoln you can slide down in a wwwwwosh — and it drops you in a basin. All that for not speaking your own language.

"Don't change yourself in any of your particulars," Phuong had said. He was practicing English with the help of an audio-tape of Dorothy Sayers' *Strong Poison,* in which Harriet Vane is told this.

"Strong poison," Phuong had said. "Maybe that is what woman is to man, man is to woman."

4. The Smell of Apples

DEBORAH sat in her ancient, rusted Saab, slightly holey from sea air and her general inattentiveness to cars, waiting. When she was twenty-one, she had taken Mount Cleveland Road, the road she was about to take now, out to the commune. The path had been perfectly clear when she had driven it in her father's Mercury.

The mountains had a cumulative effect. Now they wrapped around her all the darkness and joy and sorrow and young womanhood that the mountains had been the backdrop to. When she first came to this place in 1975 the immoveableness of the mountains had not been clear. She had thought, perhaps, she would wake up and they might have moved on as she assumed she herself could.

She had found the homestead and some of the cabins in the woods in the little valley between Mount Agassiz and Cleveland Mountain. A girl at the old farm house they called the homestead said she could stay over in one of the places that was empty. She had walked down the trail in heavy rain until she saw the cabin with a boulder for a doorstop, as the girl had said there would be. Deborah climbed up on it and pulled the handle on the door. It was an extremely heavy door and it stuck in the wetness, but she yanked it open and stepped inside where it was dark and still. There was a woodstove in the center of the room, venting out the roof, a washstand, a wooden spool for a table, and a piano. A McPhail from Boston. The floor was planks of rough wood laid diagonally. The walls were planks, some vertical, some horizontal. Wooden shelves were supported by crooked tree limbs. The rain fell against the glass that dropped straight down on the back side. The cabin looked like half a house, with a roof that peaked and then dropped to a wall nearly all window. She thought she could live there.

The homestead was diagonally across the path from this cabin. Later, Valerie, who lived there, and her daughter, Fran, brought her corn on the cob in a metal pan and a dish of white butter and they ate the corn out in front of the cabin, sitting on rusted webbed chairs among a good-sized woodpile and wildflowers that grew to the door. The woods around were mixed woods, paper birches, hemlocks, white pines. Up the road someone played a flute.

Deborah was distracted from taking in the trees by the daughter, who had come with the corn. She wore an evening gown hiked up about her waist.

Valerie was waiting for the rain to stop so she could get back to the garden. Her legs had blond hair and were streaked with mud. She was a large woman with straight blond hair and a square and stoic face like a French Canadian girl that Deborah had met at UNH, a local who called her grandmother "Memere" and when Memere came, she spoke French and pinched her face.

"You came to see Christy?" Fran said.

She said, "Yes."

Fran said, "They last about a month."

"Who does?"

"Christy's girlfriends."

Deborah shrugged and wolfed the corn, which was the first thing she'd eaten that day. Valerie brought out a loaf of bread that she had had in the pocket of her rain parka. Deborah found a knife from her new kitchen and she sliced the bread on a tree stump, yellow and rippled and fragrant since the tree had been newly cut. The bread held the taste of the tree. "She's different," Valerie said about Deborah, her mouth full of the crusty bread. "He gets back about four," Valerie said. "He thinks the fuckin' woods are mined. The only time he's sane is when he's teaching. Give him a class and he's on, otherwise he forgets he's a human being."

"I like him," Fran said.

"You would," Valerie said. "You romantic. How'd I get a daughter like you. Look at you," and she fussed with Fran's evening attire and hugged Fran's head to her large breasts and Deborah liked them both and felt fired with the sweet, brand-new corn in her stomach.

Christy did not appear to be surprised to see her. By the time he drove up Deborah was in the garden streaked with mud, so that she and Valerie and Fran looked like members of a tribe that decorated their bodies with intricate designs made with clay.

Christy pulled his truck up to the barn. There was no road to his cabin yet, and later, when there was, it usually ripped out the bottoms of his cars so he still walked the road or the trail in the woods from the homestead to the place that he had cleared with a machete, and later he cleared the path farther, to Deborah's door.

Deborah stood by the door to his truck, as if she always did that when he drove in.

"So," he said, "the beach girl."

"Yeah, the beach girl."

"What'd you ever do with that guy, that Jake?"

"I'm not there anymore."

"Oh yeah?"

"She's there," Fran sang. "She's over there. We gave her the arts and crafts cabin."

Deborah shrugged at Christy and went back to work in the mud with Fran, her bare feet leaving imprints on the muddy drive and her hair in wet strings and spirals down her back.

DEBORAH had fourteen dollars. She had a pair of jeans, aside from the muddy ones, and two shirts and her books from the classes she'd dropped, some poetry, some zoology. She had a picture of her mother, together with her father in a tiny cardboard oval frame. She had a card with her blood type, O neg, and a small, stylized bird made of smooth wood she had gotten from a Portsmouth craftsman.

Later that afternoon she rode into town with Valerie in her truck and checked out places to look for work. She asked around to see if anybody was hiring. She went in the day-night store. She went in the library. She went in the restaurant called the Milk and Honey and knew that was where she would work if she could. She told them she knew how to make curries and the guy in the kitchen said, "Sure, someday you will make curries, but everybody works here" — he had gestured to the dining room — "waiting tables." He said if they lost somebody, they might want her. Valerie told her they were all Premies, members of the sect The Divine Light Mission, who ran the place.

When Deborah got back to the cabin, she found a watermelon on the tree stump where they had sliced the bread. Fran was also there, now in rows and rows of iridescent pop beads around her waist and around her wrists and ankles. "That's from Christy," Fran said. "That's the way he cuts them. He gives them doors." Fran opened one door, which was cut in the shape of a trapezoid, through which they could scoop out the fleshy fruit. Deborah imagined Christy's large hands holding the knife as he cut the shapes of the watermelon doors. She opened and closed the doors. She opened them again and reached in and broke off some watermelon, knowing that he was asking her to go to him. "Do you want some?" she said to Fran, and they both reached in and stuffed themselves with the sweet fruit.

DEBORAH went for a walk with Fran, who loved being the guide. Fran wanted them to be alike. She put pop beads on Deborah's brown wrists and ankles, then took her hand and led her into the settling dusk. The woods here were denser than any Deborah had known. They walked up a path across the road from the homestead. In the dim light she saw three trees, birches, so close they almost touched. Here was a sprawling stand of ferns, here was a springhouse. Here was a stack of sticks, just so. Deborah would walk there for days before the details didn't float, one into the other, but were distinct and everything had clarity. The path had always been clearly marked. There was only one stand of three birches just like that, in a curve in the path.

They wound back down the trail to the old house that must have stood alone out here for fifty years.

"Thank you, Sweetie," she said to Fran. Fran was standing on the porch of the homestead now, arranging her orange cat in a derelict pram. She had misted the cat's tail earlier with Aqua Net and as the cat waved its tail, the cosmetic smell floated into the night. Fran wore shorts and a striped top, snarls in her hair; she was yawning, and Deborah was envious of her going to bed on a hot summer night, curious and innocent.

"He sits out late," Fran said. "I spy on him. He sits in a red chair and looks at the mountain."

◆ ◆ ◆

DEBORAH took the trail Fran showed her to Christy's cabin. It was narrow and quite dark and she smelled pines and the sweetness of flowers she couldn't see, and heard water Fran said ran down from the mountain. She met an owl. They both stopped moving and looked at each other, he nearly bending over looking down from a hemlock tree, Deborah staring up. It was a strange contest and she didn't want to let go of his eyes. They leaned and considered each other. She ended up leaving first, feeling the owl's eyes bore into her as she moved on from him.

The path became rocky and then opened into a garden as Fran had told her it would. Maybe a dozen kids, Deborah imagined they were students, were hanging out in the garden and in the section below the small wooden cabin where there were some kitchen chairs. Ahead of them the moon was just coming up.

Christy usually had a potluck on Wednesdays one of the guys told her. He was leaning against a cider press in the middle of scattered piles of wood and debris and metal fixtures that Christy had scrounged for future improvements on the shack. The guy was round-faced, and gentle and graceful like a bear. He said his name was Michael and Deborah liked him from that day.

She didn't see Christy. She moved through the students, helped herself to the jug of wine. Finally she saw him, looking amused and charming, one arm crossed to his elbow, his hand rubbing the beard that had surprised her because it had been soft to her cheek. He was talking to a group of students and particularly to a girl and, while he was telling some story about a prisoner, he said her name several times, Louise. Louise stood slightly sideways to him, listening with her long, narrow arms lightly folded over each other. If Christy saw Deborah, he did not acknowledge her. Louise was a tall, icy, cerebral girl, the kind Deborah would have liked to be.

Later, in the dark, the students called out aphorisms, couplets, clichés. They tossed them out across the field to each other like Red Rover, Red Rover, hurl one out and get another one back. They circled and read their own poems. Christy was a storyteller and the students deferred to him. Deborah trudged to the house, her hands in the front pockets of her oversized striped pullover, and back to the garden again, past the woodpile where she kept her wine. She watched Christy listen to Louise or another student with respect and delight in his eyes. This was a side of him she hadn't seen in Portsmouth, with him and Emil Tero. She watched him talk. Sometimes he looked at Louise, sometimes he paused to look for necessary words. Louise met his gaze evenly and didn't seem aware of his necessary words. Deborah noticed she moved her fingers slightly across the pale hairs on her forearm, began to stroke the arm that her long, tangled hair fell across. Deborah was fascinated and disgusted. She felt drawn back to the owl. Later the students got rowdier and they formed a circle around the apple press and went back to a rowdier and lewder Red Rover. It got late. The air smelled sweet and ripe and Louise and Deborah found themselves sitting in the stuffy greenhouse off the cabin. Rain began to hit against the plastic. It was stuffy with dampness and sweat. They had been smoking and now were hungry.

"Did you just come up here?" Louise asked her.

"Yeah. I did. I just came. What do you know about him?" Deborah nodded toward Christy. He was leaning back, relaxed, his mouth slightly open, moving to the music Michael lightly played on a flute.

"I'll tell you something about him."

Someone joined the flute with a guitar. It was lovely and eerie. A fog had descended around them on the mountain's edge.

"One time I was with him," Louise said. "We were driving through the Notch. You know how narrow that road is. There was an accident and we came on it and Christy stopped. There was a woman screaming. It was awful. She was holding a little child who was still. I remember her hair. I couldn't see her face but I saw her hair hanging over her mother's arm. Christy saved her. I don't know what he did. There was a lot of blood and he got hold of the artery and got a tourniquet in the right place. But you should have seen his face. He looked really happy. Or maybe vindicated. But now I think every day he has to do something like that in order to be able to live with himself."

The air was hot and so humid, and the grass had been so pure, and Deborah thought she was going to faint in the thickness of it. She moved to stand up but Louise said, "Put your head down." And Deborah put her head between her knees, rocked herself, her hands cradling the back of her neck. What had she done? Where had she come? She wanted to be cerebral, elmlike Louise, and here she was, too large to be really pretty, her mother had always said. Too awkward and large, though very good with animals and children.

She rocked and thought of her mother whom she would never go home to, as she couldn't to Jake. Fourteen dollars.

She rocks herself and remembers Helen sitting on a stone bench embedded with smooth, colored stones that Deborah's father had had shipped from Mexico. They sat on the patio in shorts, a hot night like this in their country house. Helen is talking to Deborah, a child. Her father is teaching this summer and will not join them. Helen laughs at Deborah who is dancing. She scorns her. She makes fun of the way Deborah talks. She mimics her. She says, "Deborah is going to be a star. Look at that child show off." Helen needed praise and Deborah found a way to please Helen by confessing to her, by adoring her, as if they were sisters, and it felt better than the truth. It felt good to hear her mother say, "You are my child and I love you." It made Deborah sit back and soak in her mother's love, *you are my child and I love you.*

She felt Louise's hand on her back. "I'm okay," she said. She managed to will her head to stop spinning, and she got up and slowly eased out into the night. She breathed in the smell of cut wood from the woodpile and it was good in the cooler air and she stayed because the music from the flute held her.

THE inside of Christy's cabin smelled like apples. One of his trees was always early, he said. He had apples in buckets, apples in a row along the window ledges. He wore jeans and a sweatshirt.

He said, "I remember you with your hair up. Do you ever wear it up anymore?" Deborah was looking at his books and he had put his palm close to her hair, which was coarse, almost matted, and thick and very long.

The students had gone and she had walked into his cabin with her wine.

"You should go," he said.

She nodded.

He hadn't touched her hair but it seemed husband-and-wifely intimate to Deborah, the way they stood when the others left, a premonition of the further intimacy, something she had never known in a family that had been embarrassed to be composed of physical parts, of arms and thighs. Standing there, Deborah had a fantasy, not of sleeping with Christy, but of having slept with him for a long, long time.

There were pots of food left over on a picnic table that he had, along with a desk, a mattress, a propane gas stove, and a sleeping bag beneath a large window. He dug into the pasta, gulping down forkfuls. "Go ahead," he said. "Dig in." She did and she walked around with a pot, eating cold rice, reading the titles of his books. "There are so many things I haven't read. I'm going to make some money here and take some classes, read all these books. Well, maybe not these books." She stopped. "All the books I never read."

He didn't say anything. He had stopped eating. She opened a heavy volume and read the table of contents and his notes in the margins. He sat down on a bench and watched her. She said, "How come you didn't come back?"

He was leaning against the wall, maybe still on a high from being beloved in his group. "Your innocence is frightening."

She didn't leave then either.

HE didn't hurt her. He moved incredibly slowly. He told her to take off her jeans, which she did, and he told her to raise her arms and he slid his arms up under her shirt and felt her waist and her ribs and then her breasts. She was too large, she thought, and no doubt her size was part of her awkwardness, an awkwardness she was more aware of, having left everything that was hers to follow this man. She felt Christy's warm, calloused hands on her nipples. He shut his eyes and let out a slow groan. She was kneeling then, facing him and the stars that shone through his window. He slid his hands down to her ass and she remembered hard, angry, thrusting sex and his yelling out her name with every thrust. They slept there in his sleeping bag on a mattress under the window that night, waking up very often in the heavy smell of apples and the rush that came with the comfort of their hard embrace.

THE next day was the first time she saw the college. She knew the building had been a hotel, but she had not imagined what she found. The old Forest Hills was an enormous white castle set in a hill above Franconia. It had over one hundred rooms that looked out over Cannon and Lafayette and the Kinsman range. Kids lounged on the grand, pillared porch that wrapped around the long front. That morning the castle, a pool, an adjacent lodge, the students, and there among them, Christy, were muted and shrouded in clouds. Deborah leaned up against her old Mercury in the field below and stared. Christy had given one of the core lectures. He was still wearing the jeans and the sweatshirt. She could smell apples, seeing him, and now the air of the mountain. The smell drew her to him and she could feel his coarse jeans and wanted to put her mouth there and reach up to him and climb him.

She slept with him all that winter and found a home for the first time in this college community beside the goshawks, who learned to fly on the updrafts of the mountain's valleys.

5. We Love the Things We Love for What They Are

ALL winter Deborah slept with Christy in the night and he rested some of the weight of his dreams on her by cradling her head in both of his arms and rocking her in his sleep. She went back through the woods in the morning to her cabin or into Bethlehem to the Milk and Honey where they did give her some hours over the lunchtime.

Another new girl came to town that fall. A lot of Franconia students were older and had been knocking around other places, and Sonia was one of them. She might have been already twenty-one. Her parents dropped her off up there to give her one last chance to make it through a college year. Deborah and Sonia had both told Patience the story of the day they met, and the truth of it was lost in their exaggeration and memory. Sonia said she had found Deborah working at the Milk and Honey. It was September and a very hot day and she found the place on Main Street, an old building with wood floors and wooden tables and a long counter down the length of the place. She didn't have any money so she just sat on the stoop and watched. A girl in jeans and a shirt with embroidered moons on the sleeves came out for a smoke. Sonia had laughed to Patience, saying, "The girl had curly hair, almost black, that she wore pinned up on her head in the heat. She looked healthy, kind of scrubbed. She had wide cheeks, she was quite tall and broad shouldered. She had naturally colored violet lips like something out of the woods. It was discouraging to look at her. Her focus was debilitating to me. How could anyone seem so lush, she looked fertile and really not too prepared for it."

Sonia, Deborah said, was so skinny she looked anorexic. Deborah brought her a fried egg sandwich on the dense rye bread the German bakery made. She gave it to her and said they'd probably let her work it off in the kitchen. Sonia came back the next day for another fried egg sandwich and then she washed dishes in the kitchen facing the woods she assumed Deborah had come in from. In the end they both worked there that fall.

Deborah described Sonia as the delicate one of their best-friend pairing, Sonia with the heart-shaped face. That was the time of their nude modeling days for the figure-drawing class. That was the time of Deborah being a poet because Sonia, who was an official Franconia College student, got her into Sonia's poetry class. That was the time when Leon Botstein, who had come at twenty-three years old and saved the college and built bridges to the town, which had grown skeptical of student-run learning, had already been enticed away to Bard. It was not a good time for Franconia, and everybody was pondering the future. That was the time when Deborah began to study war.

She read Vera Brittain's *Testament of Youth* in the woods, in the outhouse, in her bed, in the kitchen with the Premies when they came in from the Premie house. The book saddened her and changed her politics. She read Vera's World War I poets, and thought now she knew. She found a little book of poems by a soldier, Michael Casey, making the rounds among some at Franconia. They made her melancholy and, she presumed, wise about soldiers. A wise waitress who began to scribble her own poems and make abstract forms over chicken wire in the studio and live with a physical ache she felt in the daytime without the pressure of Christy's body.

In May Deborah stood shirtless in Christy's kitchen, in front of the mirror that hung over the sink, looking at her breasts. She studied them in the mirror. Then she looked down to verify that what she saw in the mirror she could see and touch with no intermediary. Her breasts had swollen and the dark part had gotten darker and wider. She looked up the signs of pregnancy in an old *Taber's Medical Dictionary* at the library and knew that she was pregnant. She hadn't wanted to get pregnant. It was a mistake. She had been using a diaphragm because she went through a time when the pills made her sick. But she was still pregnant. She had thought the diaphragm was in. It was one of those cases of time blending together with the late snow and the cycles of their days. She wanted with all of her being to have the baby. She touched her swollen breasts in Christy's kitchen. There had been a woodpecker pecking on the beech tree just past the window glass and the mirror.

Deborah didn't tell Christy. After she saw her breasts, she and Sonia pored through herb books to find a natural agent to make this disappear. They searched for a kind of mushroom and found them and dried them across the top of the piano and made a brew of them and Deborah drank it by the cupful but the baby stayed. They plotted with berries and Deborah ate berries that they thought might work, but the baby was stalwart and they both felt affection for him.

"Have the baby here," Sonia said. They were in the cabin with the McPhail, sitting on the floor cross-legged, barefoot and in ragged jeans and flannels because the woods were still cold. They laughed, imagining this baby and the music.

DEBORAH was a quiet and dogged student. She read voraciously, everything from Christy's political theory to books on candlemaking, which she did then too, and there were candles strung from beams all over Christy's cabin. She had already decided that she couldn't have the baby, but she hadn't figured out how to let him go.

Sonia said Deborah had a long, vague yearning that she brought with her to everything she did and Deborah said she didn't use to be that way before Christy.

She put in the spinach plants and played the old piano. Christy would have been able to hear the notes bounce across the garden on the wind. She got Thompson's piano books and sheet music at the library and picked out songs, like she had on her father's piano.

One day she went up to the old farm they called the Frost Place because Frost had lived there for several winters when he was young and his children and wife were with him. Someone had told Deborah a woman kept it open and walked people through. So she drove into Franconia and up Ridge Road, following the ridge of the foothills of Mount Lafayette, until, on the right, she came to an ordinary farmhouse, small and white with green trim. Beside the driveway was a mailbox on which was painted by hand with fat strokes of black paint, R. Frost, nearly hidden in the lupines and wild roses. Deborah left the car in the driveway, climbed the stairs of the porch with newly-painted — she could smell the paint — green rocking chairs.

A woman was inside. She was a tall, big-boned woman with disheveled blond hair turning white. She was asleep. When Deborah pushed open the front door, which had been unlatched, the woman looked up eagerly. But when she saw it was a visitor and not someone else who had pushed open the door, the eagerness disappeared.

"I'm sorry," Deborah said.

"Come in. I was only dreaming."

Maybe the woman was a docent. Maybe she was a poet. There were people working on the house. From upstairs Deborah heard hammering and the Beatles, "Love is all you need. Love is all you need." The poet was neither friendly nor unfriendly. She said her name was Rhoda and that Frost had written his *Mountain Interval* poems here. That people from Boston thought he'd gone to the dark end of the world, coming to Franconia.

Deborah sat down. Beside her was a small, slanted desk with a sign that explained that this was a replica of the desk Frost had used. The living room was fussy with fringed tablecloths and lampshades.

"You can look around on your own," the poet said.

Deborah nodded, but she didn't leave. The woman asked her, "Where do you live?"

"Bethlehem."

"What do you do there?"

"We dig," she told her. "We're digging a pond. We haul out the rocks in a wheelbarrow. We spend nearly all our time working on the pond."

It was a warm day and she was wearing one of Christy's shirts with the sleeves cut out, leather bands around her wrists. She had a tanned chest, calluses on her hands at the base of every finger, and she ran her other fingertips across these while they talked. The poet rocked and seemed to take all this in through her slit eyes.

Deborah talked about what she and Christy were doing in the garden. Rhoda listened. "What about the peas," she said. "How are you growing them?" Deborah told her about their trellis to the clouds.

She told her they had gotten some new chicks and that after supper they went out and sawed and hammered boards and limbs for a new chicken house design.

"I thought you were Sandy," the poet said. "But that was a while ago. Sandy fell in love with somebody else." Rhoda said, "Tell me some more. Tell me everything about digging the pond."

Rhoda sat with her. She whispered, "Oh, my imagination hurts me." She nodded, Yes, as Deborah talked. Give me one more word, give me more pictures for my mind. Deborah talked a long time to help the poet out of her imagination.

She told Rhoda about the baby. That was the first time Rhoda smiled.

"I don't know what you're going to do about the baby. Just don't let them put on your gravestone, she made a lot of lovers miserable."

"What a funny thing to say," Deborah said as if all the things they had said hadn't been.

"It's hard to love," Rhoda said. "There are all kinds of reasons not to. It's easy to leave."

"You said Sandy fell in love with somebody else."

"She didn't want what I wanted."

Deborah listened.

"Maybe she didn't know what she wanted. I still dream about her." Rhoda shook her head. "Go on, have a look upstairs. Have a look up the hill behind the house. How do we stand ourselves?" Deborah continued to sit with the elderly woman even when she fell back asleep. The Beatles continued to play upstairs where she would have found the bed in which Frost and his wife had slept, or perhaps a replica. She imagined an austere iron frame bed and stiff ironed sheets. And then she remembered something her mother had mentioned once. When her mother was a small child she had gone with her austere father to Vermont and while they were eating at an inn one

Sunday noontime an old man had come in, a stooped man with thick white hair, and the waitress had bent at Helen's table and told her, "Look, it's Robert Frost."

Sitting in Frost's front room, pregnant, slightly queasy, light-headed with morning sickness, Deborah's worlds melded and she became the little girl in the inn, as she had always been overlaid on her mother even when they didn't talk. She got her own experiences mixed up with her mother's experiences. Would she get them mixed up with her child's? This child she couldn't have. She closed her eyes and looked at the man's magnificent white hair. Helen had said he'd had a beaten-up hat in his hand, so Deborah gave him a hat and they talked about ponds and finding the source of water for her and Christy's house. In this way, Frost was a link to her mother to whom she did not talk, but in whose belly she would have been this same unease that she felt in her own.

Deborah was pregnant and the baby's father was a shadow man. One of the books she read on his desk in the night told about one farmer's field in the Soviet Union that was littered with the mines and bones of combatants. Was that Christy's landscape? Christy's cabin was to her the sun shining through the understory of birch leaves, although sometimes now that made her cry.

SHE was having morning sickness and Christy was having a case of disappearing into himself. Sometimes they didn't eat, but one night Deborah was ravenous. She was whistling a fragment of a tune while she worked. She asked Christy if he had any food. "Ahh," he said, "There's some rhubarb somebody canned. And some bread-and-butter pickles."

They both appealed to Deborah. She baked a rhubarb pie, thickly sweetening the rhubarb with honey and raw sugar. By midnight they had both worked up an appetite and ate rhubarb pie with bread-and-butter pickles, sitting on a flat rock in the garden. Christy held her around the waist, not wondering why she wanted such a strange meal. The mountains were under their veil of clouds, they might have been on an island. To this day, Ian craves sour.

Throughout June, Deborah learned more simple songs on the piano in her cabin. She dipped wicks into bright-colored wax and made misshapen, runty candles, something you might do with a child. She and Sonia went away for a few days. They drove to Portsmouth to see a friend of Sonia's who played in a band. They thought about not coming back to the mountains, but they did because Deborah kept bringing up the Milk and Honey they had left short-handed, as well as waking up crying, which was driving Sonia crazy, so they drove back, first stopping in Barrington at Calef's where they always stopped for bread. They lived on bread, two girls in thin cotton hippie skirts and sleeveless tank tops, prone to laughing and intense conversations over cheese crumbling on their chests and both full of dreams. They said, Maybe we'll put on makeup and go to Boston. We could be city girls and ride the T.

6. The Pond

DEBORAH and Sonia came back to the mountains on the Fourth of July. Deborah found Christy in the pond, which looked similar to the way it had looked before she left. He had put a float in it and he lay on the float naked. She watched him for a while. It was very hot and she was sweaty. She thought of the first time they made love in the mountains — on the floor by the fire, and since then they had made love in many ways and he had taken away her embarrassment about being so exposed. He liked how large she was. In the little bed she had in her cabin, she had touched her breasts; she stroked them like they were his penis and brought her tongue to the nipple as if it were the head of his penis and touched herself, missing him and pretending she could have this baby that was making her nipples large and aching.

At the pond, she took off her clothes. The pond wasn't much more than a small flooded gully, and a shallow one, but cooling, and she walked in. She touched Christy's face and he held out his hand and then she straddled him as he had often pulled her up on him to do. Maybe he would see her breasts and understand what was happening. He wanted her. He had always said she was a serious lover and now, as they slid off the float and he took her on him against the soft, muddy bank, she looked at him with eyes unsmiling and serious in sex. She dug her heels into the soft bank where they had seen polliwogs, frogs having taken instantly to their pond. She loved it there so much, and she came down on him slowly and earnestly and when he was near to coming he pulled her up higher so that her knees and thighs were in the soft mud and after a few minutes of sweet, slow rocking she came against him and their emotion became the same as the thick smell of the mud and the birch bark, and she didn't know how to leave him.

CHRISTY talked about the garden. "I'm finally going to get the corn out," he said. He was loading up the rickety wheelbarrow with the flats of the corn they'd started. He looked haggard and Deborah knew he hadn't slept while she was gone and he had spent the time with Emil Tero, over and over. How exhausted he must be. He was going to cut some of the oaks and birches back from the garden, he said. There was a rare elm that he wouldn't disturb. Deborah went through the path that Christy had kept clear, across the same stones laid through the brook, past the homestead and up the path toward the summit of Cleveland Mountain, past the same birch trees standing in three. But it was slightly more grown in today. Summer was thick and luscious. She could still feel Christy's cock in her when she walked here away from him.

She walked deeper into the woods. She walked for a long long time, putting it off. She sat in a tree overlooking a ravine. She wore a bandanna over her hair and a cotton shirt that was yellow print. She had lost weight and she wondered if she could postpone a little longer, but she put her hand on her stomach. In awe. Three women knew. Emil Tero was never going to have a little baby, so maybe that meant Christy couldn't either.

She went back to Christy's garden. She bent to help with the corn.

"I can do it," he said. He touched her face, pulled some of her curls back. They had barely talked at the pond.

"You missed me," she accused him.

He laughed.

"You always miss me. Just remember that, Christy Mahan."

"You and Sonia break loose out there in the world?" But he didn't want to hear too much about the world. He was on his knees, setting the plants in, patting them down. His hands were black with mud and she wouldn't have minded if he touched her with them. She would have liked to feel again his pressure against her bare legs, which were still muddy from the bank of the pond. "Oh yeah, we did," she said. "You wouldn't believe the things we did."

"They took the article," he said.

"I knew they would," she said. "No really," she laughed because she was really happy for him that the scholarly journal would print the research he had been doing. Christy was a scholar. He would publish a little book on landmines. There were no landmines here. What was all this about? They were fine. They were safe.

"I'm having a baby," she said.

He stood up. He looked at her through narrowed eyes the way he looked at students sometimes who concerned him. He should not pass them because they had not actually written any papers, but they vitalized discussions. Deborah took his face in both of her hands, which seemed to them both a very grown-up gesture. She held his face and felt the outline of his bones and the softness of his beard. Her head was slightly angled, her eyes felt glazed the way they were after sex. Then she started back down the path. When she was nearly out of sight he called to her. He said, "Let's go up the mountain. Don't you think we should?"

"That's all right."

"In a while. After I put these in."

Deborah left and pretty soon he would have been able to hear her simple songs from the piano coming across the garden. They were songs he knew from his childhood and he would listen to them as he worked and find them innocent and silly. They would take him back to before he was a man. He would feel an odd content putting the plants in and wonder briefly if it were possible to have more strings of moments like this second, if he were with this woman. She suspected he liked the idea of their life, that he had not slept while she was gone because she wasn't under the nylon poncho cover even while he was up and watching the night.

LATER, Deborah worked in the greenhouse, hanging the tools, cleaning out the debris from construction tools from the pond dredging. Christy came in. He stood with his large hands by his side and watched her. Christy had a very calm, very gentle way in his attempts to maintain contact, even when he was ravaged from not sleeping. But he seemed unable to think of something to say.

"Remember the bar we went to?" Deborah asked him. "Where that guy was playing Cat Stevens? That's where this band was. Sonia's friends. I might go back sometime. Or Boston. If I'm going to be a writer, or something, I think I have to live in the city. I can't just keep living in the woods."

THEY went on a beautiful trail with long cuts of timber across the river for bridges. They climbed over large stepping-stones, past flowers, trefoils and buttercups. They crossed three log bridges together. At the last crossing a sign was posted that read: LAST SURE WATER, and it made Deborah parched.

Christy said, "There's a clearing by the timberline. The view will be good."

It was steep then and the birches gave way to pines. When they got to the clearing, they rested. Deborah was overcome by the cold as their sweat dried like it does when you rest on the trail. They ate nuts and dates, and Christy was at peace and not dreaming and he tried to warm her against his chest. She could feel his hot mouth on her neck and he didn't want to talk anymore. But Deborah couldn't stop shivering, and she knew she was going to have to give up seducing him, now with lips this blue.

She was getting practiced at longing and maybe, whatever Christy had done, she would have continued to yearn. Christy knew what hurt and what, for a few seconds, didn't. The sun set and they still stayed at the timberline, on a table rock, watching what happened to the landscape in declining light and then in the dark.

And it was in the dark they began to walk, single file. Christy found the remains of a joint in his pocket and they smoked it. The moon rose but it was partially blocked by the pine trees and blue spruces and the overcast sky of the mountains.

From the near distance came the distinct sound of a screech owl. It came from high in a white pine, or some other thinly needled pine, on an asymmetrical branch that leaned down on the top of the moon. In the tree below, Deborah could see something she couldn't at first identify. Something like two tiny animals, and as the moon lit them she could see that they were tiny mice, unmoving. Then she could see their string tails but she could not see their heads.

"Look at that." Christy's voice was husky. "I heard that screech owls decapitate animals and hang them like this but I never saw it before."

They listened to the owl for some time.

"What's a mine look like?" Deborah said.

The owl called, one low call.

Christy had his hand on the back of her neck. "Just about

anything. You never knew. Could be a Coke can filled with explosives. They could stuff a 105 shell. You can make anything blow up."

They continued to walk, now with Christy ahead.

He said, "We walked in front of convoys with our minesweepers. Two guys. *Leeeft Riiiight Leeeeft Riiiight.* Looking for disturbed dirt. If you found a place, you were supposed to probe it with your bayonet. We got trigger-happy, though. We'd blow it. Or we'd let the tank shoot on it. They'd truck us in. Truck us out."

"On mined roads?"

"Everything was mined."

He was getting antagonistic. She could hear it in his voice over the roar of the tanks moving slowly behind them, coming closer.

It was very, very still on the mountainside in the dark.

"It's the uncertainty that gets you. Just when you think it's a skill and you've got it down . . ." He rubbed his thumb against his fingers in front of Deborah's face, his eyes narrowed. "And you know what to look out for." She turned her eyes to his large, powerful hands. His eyes narrowed in — disgust, was it?

"What happened?" she said, hardened, and despite the contempt she saw on his face for her not knowing more than she did, for being female and young and a student and for only using her hands on shovels and spoons.

"Was it a big mine in a ditch — command detonated? I read that had happened."

"No."

Christy's face became blank. His blue eyes weren't the story-teller's eyes. "No," he said.

"Tell me."

"Just him and me. One second we're talking, like you, now. The next . . . Two guys walking. I'm walking right here. You're walking right there. Then you explode."

She saw him pull a tolerance for her ineptness on the subject out of nowhere. She felt it in his hand he returned to her neck. A disengagement. Maybe it would have been better if he had begun to hate her.

"No," Deborah said, "I don't explode. Fuck you." She ran ahead of him in the dark. It was foolish to be there in the dark. She walked first and made her way carefully over rocks and then the timber bridges with slight moonlight, watching for the owl, imagining his head revolve, following them as the owl had done on the trail to Christy's garden. Was he interested in their heads? No, owls would not do that to heads.

"Look, I've told you," Christy said.

At the cabin he said, "Go if you want. I won't stop you. This is just a sex thing isn't it. You hang around for the sex."

"Yeah," she said, "I hang around for the sex."

"COME here," Christy said.

She went to him. She was wearing something crinoline and pleated that Valerie had found in her stuff and shaken out, since Deborah needed bigger clothes.

"Take this off." He ran his fingers across her belly and up and down the valley of the pleats. He pulled the dress up over her head.

She sat on the wooden counter Christy had just built in the kitchen. The air was cold and Deborah arranged her hair over her shoulders. She sat with one knee up, laughing at Christy's camera, telling him to Hurry it up for Christ's sake, it's cold, and showing him her teeth and all the pear roundness her belly had. He said from behind the camera, "You are a country in my head."

She said, "I know."

She looked at her husband, the man she had thought of as her husband since they met, who was shooting her. He was wearing jeans and a white shirt like he wore to class. She'd got-

ten him the shirt, an extra large because he was broad shoul-
dered. And he had a kind of love in the turn of his mouth that
Deborah now connected with the explosion of mines on roads.
She was getting bigger and bigger.

He photographed her for seven months. He photographed
her nude standing in front of a mirror and her ass and the hair
down her back were reflected in shadows in the glass and he
developed the pictures himself in the darkroom at the college
and kept them in his desk drawer.

7. Where They Used to Make Love

CHRISTY may have been the only grunt Franconia College ever saw. He was an oddity and really not much of a homesteader. But he worked hard. And he brought a toneless reality to philosophical dialogues on ethics — his stories about fragging and trip mines.

In his and Deborah's cabin at night, he was writing a book about landmines. One mine clearer takes a half hour to clear a square meter of ground.

It was very late summer just becoming September and Christy was at his desk. It was hot and Deborah was on the porch with Ian, letting him nurse even though he was a year and a half and had a mouth full of teeth. Christy was always shoving cups at Ian, Hey sport, which the child emptied down his throat; but he loved to nurse, especially between play — which he did the same rugged way his father worked with a handsaw or a book — and sleepiness, when he came and wrapped his gritty, round arms around Deborah to claim her.

So Deborah hadn't stopped him climbing into her lap, first one frog leg, then the other, where she sat in the green garden chaise lounge with the loose webbing and some rows completely missing. She had a newspaper from Portsmouth in her lap and was on the telephone talking to Sonia, who was living down at the homestead then.

She was wearing only shorts in the heat. Behind her was Mount Agassiz, looking very verdant. In front of her was the garden where Christy fought the woods to keep the space open. It was a constant battle to let in the sun. Christy had a whimsical touch as a homesteader and cut out the shape of a crescent moon and the stars on the outhouse door and also the shape of an egg for the chickens on the chicken house door. He had hung a low orange light bulb in the chicken house when the new meat chicks came and it shone out of the cut-out egg. Sometimes when Deborah and Christy had come home in the night when the mountains were fog bound, the only light around was the bright orange egg on the chicken house door.

It was 1977, almost ten years after the already mythic times when the students first opened a head shop in town and when the police raided the campus they had opened their windows and dropped bags of pot into the snow.

BECAUSE Ian still nursed, Deborah's breasts had stayed large and the nipples pronounced. Ian's black hair was splayed over her arm, which was muscular from doing construction and hauling water. She and Christy had done a lot of the interior work on the cabin, and they had got the idea to plaster the walls. Sitting on the dilapidated chaise lounge, Deborah was conscious of the sleepy weight of Ian's body. Her hair was still up in a knot at the back of her neck, the way she wore it to cook at the restaurant.

"So hold off for tonight," Sonia said on the phone. "I'll hide everything under the porch. Whatever they find I'll say it's Swede's."

Deborah didn't answer. She kept looking at Ian's black hair. She had never seen anything so beautiful.

"What's wrong?" Sonia said.

"Nothing. I won't come."

She pictured Sonia. Sonia almost always wore black. She wore a black jersey all summer and all winter with worn, brown cords. Her hair was reddish blond. She had developed a sweet and lazy and easy smile when she talked about her family that never wanted her to come home. She was Deborah's one real friend.

"You okay?" Sonia said.

"Oh, yeah. I'm going to put Ian to bed. Catch you later, Chicky."

Dennis, the dog, walked up to Ian and Deborah with his too-long choke collar dragging and rattling while he circled them and finally settled, spotted belly up.

Deborah hung up the phone. She tore an ad from the classified section, carefully so that none of the words were torn. Still holding Ian, who was dozing, his head heavy on her shoulder, she folded the newspaper and put it under a stack of books where there were several more newspapers. She looked at the ad again.

Baker, full time, Ceres Café, must like good food
and play well with others. Midnight–6.

She wished she'd read the ad to Sonia and maybe it would have seemed funny. But she hadn't read any of the ads to anyone. She looked over the bookshelves where she kept books of Frost and her own scribbling and realized her journal wasn't there. She'd left it at the homestead that afternoon. She slid the ad into *Mountain Interval* and looked at Christy.

"Cops are coming," she said.

"Coming where?" Christy said.

"A raid. That was Sonia. They got some tip there was going

to be a party at the homestead so nobody's going down there after all."

Christy was soaked with sweat. The material of his shirt stuck to his belly and chest so that Deborah could see the darkness of his chest hair through it. He leaned against the wooden counter, his arms across his chest, his hair in a ponytail.

"A guy in Littleton was selling used pumps," he said. "It's a thrown-together operation but I bought one. He was selling them for two bucks. How could I resist?" He grinned at Deborah that boyish grin, self-effacing and charming and erratic. But when his habit of the grin and the cock of his head died, he kept watching her. Deborah didn't understand what he was seeing, but she knew he didn't like her out of his sight.

"I could have resisted," she said. "I'd have bought a loaf of bread at Calef's." Calef's, which was in Barrington and not in Bethlehem at all. Her mind went to Calef's, and the warm bread they sold. Sometimes her mind wandered to going there for a while, to Barrington, when people talked about the college closing, which they did all the time. The college had closed more than once. But the faculty and students never left. They protested the closing and waited it out. Even the time when the president was fired and the faculty quit, no one really left. It was like a long winter break, a time when no one left either.

"Christy," Deborah said, "would you do something? Go down to the homestead and get my journal. I left it there when I was with Sonia and Val."

He got up and stretched and said, "Did I tell you what I know about plumbing?"

"Plumbing," she said.

"Don't lick your fingers. Water rolls down. Payday's on Thursday." He grinned at her, and then said, "Stay home tonight."

She glanced at him. He was talking and talking. He didn't do that so much. "If you want," she said.

She spread the ripe tomatoes on the counter because tomorrow she would make the winter's tomato sauce. Tomatoes covered the counter like a bright red sea. Christy and Deborah had not been sexual. He had not wanted her to touch him. They had begun going elsewhere.

He climbed the ladder to the loft, the ladder that they had planned to replace with stairs after the baby was born. The stairs lay in parts in the shed outside the back door. Deborah followed him up the ladder.

"I dug in a line down to the pond, from the side of the mountain. Might be there. We'll dig again tomorrow." His eyes were bright and urgent and he was focused on the spring that Deborah knew the pump was for. He stretched out on the bed, his legs sprawled, his kneecap pressed into the ragged jeans that she would have liked to press, to feel the coarse fabric and press her hand down his thigh.

He'd been exploring for a spring nearer the cabin. None of the people who built the cabins built them on springs. They'd all had to pump water from someplace, but Deborah and Christy were still hauling water.

Christy's mind stayed on the pump, considering where to work down the next line from the mountain, tracing the land with his mind looking out for damp moss, a sign of surface water.

Deborah stayed at the foot of the bed, facing the window and rocking Ian.

Christy was good at taking things apart and he did this with excited eyes and then after he had taken them apart, he put them in the garden where they waited for new parts or to ripen. They joked about this. He had scrounged a stainless steel sink. They were using a large, deep, industrial porcelain sink that required leaning far over. It wasn't convenient for dishes, but once they had gotten into it, just fitting, and sudsed each other after a sweltering day nailing shingles over the plywood roof, and rinsed with rainwater. Now both sinks lay in the garden, surrounded by pipes. Maybe none of them was right. It was still August and they used washbasins and plastic jugs on the porch and there seemed to be no danger of running water.

They had managed the bed for Ian at the foot of their own with a crate at the top to keep him from rolling out. Deborah couldn't imagine the cabin with stairs now. If there were stairs it would seem like somebody else's cabin. She had always wanted a window over the kitchen sink and to find a spring nearer the cabin and to have running water. But now everything was fine as it was.

She wondered if now was the turning point, now that the college might close. That this ripe summer would finally crack like the birch that the lightning split. "Just thinking," she said. She laughed and turned away. His eyelashes curled like a boy's, and his jaw was hard. "That we wouldn't recover from running water."

"Right," Christy said. "That's the country's problem. Too much running water."

"Aren't we okay? Can we live without running water? On the edge of running water?"

Helen referred to Deborah as the goatherd. Helen's face was lovely and composed, almost charismatic, so that Deborah had always been lulled into taking her words deep inside her. She offered the word "goatherd," so Deborah was one.

But it was here Deborah was first drawn to hotels. She could have been the hotel on Main Street with faded green letters that read THE ALPINE, gone back to nature, its windows open to summer rain. The hotel had to be a she, Deborah thought, like men call a ship a she, and this she-hotel became sophisticated and fed off the rain and the pine needles and snow. They etched her and she became a treehouse, a tree that was a house. Maybe she could suggest this to Helen in order to confirm her concerns for her.

Christy said, "Let's think about water."

He sat down on the bed and pulled Deborah's hair back from her face. The curls were thick and in the heat he had to peel them from her sweaty cheek. She could smell he'd been drinking but she wasn't brave. She wanted him to tell her to put the baby down. She wanted to curl into his wet shirt and she would be able to feel the cotton and his sweat against her breasts.

She pulled her shorts a little way down. A wide indent showed across her stomach, left by the waistband of her cutoffs. His eyes fixed on it and she thought, Now. He said, "You smell like the night and marijuana."

"Yes."

He touched his hand to the indent on her stomach. She shut her eyes. She lay back against the wall on the feather bed they were thinking of ditching. Ian slept. Deborah let him sink into the feather bed beside her. Christy's hand stopped but he didn't take it away. She would have done anything to feel the weight of him on her. He said he thought he'd be going for a walk. It was a physical pain. Her craving for his weight.

"Christy," she finally said, "if I stay here, would you get my diary?"

"Where is your diary? What time is it?"

"Nine. Ten. I don't know. Sonia said they all cut out, and they took everything, but I remember I left my diary."

"Why'd you leave it there?" he said, but he wasn't listening. His hand moved to her pubic bone.

He told her they had packed water up Nui Ba Den. They had packed it in canteens with camouflage fabric covering. In Bethlehem they carried water in five-gallon plastic jugs, their fingers hooked through the rings, and water spilled over and onto their jeans. Deborah imagined being at the sink washing zucchini and beans from the garden and water trickling over the woven bracelet she always wore on her left wrist. Christy would be on the mountain, tracing the mines he had laid, mentally disarming them. He would come home exhausted.

At twenty-three, Deborah was more serious than she wanted to be. When she heard Michael's music in the night from the new cabin he was building, it seemed more solid than her life. She did too much pot or none at all and, instead, drank an echinacea infusion and fasted, sometimes for twenty-four hours, but now she was coming out of a forty-eight hour fast. She felt paper-frail and at the same time supersensitive. Christy's hand on her pubic bone almost made her come.

"You're beautiful," he said, his smile gone.

She shook her head. She was feral. She was a hotel. She imagined her hair gone in patches like The Alpine's paint. But she was moved that he had called her beautiful. She believed what Christy said, as well. She went to other men for something else.

> Plumber's Assistant. Long hours, hard work. No
> Benefits. Pay not bad for the right man.

She had cut out mostly outdoor Help Wanteds and pasted them in her journal. They were all from somewhere around the seacoast, where she might go back to the university. Outdoor places and food places. *Donut Maker*, or *Hard Worker To Build Lobster Traps*.

Christy poured wine into one of the jam jars they used to drink from. He poured Deborah one, too, but she could barely tolerate the smell of the wine. It made her queasy, not having eaten in so long. She left it on the crate beside the bed and lay, still coiled and breathing hard and chilled even in the heat without Christy's weight.

"I was looking through *The Stranger,*" he said. He took a drink of the wine. Deborah felt his jeans against the fleshy part of her arm. He touched her hair once on her forehead. She slid down the wall.

"Now you're gonna say everything's always existential," she said.

He said, "Don't you think so?"

"I left it by mistake," Deborah said. "I don't want cops reading my diary."

Ian woke up. He was confused and started to cry. Christy held him then in the dark until Ian's eyes couldn't stay open.

"Why won't you touch me?" Deborah whispered this and if he didn't answer she could think he didn't hear.

He didn't answer.

"No." She moved to him and pressed her hand down his thigh and against his cock. She leaned down and pressed her face into him. Very slowly she unzipped his jeans. He stood up but he didn't leave. He was very hard and she took his hardness into her mouth. "What did I do? Christy, please." He was wet with her tears.

"Deborah, stop. Stop."

"No."

He pulled her away. "I'm going to go."

"You stop!"

They didn't fight. This was extreme for them.

And then he wasn't with her anymore and she wasn't with him. She stopped.

She got up from the bed and stood by the open window, trying to know this as solitude and to savor it. She listened to the wind chimes Ian and she had tied together with pebbles and shards of colored glass that Christy had found at the fire ruins of a hotel.

"You could get it, Christy," Deborah said after a while. "If they read it, they'll know everything. They want to bust everybody."

Christy took a drink of the wine and knelt beside her.

"What are you looking for?" she said. "If you'd just get it." She felt dizzy.

"No problem."

"Everything will be okay," she said.

"I'll go," he said. "I just want to see about the stove. Something's keeping the front burner from lighting up."

"It's okay, we'll use the back burner."

"I'll take a look."

She pictured the stove in the garden and laughed, or cried, both at once, in the same contractions of muscles in her throat.

"Why don't you eat something," he said.

"I know, I need to eat." She pulled her shorts up all the way and put on an olive drab T-shirt of Christy's from the army that she had found in the homestead and had taken to wearing.

Christy rappelled down the ladder. She could hear him pour water from the jug. The rattle of pills. His footsteps taking the three wooden steps to the outhouse, the door bang. She heard Ian's shudder-breath in his sleep, like he had a number of cares; possibly one was the sink in the middle of the garden. The outhouse door banged again and Christy set off down the trail, soundless. He'd be point man and soon he'd come upon the Buddha that Deborah had set on a flat rock along the trail.

Christy could have walked the trail blind and often did. He had drunk what he usually drank in a night. She had heard him take some downers, some Seconal, so when he got back he wouldn't stay awake staring at the cedar boards of the roof.

Dennis would have followed Christy squarely in his squat, composed way. They would both place their feet carefully. It was their jungle. They stalked it for mines. Every time they walked it they were prepared for new mines that someone had imbedded in the decaying New England soil.

8. Water for House, Garden, and a Pond

DEBORAH sat on the porch in the dark in the heat, thinking of mines. She had come to know them indirectly, first from bits of stories Christy had told her at the Hammer in the city. They had proceeded from that day to use each other in their attempt to make sense of a mine designed to bounce waist high on a man, explode, and lay bare the man's intestines, his testicles, his fist-sized kidneys, and pour his blood in the dry dirt. All she knew at first was that Emil Tero had been twenty, the same age she had been that day.

Christy would be walking across a stone wall, between the stands of birches, through the pine needles, beating down branches that threatened to take back the passage. At one spot his boot slipped on wetness on a sharp rock.

The homestead was a house that a woman named Jenny had bought, as well as the land all around. She started a commune and a family grew at her place, students and other people who came for the college, but were seduced by raising goats and growing corn or the drugs, and maybe got through one semester but stayed on in the woods. Some of them built their own places deeper in the woods and up the mountainsides, like Christy. Jenny wasn't there anymore, but some of the original people were there and they kept the electric in Jenny's name.

Christy would be almost at the door of the homestead, which was overgrown with trees and shrubs. The window at the back bedroom was cracked and the bottom corner of the ledge was missing. The wood floor in the entryway was soft under his boots. His long hair clashed with the floral wallpaper on the bedroom walls. The cops who were reported to have planned the raid were sick of looking at all the longhairs the college had brought to this town. Sick of drugs. Sick of the kids from the suburbs.

DEBORAH got up from the chaise lounge, checked her son in his bed, and went to the bottle of pills that she had heard Christy open.

CHRISTY stomped in with Dennis, a poor display of a mine-tracking dog, squat like a hound, devoted to women, looking for Sonia who would come in with her sweet and lethargic smile. But he and Dennis had found Emile Hudon — another Emile, another New Hampshire kid — before they ever saw Sonia. Emile was leaning up against the old refrigerator in the entryway. He'd turned his flashlight on Christy and slinking Dennis. "You folks fuckin' hid it good," Emile said. He was a town cop. A young kid, French Canadian, the good-looking one, Sonia and Deborah and the other women at the Milk and Honey said.

Christy shrugged. He walked over to the shelf where there was a five-pound tin of coffee, a can of diesel oil, the business section of the *New York Times,* for the women who were talking about getting small business loans. Christy had seen them clustered around a table, making lists, divvying tasks.

Emile was angry. There should have been tons of stuff. Christy's eyes roamed the shelves looking for Deborah's diary. "Late for a walk," Emile said.

"My wife gets these cravings," Christy said.

Emile's eyes followed Christy's search.

"Um," Christy said, stopping on the black and white composition book he knew she wrote in, beside a gallon jar of peanut butter from the co-op. The notebook was partially covered with a marbled-paper cover that Deborah had made in the college studio with a master teacher. Christy took it down, taking the peanut butter, as well.

There was something impenetrable about Christy to Emile. It was partly the powerfulness of his hands and his arms and his remoteness, together with something deferential when he talked, and then also the idea of a man, even a hippie, seeking to assuage his wife's craving — and also because he knew Christy had a wife who loved him. Emile knew Deborah very well. He went into the Milk and Honey often and one time they had left together.

Emile noticed the book. He didn't read many books and that separated him from the hippies, who were kids from the suburbs, places he had never really seen. He grew up knowing building, skills Christy was not picking up in any progressive way, but was learning slowly by trial and error from library books and hanging around at work sites.

DEBORAH knew all this about Christy and Emile. The story became common knowledge. When they met up at the homestead, she had shaken the remaining pills into her palm. She took a few and pushed the rest into her pocket. She pulled on a blue shirt over her T-shirt and then went to sit again on the porch. She was exhausted but was also attracted to the Buddha in the woods.

*   *   *

CHRISTY had been fascinated by Deborah's eyes when he first met her. They had seemed maternal and sexual, he said, and when she said that was a line, he said she just didn't know. He described the dress she had worn when they met. He said when the sun shone through it, he could see through the thin fabric. When he was away from her, which he often was even when she was there, he held that in his mind as he worked. Christy Mahan talked about China which was opening to the West. Why would China do that? he said. In a war of all wars? When they slept together he had cried. His body was dense and knotted with bone and muscle and words not said.

THAT night when Christy and Emile Hudon met in the homestead, the old Forest Hills Hotel building was getting ready to open for the last time, as a hotel or a college or anything it might have been to the next generation holding up the times of their lives to the light. There had been rumors the college wouldn't make it since the day it first opened, bearing the weight of millions of dollars worth of loans, and the first question that would serve as the core curriculum was posed, and the first girl decided she wouldn't set foot outside of the college building from the first snowfall in October to the last one in May.

Christy held Deborah's journal in his broad hand. With the other hand he took a pack of Winstons out of his pocket. He offered a cigarette to Emile whom he didn't treat like the rest of the cops, as Emile didn't treat him like the rest of the hippies. Emile took it and they sat on a stack of abandoned tires in the corner of the porch. Christy lit their cigarettes with a kitchen match from a box on the shelf behind the refrigerator. The porch was a darkly shaded room even in full sun, boarded up on three sides and turned into a junk shed. Christy vaguely wondered where Sonia was hiding out. She was a funny girl.

Sometimes she hung out with everybody, smoking, walking her languorous walk, her easy smile electric in the room. Sometimes she shut down and at those times it was only Deborah she talked to, and sometimes they didn't talk, just worked the garden together.

"Emile, how come you're a cop?" Christy was getting drowsy. He'd taken the Seconal too early, not thinking much, a few, only trying to dull his head, he'd take ten minutes, just a ten-minute break from his racing head, from turning the New England woods now dotted with Indian pipes into minefields.

"Why do you put up with this shit? People calling you dick-head." He looked at Emile's chiseled cheekbones and the brown eyes the women talked about.

DEBORAH was getting very sleepy but she wanted to talk to Christy before she gave in to it. She checked Ian again. He slept on his belly with his knees pulled up and his haunches in the air. She set out down the path toward the Buddha statue. She was weak from not eating and sleep was filling in her arms and legs as if they were hollow.

EMILE shrugged. "Didn't have a choice. My uncle was a cop. He got killed on duty and from that day I knew I was one."

It was Emile who found the acid. It was in a baby food jar, a couple of tabs of purple Owsley, pills smaller than an aspirin there along with a hash pipe, somebody's stash. Emile found it under the floorboard of the porch with his flashlight. He tossed the jar over to Christy, saying What the fuck. It would have to have been antique acid, Christy had said. Maybe acid that went back to Jenny's day. Emile and Christy talked for a while longer. Christy put the jar beside Deborah's notebook. Soon Emile left. After that, Christy went to see if Sonia was in her room to show her his lucky find.

She was in her bed. Maybe she was already stoned when

Christy showed her the acid. She came out and they sat on the tires, looking at the little purple pills. "What are we going to do with them?" Sonia said.

"I don't know. I guess we don't have any choice." They split the pills between them.

Now it's Bethlehem lore, the antique acid Emile found under the porch and left with Christy. Things happen. It was good acid. Soon Sonia and Christy were someplace else in time and space. Later the incident made Deborah imagine them riding time and, in time, their bodies rode each other. When she got there, she couldn't find Christy. She didn't know if Sonia had even hung around. She went through the kitchen calling. She saw them in Sonia's room on the mattress that was on the floor by the window and the wall with the Indian print wall hanging. On the windowsill were sticks of incense in the small brass candleholders she and Sonia found at the flea market. On the mattress Christy held Sonia in his arms. He actually covered most of her. His shirt covered part of him and her arm, which was thin, not muscled like Deborah's. His hand was on her hair, which was straight and smooth and pale, not curly and coarse like Deborah's. Maybe they were sleeping. Maybe they were in slow motion in time. Deborah turned around. She was only in the wrong place. She felt sick to her stomach and a noise — not a scream, more of a steady electrical hum — came out of her throat, as if a noise could hide her husband's white shirt barely covering Sonia's pale, blond bush.

The Seconal had filled her legs so that she had a hard time walking home. Dennis was with her. She was aware of Dennis's brown-spotted body and of dampness on her cheek and above the slender birches and a warm breeze that brought with it the smell of newly cut pines from down the road and something in her began to let go.

At home she fell asleep on the couch with Ian, but in the dawn she woke up. Ian and Deborah were alone. She didn't want to be awake. Ian was still sleeping. She knew he would sleep for a while and in a while Christy would come back, but she didn't want to be awake now or when Christy came back. She found the other Seconals she had shoved in her pocket and she took them.

Much later she was aware that there had been or was — she wasn't sure — a lot of barking and pounding but she couldn't get up to see what the matter was because a paralysis had penetrated through her muscles.

She was aware of Christy's voice. You don't know who you're talking to, Christy whispered.

You're talking to me. You don't know who you're talking to, he kept saying softly, barely audibly.

He pressed on her ribs through his own T-shirt that she wore. She thought he would crack her ribs and she thought she could accept that too. It's me, he said. You don't know who you are talking to. Don't do this. Deborah. Don't do this.

He pressed in a steady rhythm on her. His mouth came over her mouth. She pulled away from his grip and she smelled damp moss on him and pictured the moss growing on Sonia's floor.

"You got her going." That was Emile's voice. "You bastard. You *bastard*," Emile said. "Why do you keep that stuff." Deborah was breathing from high in her chest, short, shallow breaths. But Christy didn't stop. He wrapped her chest and hips into his arms. He continued to breathe into her, now in shallow spasms.

"She's breathing, man," Emile said. "Maybe if you let her save your life like that, she wouldn't go whoring in the night."

Christy was gone. There was a scrambling on the wood floor. Deborah rolled over and vomited a thin stream. Christy was back and lay down beside her. He pressed the green cotton of her T-shirt over and over with the heel of his hand across her ribs. He stroked her face the way he couldn't do in their bed.

Deborah rolled on her stomach. Her head fell across his knees and she felt his coarse jeans on her cheek. She felt less nauseous. Now she floated, face down, her hair across her husband's body. He held her hard and rubbed her back the way he had when she was in labor and he couldn't go with her and hold that pain. She had back labor and was in a lot of pain, though afterward she only remembered that Christy had rubbed her back and he and Sonia and Valerie and Michael ate M & Ms by the handful while they waited for that baby.

Emile in the meantime was struggling to get up. Deborah thought Christy hit him and he had staggered back into the kitchen and they were all floating. Emile said, "You goddamn hippies," and he came and sat by Christy and Deborah as if to plot about the essentialness of living, made slightly more real by the image of a trickle of water that was seeping from under the Buddha's foot, something Christy kept talking and talking about in Deborah's ear, maybe thinking it would help them.

9. Winter at Half Past Three

DEBORAH slept all the next day. She had nightmares and she remembered Christy being there and saying it was just the drugs talking, trying to get out of her blood, but the dreams were terribly real. Ian screamed for her and she couldn't find him. In the dream she ran from the garden to the porch to the greenhouse under the clear tarp, through the woods to the Buddha on the rocks. It's okay, he crashed with Dennis in the beans. Christy talking. In Deborah's dream she turned and ran into the beans that were late and past their prime and she woke up, her chest aching from dry tears and the relief of Ian in the beans. Christy, beside her, looked at her, his eyes narrowed in concern, his lips taut and at an angle, and he leaned into her with also a glint of satisfaction because he knew he'd brought her out. Like when he looked at the shape of her body where the quilt was over her pubic bone, he knew he controlled her there. For a second they both understood each other completely.

He didn't say anything except that he was going out then,

and Deborah didn't say anything to him. She watched him leave, with his index fingers curved through the handle of a water jug. She let herself cry wet, exhausted tears that came with the relief that Ian wasn't dead. Oh, damn, but she had felt the loss of him in all the corners of her body. What a cruel dream. She was a cruel woman to dream such pain.

At the Buddha, Christy found a wedge-shaped rock below the flat rock that was damp. He followed the rocks down and found many that were cut sharply and a trickle of a stream slightly leaking through the cracks of the rocks. He put his hand in the wetness.

That night Christy wanted to talk about the Buddha. Ian was asleep. Deborah lay on the couch against a pillow, her eyes following Christy as he cooked. Her hair was down and it was wet with sweat around her face. He said he remembered a Buddha in the shrine near Nui Ba Den. He said the women took him rice and that the Buddha had bowls of rice that the monks came to eat.

"Tell me about the girls," Deborah said.

He looked at her, and she knew he was trying to understand what she wanted.

"Did you fuck them?"

He said now he was sure he'd found a spring beside where they'd put the Buddha. He was going to go back tomorrow and dig again and see if it was still there.

"Yeah," Deborah said, "because springs are fickle. Some rock will shift and it will disappear. Tell me about the girls."

"They were quick," he said. "And cheap."

She lit a joint and tears streamed down her cheeks. "Go on." She held his eyes in a way that said, You will never touch me, even while to watch him was sweet. She also thought he taught history because he was in pain, and he was trying to lose the pain in something bigger, but she didn't think that was working. "Tell me."

His hands shook and he put down the knife he was using. "Tell me," she said again. He came and sat down on the chair beside her. He spoke softly but his hands shook even in his teaching pose and his eyes were a blue too bright. "They came out to us at a café where they sold warm bottles of coke." He spoke methodically, an old story he had already heard. "I took one behind the shack. You could smell fish and *nuoc cham*. I couldn't stop even when she cried. The older girls taught her a lot of tricks."

"So you fucked a virgin?" Deborah said. "But it was the older girls' fault."

He looked at her for the first time.

"I don't know, Deborah."

"Tell me."

" I remember the nuns always said, 'Leave room for the Holy Spirit,' to the boys at the school dances."

"So you didn't sleep with them."

"No."

"But you raped that girl." Her eyes gleamed.

Christy left. She felt a sickly satisfaction. He was only a man. She also became the girl. It was her, Deborah, that he followed behind the shack and she would learn the tricks and he would not be able to stop. They would do it against a tree. She would be anonymous and he would thrust into her. They wouldn't be able to stand and they would fall down and he would tell her everything he had never been able to tell her with his thrusts. Her imagination was without limits.

THE rumor started spreading that the Milk and Honey would close. The place wasn't making it. They gave away too many meals to kids who looked hungry. Sonia and Deborah both worked breakfast and lunch on the day the rumor was around. Deborah's fingers were yellow and smelled like saffron and other spices because she'd been filling the jars from the plastic bags of spices. Sonia and Deborah had some tea after they got off and they hung around outside, taking in the Milk and Honey and, across the street, the antique shop. Sonia was wearing black as usual. Deborah was wearing a long, straight dress she'd found at the flea market. She had taken the sleeves out, so she felt the smallest breeze across her chest. They sat on the curb. Sonia was pulling her hair up off her neck and Deborah took the comb out of her hand and secured her hair but for some that dangled around her face. Sonia smelled like ginger. She'd spent the morning making ginger cake and they had served ginger cake with cream. They looked at the row of Buddhas on the porch of the antique shop. They sat among the driftwood and glass bottles and watering cans and dinner plates from the old hotels, whose names were printed on the rim of the plates, the Top House, Maplewood, the Forest Hills. The Forest Hills plates were decorated with sprigs of pine boughs and their cones. The Buddhas sat cross-legged, their eyes shut, their hands in repose, like the one Deborah had bought for Christy. She had gone in and bartered with Mackie, so many chicks for a stone Buddha. They had settled on two dozen.

The next day she had enticed Christy down the trail and there was the Buddha on the rock. It had made Christy shiver. "It's that rock you like," Deborah had said. "You always said this spot needed something to celebrate it." And he hadn't answered, because she'd done that for him and he remembered how she'd walked him there, light-footed in Keds, and he had liked that lightness, but the Buddha made him shiver.

"I don't know what happened," Sonia said.

They were smoking a Marlboro.

"It happens all the time," Deborah said, but they both knew Sonia was different. Deborah had been fascinated with her body that day at work. What did her body have that Deborah's lacked? They had seen each other's bodies plenty of times. Sonia had been with her in the cabin when she was in labor.

They swam naked in the pond together, all of them had. They worked in the garden naked. They took rain showers. Sonia was slight. Deborah was taller, large-boned, more slow-paced, and her breasts had caused her mother to buy her boy clothes and a boy haircut so that she had been taught to be ashamed of the femaleness. It was Christy who'd liked her body and wanted to photograph it. But now she was aware of Sonia's narrow ankles and wristbones. Had he held her heart-shaped face in his hands?

"If he didn't love you so much," Sonia said.

"What's love?" Deborah said.

They sat on the curb for some time. They smoked another Marlboro.

"I can't imagine this place without the restaurant," Sonia said. It was late afternoon. They looked back behind them. The benches in the window of the Milk and Honey were empty.

"Maybe it was never meant to be here forever."

Deborah studied her then very closely. She studied her brown eyes. She imagined touching her, as if Christy and Deborah were one and if Christy had, then Deborah had. She looked at Sonia's hands. They were narrow. How could he do that? Had she touched him tenderly? Had it been lost in a trip and they were just both lost? Had she come? Some more of Sonia's hair spilled over her cheek.

"It was nothing. It was the acid." Sonia shook her head and laughed and her pale red hair swung around over her face with the pale freckles.

Deborah shut her eyes to the sun. She breathed in the warm, dusty air.

"I'm pregnant," Sonia said. "I know it's Swede's. I was already pregnant."

Sonia's eyes were still crinkled from laughing and Deborah saw the crinkles disappearing.

"Jesus, Sonia."

"I want to get out of the homestead. Tell me if you hear of a place."

"Swede's building that place with Michael."

She shook her head. "I don't want to be with him."

Deborah reached down and found her car key in the big pocket of her skirt, shaking her head at Sonia. For just a second, Sonia buried her face in Deborah's neck and tangled hair.

Deborah took the cigarette from between Sonia's ginger-stained fingers and ground it into the dirt. "You have to quit this shit if you're pregnant." They both knew she was having the baby and that everybody's life was about to change.

WHEN Deborah got up the next morning, she cut her hair. It had been down her back in thick strands. It was coarse and wiry curly. She cut it in the bathroom — the room Christy had built as a bathroom. Inside was a high plant table and on that a mirror swinging between the legs of its wooden base. She stood in front of it in Christy's white shirt — she had always been incorrigible about borrowing his clothes. There wasn't a door on the little room, so she had strung beads and they had laughed because Christy said it was like a Saigon tearoom.

Ian was sitting in the wooden bowl she used for chopping cabbage. He curled his pudgy legs in and swung the bowl side to side on the cabin floor, making a loud, wood-grinding sound. Christy was at his desk in front of the window, surrounded by books.

Deborah lifted the scissors and began to cut. She thought of the job as the night-shift baker. That made her think of the book she read over and over to Ian. The little boy who worked at night with the bakers — he fell down down down through the milk into the night kitchen. She cut her hair while Christy read. She cut her hair so that little shoots left from the long strands stuck out behind her ears.

Christy looked up and saw her watching him.

She looked so different that he seemed not to connect her with his wife. He was a boy. She could see he was afraid. So many rumors of things ending. She didn't help him. She stepped into a skirt and buttoned it over the white shirt. It came to her ankles and swallowed her. Since she had stopped eating, her hips had gone away, though her breasts hadn't. She put on a pair of thin Keds and tied the laces. He stared at her.

"Oh, forget it," she said. She loved wearing the Keds. She was a doe instead of a hotel. "Oh, forget it," She said again. He was a boy. She wished he would say something. She smoothed the hair down on his head.

"Plumber?" was all he said.

"Plumber's assistant," she said.

So he had looked at the black and white composition book where she had copies of R. Frost's poems and phone numbers for Portsmouth jobs, pages of Portsmouth jobs. Then with a large sigh, "Oh, shit."

It felt like she was driving steadily to the edge of a cliff and, breathless, she stopped. Ian and Dennis were in the cupboard making a din among the potatoes.

That's when she got the idea to work like dogs on the spring. They'd quit this melancholy. She would be a plumber in Bethlehem.

"Oh, forget all that," she said. "Come on." They all went together to the Buddha.

They went the next day and the next and every day the leak was still there. They dug in the black dirt. Deborah loved the smell of it. They found the opening to a spring. It seemed to go deep into the earth. By the third day, with a pump and a medley of pipes and hoses and joints and clamps, they brought water as far as the garden. It was an enormous victory.

That night after Ian was asleep, Deborah went to Michael's where he was just beginning to stay in his new, raw cabin. She didn't stay so long because Swede came back. There was room to stay. They had built a three-story cabin with lofts on the second as well as the third floors, though at that time the lofts were only roughed out and hazardous for sleeping. Deborah walked home through the woods at midnight. The moon was a sagging balloon and veiled in clouds.

At home, she climbed the ladder to the loft.

She unbuttoned her blue work shirt. She stepped out of her cutoffs and pants and slid the shirt off. She left them in a pile, feeling too tired even to put the clothes on the stool by the chest. It seemed such a long walk home and her thighs ached and her calves ached. She came into bed. She lay down beside Christy who had not moved, had not shifted in any way. She suspected he was awake, but he did not talk to her. When she was in this bed, she gave in to her exhaustion. Her muscles gave way. If she'd been standing, she would have sagged like the moon and would have had to wait for Christy to help her stand and come into the bed.

She shut her eyes and relaxed into the hollow of the feather bed. She leaned slightly toward Christy. She fell asleep but then woke to the small change in pressure on the bed. The feather mattress was on a wooden frame and did not squeal. She didn't hear a noise, it was only a sense of space which felt like abandonment that woke her. Christy had gotten up.

She ached for this bed and she ached for him to reach over and take her hand and put it on his chest so she could feel his heart beat. She shut her eyes to keep herself imagining. She listened to him move around the room. She imagined his troubled mouth, the way it did not curve. When he stopped moving she opened her eyes to see where he had gone. Had he gone? He stood by the door. He was bent like an old man in grief. She gripped the quilt in her fist, struck by his pose. He had picked up her clothes. He held her shirt and her underwear. His shoulders shook, such an ungainly, tall, and old man, thirty-one years old, his head buried in his wife's clothes that smelled like sex.

He went downstairs as he often did in the night. She switched on the light. She pulled a T-shirt out of the chest and put it on. She lay surrounded by books. She wouldn't give in to this. She had resolved to use this solitude. The light from the lamp made a yellow circle around her. She picked up a navy blue bound book the size of a prayer book. George Eliot.

"Whore!" Christy roared coming back up the ladder. He stood just outside the door as if it were barred and would require shooting in. Deborah meant to lay the book by the bed and ignore him. He would have been drinking before she got home. There had been the smell of wine. That was his smell.

"Whore!" he said again.

"Go downstairs," she said. "Go back to your desk or wherever you go."

He forced his way through the wide open space in the dark between them. He threw the lamp and its yellow glow against the pine wall boards.

"You're going to do that?" she said. "Why don't you hit me. Come on. Come on, why don't you hit me. It would give me some relief. Come on." She took his fist with both of her hands and beat and beat and beat it into her stomach. "Come on."

He got on top of her and held her arms above her head. "Please," she said. "Give me some relief." He held her wrists with one hand and unzipped his jeans. She took him. She saw what she had done. "Come on," she said softly, "I am a whore." He fucked her and she was wet from sex and the tears that made her mouth salty and made his hand slick pressing up and down on her cheekbone and jawbone as he thrust.

The sheets were wet. Christy had taken out the black and red wool blanket and the nylon poncho liner they had slept under the first winter. Christy was sweating. His body put off a lot of heat and his shoulders and chest were wet with sweat. They lay gasping on the wet sheets.

"I dreamt you were dead," he said. "You were pregnant and you hemorrhaged."

They were still sweating. Christy's lips, which were playful when he was a storyteller with students, were straight and stiff.

Deborah didn't say anything. She hadn't caught her breath. She could say, Getting pregnant is not the same as dying. Getting pregnant is getting pregnant and people bring us little shirts and sleepers and people are happy. She had said this at other times and did not bother now.

"Are you pregnant?"

"How could I be pregnant?"

"Christ, how could you not be pregnant."

She sank into the feather bed.

"What does that mean, Christy?"

She turned to him. His back was to her and she ran her nail down his sweaty spine. She pressed his scalp and his jaw through his beard and he stayed and he held her.

CHRISTY bought a bigger pump. One morning when Deborah was coming back from the outhouse, bleary eyed, her arms crossed against the chill of the new season in only a sweatshirt, she paused in the doorway, watching a waterfall come out of a faucet in the sink. The faucet was porcelain and curved like a swan's neck and anachronistic, a touch of the Maplewood Hotel or the Profile House in their hippie cabin.

"You've become the scrounge artist," was all she said to Christy.

That day she planted more daffodil bulbs, all around the chicken house and around the plastic-roofed greenhouse and below where Christy was going to put in a picture window facing the garden.

In January, a few days before the new term was going to begin, when Christy was getting ready to teach his classes, he came home and told Deborah the trustees had closed the college. They had just decided, and they would not even open for a final winter semester to finish the year.

Deborah was washing potatoes and her hands were red from the cold water. "What are we going to do?" she said.

Christy shrugged as if that didn't concern him. He went and sat at his desk. It occurred to her he had everything he wanted in the cabin on the mountain in the little town with the head shop.

He cracked jokes about the college. He predicted another renaissance.

But the college really did close, never to reopen — like the Forest Hills Hotel had. In the days of the college, elderly couples who had honeymooned at the Forest Hills Hotel in the 1920s came back to revisit their honeymoon and found hippies grazing on the lawns. Years later, students would come back to see their old college and find it not only closed but razed. But it didn't disappear. It was only having a metamorphosis. As the end of one thing becomes part of the next; not that that premonition did any good in a cabin in the woods where the sun set at half past three, before the suppertime clatter can begin in the kitchen and all that's left for a family is to sit in different corners of the house and watch for the moon.

Deborah said to Christy, "I'm building a new cabin. Up the road. Sonia and me. It'll be a women's cabin."

Sonia didn't actually know this. Deborah had just found it out herself standing in the kitchen with the potatoes. Christy took her hand and tried to draw her away from the sink. Her hands ached from the cold running water. "Come on," he said. He dried her hands on his shirt. "Come on." He wanted to go upstairs and finally she went. They lay on the bed. He held her head to his chest and his broad hand tightened on her hair. He talked about the roof. He said he was going to scrounge some of the asphalt shingles they were tearing off a place in town.

"Let's go back to when you asked, 'What are we going to do now?'"

But she couldn't. Now he held all of her body tight to him. She said, "Think about what you would do if you had me again," and in the dusk they made love.

10. The Women's Cabin

THEY did it with hammers and crowbars and muscle.

In the morning Deborah stomped down the snow in Christy's great big military boots while she was poking around the shed off the back of the homestead. Then she got a crowbar to see what it would take to pry free the two-by-four that connected the shed to the back doorsill. The screech the nail made coming away from the half rotted and frozen wood was horrific.

"Swede!" That would be Sonia, screaming from the other side of the window, which was not three feet from the opening to the shed. "I'm *sleep*ing. Leave me *alone*."

"I don't give a rat's *tail* what you're doing. Get out here, girl, if you want a place to live."

The shape of Sonia's face appeared in the window. Her breath began to make the slightest hole in the frost and then Deborah saw her round mouth, then the freckles on her top lip.

"Do you know the place by the three white birches,"

Deborah shouted in to her. "We're hauling this shed up there."

Sonia shuffled out, her parka over her long underwear, in oversized boots that came to her knees, from the stash of communal boots of various sizes and makes that had accumulated in the entryway. "Why're we doing that?" She was drawn, her eyes were pink from no sleep. She was thin, though she had begun to show.

"For a cabin."

"We are?" Sonia said, yawning, not focusing. Deborah was a dream. She slouched tiredly, her hands by her sides, one hand coming round Ian who squealed in delight. He thought they were dancing and jumped up and down hard on the snow.

The sun had just gone behind a cloud. They could smell the pine needles from the Jack pine. It was so cold the small hairs on Sonia's ears took on the white of freeze. Deborah continued with the crowbar. Ian was bundled in two sweaters and leggings and a snowsuit. Sonia smiled her beautiful if tired smile at him and they waved their arms and swayed like the Jack pine.

"The trail's under two feet of snow," Sonia said.

"We'll plow," Deborah said. She was euphoric. She had a plan and continued to pry away with the crowbar. "Did you know that in Cu Chi the Vietcong had tunnels right underneath the base camp?"

Sonia sat down slowly, cross-legged on a tree limb in the snow, and her hair fell over her face. She pulled her shirt over her boots and her knees to her chest. "No, what did they do in the tunnels?"

"They had hospitals, they had stockpiles of rice, women had babies in the tunnels."

The shed came away. Deborah was sweating in her long underwear. As the shed pulled away, four-inch nails exposed themselves. She grabbed Ian away and he cried out in frustration because he only wanted to dance. There had been a rotted step into the shed and it too came apart. Under the step they saw a box. It was red and when Deborah picked it up she saw it was a red tin like the one she kept Christmas cookies in. This was her tin, only now it was badly rusted. Something heavy was inside and they all leaned over it while she opened it. Inside was Christy's Spec 4 insignia, the ones he wore on the tabs of the collar of the fatigue shirt that showed, with the shirttails tucked in, how skinny he had been. Deborah had seen a snapshot, Christy in front of some headquarters building in Cu Chi, RVN. Also in the tin was an object wrapped in fabric, a fabric that she had cut up in squares to make a patchwork quilt.

She unwrapped it and held the object in her hand. "Jesus Christ," Sonia whispered. It was cold, round metal and solid and heavy in her palm. "Jesus Christ," she said again, "Is it ticking?" She had slowly risen from the snow.

"What is it?" Deborah said, although she knew.

"Isn't it a grenade?"

She raised her arm like Sonia and Ian had raised theirs, dancing, and threw the grenade deep into the woods, south of the outhouse and beyond. She and Sonia waited and listened, which made Ian very still. His red suit matched the red tin, its lid beside his small boot in the snow.

The stillness was huge and took on the dimensions of an explosion. It was like the day Deborah knew Christy had read her Help Wanteds and then they didn't say anything, only went back to the woods to dig for the spring.

"It wasn't real," she said. "He keeps things. He keeps Vietnam."

They both started laughing because their hearts had stopped and now Deborah sounded like she was jealous of the grenade, that Christy had kept it, that he had taken the time to wrap it and stow it.

She could imagine it in his big hands. She could feel his lean body. She could feel his hard thighs and she ached. She loved the oblivion of the snow but kept being drawn back by Ian's red snowsuit.

Sonia went to put on the black jersey and brown cords which hung on her thinness in places and pulled tight over her belly. Deborah went in, too, and made coffee in the kitchen.

Sonia said, "That smell makes me sick."

"What?" Deborah said.

"The smell of coffee."

Deborah poured a cup and put the pot of brewed coffee out with the boots, spent batteries, and everything that would never go away.

"You're moving out from him?" Sonia said. They sat at the table. Sonia ate chowder crackers out of a box. She put them on her tongue and let them disintegrate.

It began to snow.

"Yes," Deborah said.

Sonia nodded.

Ian had found the house's cat in a pile of blankets beside the cookstove. From that moment on, he never took his eyes off the cat. He lay on the floor and inched forward, as if he needed desperately to lie in those dirty blankets with the cat.

Deborah said, "We could think about hens."

They watched Ian.

Ian sucked in his breath every time the cat opened its eyes to see if the pest was still there. He said, "Pa dump pa dimp pa dump," which he would have known as cat language.

"You're sure you want to do this?" Sonia said.

"This, or back to Durham," Deborah said. Puddles of melted snow formed on the wood floor. The kitchen smelled like old onions and garlic and wood smoke. Deborah paced. She hadn't taken off her watch cap or her Mickey Mouse boots and she pounded around the room.

"Okay," Sonia said.

"Isn't the yucky part over yet?"

"Oh, yeah." Sonia had lit a match and heated a kettle of water over the stove. She poured water into the sink and rinsed out a washcloth in it and spread the cloth over her face. "I miss my job," she said, muffled. "I miss hanging out at the restaurant. And now I can't even finish my sophomore year."

Deborah said. "Were you thinking of transferring? Or going home?"

"Yeah, I've been thinking about going home. I'm just not sure where it is."

Deborah shrugged. "Here it is."

Sonia said, "I thought when my parents dropped me off here, I'd fallen off the world." They watched the snow while Ian tamed the cat. She began to laugh.

"What are you laughing about?" Deborah said.

"At home we have a maid." They found this hysterical and Deborah went and got the basin of warm water and put it at Sonia's feet and curtsied and Sonia heaved off her boots and put her feet in the water, still laughing. "I want to be the maid," she said.

"No, I want to be the maid."

"Okay, you be the maid." And they laughed and lit candles and waited for Sonia to feel less pukey.

They had twenty-five dollars together. They made plans and numerous phone calls. Sonia got some energy by midday and she borrowed Swede's truck because it was sitting in the clearing and had the keys in it. While Ian slept they plowed part of the way up the logging skid trail. Then they got out of the truck and walked the next part.

They had come to the three white birches that stood so close together that they almost touched. The snow came to Deborah's thighs these few hundred yards higher.

"I want to do it today," she said.

"I know," Sonia said, but without hope.

The trees were rimed. There was only white winter and the

college was closed.

"What about that?" Sonia asked.

Above them was a place that had been hammered together. Maybe a studio. Maybe once goats wintered in it. They forged farther up Cleveland Mountain to this ruin. It was barely held together in the woods within overarching branches of wintering trees. The front door was made of slender split birches nailed side to side. Deborah opened it. When they stepped inside they saw spaces of light through the door, but the wind calmed. Light poured in a side window that needed a pane. A washtub sat on a timber table below the window. It lacked a stove, but there was a place to cut in the back for a stovepipe. It would do.

Sonia smiled. She leaned against the timber table. She said, "Are we really doing this? You're so tough. Sometimes I think you know you're always setting yourself up for something to hurt and you're not going to let it happen this time, but it always happens. And you're golden, not like most of the hippies. How did you get that way?"

"Shut up, Sonia."

"I just wonder how a person gets that way."

"Yeah, well, how did you get that way?"

That was when they were both twenty-three years old.

THEY scrounged a stove and an already-built window from Mackie's shop. It was their third winter in the woods and they had become good at scrounging. They brought their sleeping bags, coffee, rice, Cheerios, rolls of insulation, Deborah's truck full of tools, Ian's bears, a black skillet, utensils, Sonia's plates with medieval designs on the border.

At first they were intrigued with time. How interesting not to have men set the pace for how they spent their time. They worked all the time. When a partial thaw came, Deborah got a hold of a Bombardier tractor — she hadn't thought they even made them anymore — and they hauled the shed up the mountain. It fell apart on the way up. That's when they got the idea to haul the piano up, too, out of the craft cabin where Deborah first stayed. They did haul it up, though it took the whole day. They situated the piano on a temporary foundation in front of the shack and nailed up the shed walls around it. It was primitive compared even to the other cabins. It was little more than shelter.

At night Sonia sat up with the Aladdin kerosene lamp and planned the future grounds in her nightgown and a plaid coat. She got into the idea of the women's house right away, maybe because the baby was growing in her. She was going to put in a weeping cherry and a Chinese redbud and a Japanese pagoda tree. She craved beauty after they hauled that shed up there.

They were on the side of Cleveland Mountain. Christy and Deborah's cabin was deeper in the foothills of Agassiz. In the night Sonia planned the spring. She read to Ian. Deborah remembered very little of the winter except muscle-aching fatigue and new blisters on her hands.

Sonia had it all worked out. She'd have the baby in the late spring. By then she'd have a fox she would leave food out for, several infant birds she would feed with a dropper, and she would make a pool in the back where frogs would come to sing at the first sign of muck. She planned where she would rototill the garden, which was going to be four times the size of the cabin. Like a demon, was the way the men described how Sonia carried on at the women's house. People said she was probably a good shot, too, if she had to be, because the woods had made her dexterous. Maybe they imagined the women with rifles, standing guard on the extension of pine logs that could become a porch if Deborah would hammer a floor over the logs, but she didn't keep working the way Sonia did.

They had cut themselves off. Sonia taught herself to play the piano. She didn't use the piano book. She sat down and worked out songs from some memory in her ear. Valerie came up and she brought them ice cream from Littleton which they ate with one spoon, sitting on the pine logs swinging their legs and passing the cardboard carton of ice cream among them the way they passed a joint.

Deborah remembered the ice cream but somewhere she got lost in the move. She worked very hard.

What Deborah remembered was wood. She didn't know when winter thawed up, but it began to, and she began to work. The woman who had the goats or whoever it was that first built the shack had done something wonderful. She had built the roof with alternating butt ends of sawed-off trees, so that the logs lay narrow, wide, narrow, wide up against the pine planks that were the wall. So what Deborah did, with Ian playing on the floor, was make a form out of chicken wire and place it over the ceiling, but not covering the butt ends. She began to spread plaster over the walls and ceiling. She worked the plaster from her hawk to the trowel and built the rounded ceiling layer by layer, her arms aching with fatigue. She stood back to survey the corner she had finished. Okay, she thought. The plaster lay smooth over the rounded form with the butt ends of the trees still exposed so that the place began to become a cross between a Strawberry Banke low-ceilinged kitchen and a treehouse. By the spring they had two rooms they could live in. By the spring Deborah had not slept with Christy for three months and never stopped thinking of him.

11. Birth Story

Sonia and Deborah's was, inevitably, a different house. It wasn't that men never went to it. Christy went the late May morning when he woke up with the smell of Deborah thick in his bed and his longing for her in the dawn kept him from being able to fill his chest with air. The longing pressed him down, it pressed on his ribs.

He fought the desire. He knew he would only look at her and there would be nothing further he would be able to do. He worked in the garden, clearing suckers that were trying to take root, mending the chicken wire around the garden that the rabbits would soon favor, but his breaths were too shallow. He resisted her until almost midday. Then he walked up the trail to their cabin.

It was a very warm spring day, as it had been for three days now. Despite the warmth, Christy wore the crumpled white oxford that distinguished him from other hippies. He had rolled up the sleeves and unbuttoned it over his chest. His chest hair was wet with sweat. His beard had been too hot and he'd cut it back to coarse whiskers. His ponytail exposed his neck but the warm breeze clung to the skin. Swede had been cutting pine trees to bare the land further up the old logging skid trail and Christy wore the warm, strong scent of pines on his flesh. He wondered if Deborah and Sonia might have melted in the early heat and all he might find was the remains of the velvet, tasseled couch that he thought gave their cabin the feel of a brothel.

As he always was in the New Hampshire woods, Christy was conscious of his footfalls. He was conscious of the texture of the dirt. Now the soft bed of pine needles. Now the hard, dry dirt impacted with roots. He was conscious of the sound of his boots or the soundlessness. He was conscious of the rhythm. In the woods he had continual chances to be more cautious, but he seemed never to be cautious enough.

The first part of the cabin he saw was the trapezoid porch. It would be the base of Deborah and Sonia's trapezoid room. On the porch were a table, a bench, a mattress on its side still made up with two sheets, and that purple, velvet-covered sofa that stood on claws. The stray setter dog they had adopted, Cody, startled at Christy's footsteps, but he didn't get up. He thumped his tail and his eyes followed Christy as he made a path through the household goods.

In the cabin, Christy found Sonia on her hands and knees with a paint roller. She leaned forward with the roller and rolled white paint across the cabin floor. She was heavily pregnant and was awkward as she had to stretch her arm high and then way out in front of her.

Christy leaned against the door. Sonia's pale hair was caught up in a cloth of some kind. He couldn't tell, maybe a T-shirt she had wet and wrapped around her head for relief. He was in a position to see a part of her finely shaped jaw and cheek. He imagined Swede with her. Swede was a sculptor. He was a square, muscular block of a man. He made animals of wood and over large wire frames.

"I want everything white," Sonia said to Christy.

She had turned and her freckles were splotched with white. He said, "You got it," and rubbed her cheek with the heel of his hand. He did not know why he did that. It caused a rush of grief to wash over him and he felt encumbered. He didn't know what that meant or why he should feel encumbered at this moment more than another. Only that he wished she had not gotten paint on her face because it had made him touch her.

Sonia wore only a white shirt over the black jersey she always wore, though it didn't cover much of her. The white shirt was unbuttoned so that her round pregnant belly was bare and it was glistening with sweat.

She paused and placed her hands in the area between her groin and the base of her belly. She closed her eyes.

"Get out of here," he said. "You shouldn't be breathing this."

She had all but covered the floor with the white paint. She walked slowly out on the porch and lay on her side on the purple velvet couch by the dog whose breathing puffed out its cheeks and blew the tan fringe that hung from the sofa's bottom.

Christy finished painting the floor. He could tell she had painted some of it other days. Maybe she and Deborah had been sleeping on the porch these last nights.

"Pretty white," he said.

"Good."

Sonia got up and then bent over slightly and he could see the sweat drip off her belly and down through her hair. He turned away from her but she leaned into him and just barely rested her forehead against Christy's back. She exhaled slowly and for a long time. Afterward she sat on the edge of the porch and swung her legs like a child.

"At least it's white," she said. "Pretty soon I can put out the things."

"Thought I'd see how you two were doing," Christy said.

"You don't have to explain."

"But that's what I do well."

She said, "I've been trying to reach Deborah and Val."

"Where is she?" Christy asked.

But Sonia was having another contraction.

"How long since they started?"

"The contractions? This morning. You know, Christy, she loves you way too much." He knew she did not mean this in any good way.

He stood, with his cynical smile, watching her from the doorway. Ethereal, fragile Sonia. She was not large, her pelvis wasn't large, she wasn't large anywhere, except now with her enormous balloon belly. "Are you sure you're old enough to have a baby?" he said.

She would hear nothing of the hospital. Val's had two babies, she had said. Deborah's had one. We can do it ourselves. She didn't want Swede, then, either.

"Did you come to save me?" she said. "Did you come to take me to the emergency room?"

"If you want," he said. "But I'll have some wine instead." Maybe he had forgotten Sonia was pregnant, he thought. He had not paid attention.

They had bottled some dandelion wine last summer. It was too sweet, but Christy knew that would be all they had up here, and he would be able to drink it.

Christy went in the cabin. He skirted the white floor and found a bottle of the wine in the bottom kitchen cupboard.

"How was it when Ian was born?" Sonia called after him, though she had been there.

Christy uncorked the bottle and poured some of the wine in a thick glass. He set the opener and the bottle on the dark wood slab the women used for a counter.

He couldn't remember, specifically, about when Ian was born. He remembered images. He remembered the black, slimy mop of infant hair. He remembered brushing Deborah's hair. She had liked to have her hair brushed between contractions. He thought she had asked him to brush it, and he had, but his image was of watching someone brush Deborah's long, black, curly hair. She had closed her eyes. It was like watching other lovers in a porn flick.

He found some peaches in the refrigerator. He peeled one, cut it into slices in a white bowl, found a spoon, and brought it to Sonia.

"Why did you do it this way?" she said. She took the bowl.

He shrugged, still with his cynical smile. He drank the wine. Checked his watch. "So Deborah's at the store?" he said. He knew they were stocking the new store.

Sonia put the bowl of peaches on her belly. "I read that if your baby dies, after that if you were sexual again, if you wanted to have sex with somebody, you'd feel like you were betraying your baby. So you'd feel bad. Sex would bring this onslaught of grief. Do you think that's true, Christy?"

"Could be," Christy said. He laughed and shook his head. "Sex brings you sweet relief, then it goes in for the kill. Sure," he said, "could be."

"It was so dark in the cabin, the floor was dark and there's only the one window. I dreamt someone said to me, I'm sorry, but your baby has died. That's when I had to make it white."

Christy took a swallow of wine.

The sun had faded while they talked. In the distance they heard thunder. "Look," he said, because he was trying to get out of there now. But he didn't want to give her platitudes. That made him despise himself.

Sonia got up and began walking back and forth on the porch. "You're supposed to help me walk," she said. It occurred to him that she was not as composed as her eyes, which were without emotion, had implied, that she was frightened. It occurred to him that she was actually in labor.

"Oh, my God," she said. She put her hands on her belly. "Oh

my God, that's a strong muscle. You should feel what it does."

Christy checked his watch.

"Look," he said again.

"I never liked you," Sonia said. "She loves you way too much. You love yourself way too much. You think you're the only person in the world with pain. Fuck you." She kept walking. He said, "Why are you walking?" She said, "To let gravity push the baby down." He said, "Lie down, Sonia. You aren't ready to have gravity push the baby out."

"How do you know I'm not ready?"

"Nobody's here, Sonia. Where's Deborah?" he said.

"She and Val went to a household sale."

"Where?"

He realized the contractions were steady.

"I'm not sure. Someplace in Vermont. This wasn't supposed to happen today."

Sonia shut her eyes again and this time he wondered if she were praying. He had never understood her. She had been elsewhere. She was a formal girl. Even though she was before him bare — from just below the tits down — and pregnant, she still maintained a sort of formality with him. She gave "fuck you" a formal sound. He could call her couch a slut couch, but she would have a formal brothel in which men found themselves being given head with decorum. Sonia was one of the wealthy, lost girls who had come to Franconia College after strings of failures other places, and whose families had washed their hands of them.

"Okay, so why don't I drop you off at the doc's. They can check you out."

This she ignored.

He wondered if her thought was that they would take their chances. He wondered if she intended this for both of them. He thought it was foolish and admirable, and the child would be a feral child like its mother who had roamed the main street in

Bethlehem, her long red-blond hair like a pony mane. And then he saw the child dead. He would have to say, I'm sorry, but your baby has died.

"I'll make some phone calls, Sonia. We'll get somebody up here. Where's Swede?"

By this time she was preoccupied. Lightning struck to the north in the direction of Cleveland Mountain. In the few minutes since Christy had come, the sun had vanished and the sky turned black.

Christy had his soldier ghosts. They were his old friends. They were his only friends. They were good in catastrophes. They did not assist him with Sonia's wet, ecstatic face.

She said, "Put water on to boil, to wash us."

Christy said, "Sonia, we're not doing this ourselves. What would you have done if I hadn't shown up?" He went inside. He forgot about avoiding any part of the floor. He dialed Swede's number. He waited for the telephone to ring and when it never did, he hung up and listened and realized there was not a dial tone. Something had happened to the telephone. Deborah and Sonia's line had never been reliable since they had installed it, and the lightning in the sky could have assured its uselessness. The stove was fueled by a small gas tank in the back, buried under Sonia's Japanese lantern bushes. He struck a match and lit a burner, relieved that the gas worked. He filled the kettle with water and put it on to boil. At least he could do this.

When he returned to the porch, Sonia was saying — as if he had not left — "I would have liked to be in love, if only for the birth."

Sonia looked too much like a child to be so large in the belly. Her freckles spilled over her lips.

But she was in distress, breathing erratically. Christy's first intention was simply to bustle the girl down the skid trail and into his car. He was comically putting thongs on her dirty-soled feet and trying to pull shorts on over the thongs, but he couldn't get them up. He went to turn the kettle off. When he got back, the sky had opened. Rain came down hard on the outer edge of the porch over which Deborah hadn't extended the overhang of the roof. As they watched, the trees began to lean in the wind and the rain fell in torrents. Christy still tried to bundle her in his arms. He was carrying her, his hands holding her tight around the thighs and her bare buttocks across his arms because the shorts had dropped. Sonia screamed. But he had her down the porch steps. And into dirt that was rapidly turning to gullies, it could not absorb so much hard rain this fast. Sonia screamed and convulsed. She gripped his forearm with both of her hands with extraordinary strength. "Christy — it's coming. Oh, please." He was down the first twist of the trail beside three birches whose thin trunks bent slightly in the blowing rain. "Okay," he said. "Okay. Okay. Okay." He had turned around. "All right," he said. "All right." All right. All right. He didn't know where he was stepping. Sonia blocked all of his view of the terrain. "All right." She said the baby was coming and he let her down on the porch again and didn't haul her screaming into the car far down the trail.

Sonia stood panting and dripping, now absolutely naked except for the jersey. She had lost the white shirt in the battle on the trail. Christy stood panting and watched her.

She said, "This morning Deborah and I laid out in those lawn chairs like teenagers at the beach." She pointed to two chairs with ragged webbing that were taking in the rain, their backs to the cabin. Sonia held on to the beam that supported the porch roof and was sweating terribly. Christy found a washcloth, one he recognized as having once been his. He poured springwater through it and wrung it out. He brought it to Sonia who stretched her head back and dropped the cloth over her face to cover it completely. He brought her a dry black shirt.

"I'm going to run down to Swede's cabin." Christy said. "I'll get Swede and I'll call the store again."

But then a contraction began again and some of the things Deborah and the midwife had asked him to do came back to him. He thought she had not wanted to lie down. He pulled the mattress up to the cabin wall where the rain didn't come in, or only a little that a gust of wind from a contrary direction splashed on them. He folded it into a chair with the wall supporting the chair back. Sonia knelt on it and Christy rubbed her back. His hands were very large. One of them stretched between her hipbones. He found some baby powder and worked it across the small of her back with the heels of his hands until the contraction was over.

"That's it," he said.

"What do you mean, that's it?"

"That's it. That's all I know." Christy was shaking. He picked up the glass of wine and turned his back so she wouldn't see his hands. The wine was warm and a wave of nausea washed through him. "I stayed at the other end. I don't know anything about this end," he said.

Sonia had leaned against the back of the mattress, her arm cocked over her head, her knees bent, her legs open.

"Am I supposed to push?" she said. They were still now. Her voice was hushed and quickly lost to the torrent of rain.

She reached her fingers over the pale hair between her legs and he saw them explore. "Christy?"

He saw her vagina wide and red through the pale genital hair that she was opening, and her wide, curious blue, blue eyes on him, and he said, "Oh, fuck it, Sonia." He went to the porch railing and he vomited the wine and the wine he'd had before he came.

She had another contraction and he didn't go to her. They were coming one after the other. She called to him and he didn't go. He watched the wind and the dangerously bending limbs of trees.

When he looked, she was on her side. She was inhaling deeply and when she exhaled, she let out a long soft cry. Not a scream, a cry, as if to practice the letting out from her body. And with it he saw tears pushing out of her eyes.

He saw that the contractions came like waves. He saw her come down from this one.

"I have to go get somebody," he said. "I don't know what to do."

"I'll tell you what to do," she said.

"Sonia, you never had a baby."

"I read it in a book from the library."

That's how the hippies learned how to do everything in the woods.

"It's messy, it said. There's going to be a terrible wet, bloody mess." She began to name things for Christy to find. Blanket, towels, get the tarp she'd scrubbed down from the greenhouse to put under her, all the pillows, boil the water, let it cool to clean us, brew the thyme tea, it's on the window ledge, don't go, Christy. I'm so thirsty. So he attempted to find things and to not leave her at the same time.

"Put your hand here," she said. She was standing. She took his large hand and put it on her shoulder. "Hard," she said, "Press." He tried to put pressure on her thin shoulder. "Now take my hand here." She held his other hand at her belly. "Now the next one, hold me like this. Breathe with me."

"Yeah," he said, "I'll get some water."

"Make me ice chips," she said.

She didn't let go of his hands. "And the next time," she said, "tell me it's okay."

"What?" he said.

"Everything," she said. "Tell me everything's okay."

"It's not," he said. "Everything's not okay."

"Say it," she said.

"Sonia."

"Say everything's okay."

He said, "It's okay." It wasn't something he had a memory of ever having, the sense that anything would be okay.

"Tell me I'm doing it good. Tell me I'm doing it just right."

He pulled away to go smash some ice.

Sonia had asked for a pair of white socks. She had put these on and she wore these with the jersey.

She instructed Christy to walk her and as they walked up and down the porch, she put her weight on Christy. They stopped for contractions. She took Christy's hand and put it on her shoulder. He pressed. He could feel the tightness in her and he pressed round and round and, under his hands, she loosened and softened. She watched his mouth and followed his breaths so he became aware of his own breaths and lengthened them. When she lost her focus and bent to the pain, he held her tight and drew her back to his long breaths. He found the rhythm and saw that she began to hold on to it. "Tell me," she said, between breaths. "Tell me."

"You're breathing fine," he said.

"I'm doing it just right," she said.

"Yes," he said.

Christy rubbed Sonia's back sometimes. Christy imagined himself as a doctor. If he were a doctor he would worry terribly about his patients. He would ask a parent how his child was, a child he had seen the day before in his office, and the parent would say, Oh, he's fine, the fever's down, and Christy would say, But are you sure he's fine? How can you be sure? He never stopped being terribly worried.

It had begun in earnest by one o'clock. Christy knew because he had been looking at his watch.

Sonia had told him to measure her. She had stretched from

the size of his closed fist to almost the width of his palm. Sometimes she sat on the mattress now covered with the tarp, propped forward with all the pillows in the cabin behind the small of her back.

It rained and they worked so hard in concentrated spans of time when they were the only people and Sonia watched Christy's breath. If the sun had still been spilling over them, its angle would have increased and splayed them with long, low rays. But in the continued grayness, an unease came into the cabin.

It was palpable, the unease. Sonia had wanted the thyme tea and Christy made it. Sonia, by then, was pushing hard. Christy was grimacing, standing bare-chested, having taken off his sweat-drenched shirt, his hand on her left foot and her feet pulled up tight to her body, her knees wide. She had been pushing for a long time. She began to cry. "I'm too tired," she said, crying hard. Her freckled face was red with anger and exhaustion, and Christy wiped the wet strands of hair off her face with the cloth and nodded to her and held his hand hard at the small of her back, still nodding to her, his own lips straight and focused.

Christy knew many things could happen. He thought of them all. There could be a knot in the umbilicus. It could tighten as the baby descended through the birth canal. Christy imagined ways to lose a baby's breath, a snuffer being held over the flame of a candle, or a cork dropped in a bottle of wine. That quiet.

"No," Sonia said, "no, I'm not."

"Not what?"

"I don't want to do this anymore. I want to go home."

He knew what she meant. The place they were in was not familiar anymore.

"You're cold," Christy said.

"They give you a hot blanket in the hospital. That's what

they do in hospitals. And you can relax. And they'll take the baby out."

He knew the baby was dead. He knew he should have dragged her to the car and left her at the emergency room and they would have gotten the baby out.

He dropped a blanket over her.

"Let's go," he said. "Maybe we can still go."

But then he saw what he knew was the top of the dead infant's head and it was going to be born. He put his arms around Sonia's shoulders as she had taught him to do, and she had taught him, if he should see the head, to tell her to pant. Now she could breathe the baby out.

If she had changed her mind about going to the hospital, she couldn't talk about that now. She held on to Christy. "Tell me, Christy. Tell me," she shouted at him. She was working so hard.

He said, "That's right. Relax." He rubbed the inside of her thigh hard and steadily. "That's it. All the muscles are relaxed and the baby wants to come out."

They were in a tight knot, there on the porch, Christy on his knees, his long thighs bracing Sonia, and Sonia wide open and in some other place he clearly could not go, despite the fact they had been physically almost one person for so many hours now. Christy's hands had been wet with her blood and water, when her water broke some hours earlier. "Breathe, Sonia," he said.

"Is it coming?" She was breathing hard, like a runner. They were wet with each other's sweat. And Sonia shivered at the same time.

Christy put his hands to the implausibly large head and mass of mucus-covered hair.

"I see the head," Christy told her. And then something let go in Christy. Despite himself, he watched the head grow larger and larger. He whispered, "It might be okay."

She laughed out loud. "That's good Christy," she said. "Say it again."

Sonia's hair was wet and Christy pushed it back from her face so that it swung behind her. He wiped her down with a towel while she worked, panting the head out. "Think of a kid," he said.

"Tell me I'm doing a beautiful job. You forgot to do that Christy."

"It's beautiful," he said.

Christy put the towel down. He considered the head. He touched it. Then he put both hands to it. It seemed to turn slightly and slowly begin to push out as if the baby were pushing itself out, it wasn't just Sonia giving birth, it was this head. And then he wondered at the possibility of its being alive. This he refrained from saying to Sonia. To Sonia he said. "Good God."

"What does that mean?" she screamed at him.

He held his hands on the head because it was coming out.

"You're beautiful," he said.

She panted and now pushed. Christy was fascinated by the head. Here came the head. He held it gently as the baby pushed through. He felt the warm mucous hair. The baby came down and the head was born and as he held it a shoulder slipped out and then another and he caught the wrinkled mass of flesh and fluids. He turned it and held it across his arm. The baby had enormous black, open eyes.

"Look at that," Sonia said. She reached her small arms between her legs and down to them. "Let me see what her name is." Christy put the crumpled, weighty mass up on her belly.

Then he went down the porch stairs and into the woods.

Christy stood in the woods not far from the outhouse where the smell of lime was enhanced by the heat and the rain and the humidity. If the baby was dead, he would have to go back and take the baby away from Sonia. He would have to take it to the hospital. He would have to get it a death certificate. He would have to hold the baby again — a good-sized baby, probably seven full pounds — and he would have to push with his fingers into her chest. He would have to breathe into her, over the tiny mouth and nose together. He would do this for many minutes. He would have to see the black, open eyes and inhuman skin.

He heard Deborah's voice. He heard Deborah laughing. She had a low, rolling laugh. Val would have said something droll. They would have finally come back from some dark, cobwebbed attic of the elderly while he had touched a baby's head. He heard their footsteps on the porch stairs.

He lit a joint. After a while, he sauntered out, his long legs brushing through the tall, wet grass. He sauntered back to the porch. The women now were all busy. There had been the matter of the umbilicus and the afterbirth and the blankets Sonia had got at a flea market and washed and dried at the laundromat to make them soft. They had been thin blankets made of flannel.

He was suddenly aware that it was evening and that the rain had stopped.

Valerie and Deborah were on either side of Sonia, their arms around her waist and shoulders. Christy watched the child that was still and lay across its mother, though now wrapped in the flea market blankets. The last thing that had been spoken were Sonia's words, "Let me see what her name is." The words hung in the air.

Sonia had worked so hard. She still wore her black jersey, now pushed up, and she placed her hands on the baby's shoulders so that they all saw how black the little girl's hair was, the same as her mother's shirt. Sonia lay back and shut her eyes. In the stillness that had come to them, Christy became aware that his son stood at the foot of the bed. Christy was certain you could feel when a person disappeared. He was experienced at this awareness. His son might as well know it too.

"Give it to me," he said.

Deborah and Val watched him. They seemed attracted to the sound of his boots as he sauntered. Things in the room stood out in detail, the line of his thigh as he walked, the black skillet hanging on a nail, the nail.

"Give it to me."

He glanced at Deborah. She was sitting on the floor, her skirt hitched up over her thighs in the heat, holding Sonia's hand. She was looking at him with the eyes of the girl Deborah he met in Portsmouth and made love to on a breakwater at Hampton Beach. The girl who would sleep with his shirt after he left her and vowed to come back and he hadn't, so she had followed him up here.

His eyes dropped to Sonia. Her eyes were shut. When he looked at the baby, he did not understand what he saw. It was wrapped in the thin blankets. He could see its hand slung over its mother's breast. He understood first that it was not a still baby. He was aware of a slight rhythmical moving. He moved closer and he saw the baby's full mouth fastened on Sonia's nipple and the baby was suckling. As he looked, the baby opened its black eyes and seemingly gazed at Christy's face while she sucked.

Sonia's hair had dried somewhat and she and the baby were nestled on the mattress that Deborah had laid flat for a bed and Sonia took up an eighth of it. She put her hand with the fingers with the short round nails and moons gruffly on Christy's neck, hauled him down to her, and kissed him on the mouth.

"Do you want her?" Sonia said.

He shook his head.

But Sonia sat up and put the baby against his belly so that instinct lifted his arm and he supported the baby and the baby's head, which was very heavy, the hair very black against his skin, and he could still feel the wetness of the water and blood that had brought the baby to the world. He felt the living weight of the baby and the helpless pressure of her against his arm.

It hurt him so much. He had never hurt this much. It was piercing like a shotgun volley that hit his chest and belly and groin. It was physical, exquisite pain. He studied her as she tried to suckle him.

He gave her to her mother.

He had been weak. Deborah was well rid of him. The world was well rid of him. The baby — what was her name? — he wished the baby would not have to understand him. He walked down the trail. His words beat steadily in his head like his boots on the ground. He walked up the rutted road to his own cabin, which had been his family's cabin, his and his wife and son's. At home, he got the scythe and laid into the branches that threatened to shade the garden. He swung it fiercely and cut back the brambles and thick snakeweeds, and the smell of desiccated flora filled the warm humid night until he felt a hand on his back. He turned. It was Deborah. She took his hand and led him to the pond they had built for the frogs below the house. It was dark and they couldn't see each other's eyes.

"I came to say good night," she said. His wife. He began to cry. He could not remember crying, although there must have been times. He could feel her hands working his muscles. He could feel her hands move up from his waist, massaging him. She unbuttoned his shirt and took it off. He touched her hair that she had cut short, one of her steps to leaving him. He touched her earlobes and followed the curve of her jaw, which was more familiar to him than his own.

He put his hands on each side of her head. "That's good," she said and he wondered if she meant the terrible cries that were coming out of his body. "I don't understand," he said, although he did not know if she could make out his words. "It's just emotion."

"Yes," Deborah said.

He pulled her down to the ground. He needed to cover all of her. He took her tongue into his mouth until his sobbing wrenched him. Still he couldn't get close enough to her and he lay on her in the tall weeds, stretched his leg across her thigh and cradled her and devoured her and wept. And still it was no relief at all. That is when he thought most of giving up. How exquisitely the desires came together.

12. The Sleepers in This House

Sonia fell in love with the baby. She said she had never been in love before. She worked hard to make the cabin a safe nest. She worked for hours in the garden without pausing, her hair falling over her shoulders and growing paler in the sun. She made a compost bed, she hauled night soil from under the outhouse to fertilize the pumpkins. She mulched the redbuds and cherry trees that bloomed late in August. The men down at the homestead and in the pottery studio could hear her at the piano. She made up songs that sounded like thunderous waterfalls or lightning storms or the staccato pattern of falling leaves. All that summer she put in shrubs and perennials, she grew cuttings from Swede's garden, or Christy's, or friends back in the Easton or Littleton woods. She put in a ginkgo and a pagoda dogwood. She planted beds of black-eyed Susans to see what would come next year and the next.

Swede began ambling up the skid trail in the early evenings. He brought up his guitar and played for Patience, twisting his lips around and scrunching his eyes when he made the high notes. He told her stories about her mother and he brought her little clay animals he had made. One time he brought a clay donkey, later a clay goat. He made a row of them on the window ledge for her to look at, and then shuffled his feet and shook his head, as if he was figuring out he wasn't just a hippie kid from Long Island anymore, because of her. But he wasn't sure what he was.

Christy never came back. Sonia sent him baked custards, which he had always loved. She sent him oatmeal raisin bread and biscuits and chicken, but he never came back, and Deborah thought she had fallen in love with him like women do sometimes with their baby doctor. So Christy never saw the sight of the women on the porch. The babies and the moms and sometimes Swede and Val and Val's girl Franny whom Deborah still adored. He never saw the round, jowly baby with the cap of black hair that didn't lighten as babies' hair usually does, swinging back and forth in the windup swing on the porch where she was born while the rest of them ate ice cream or a cobbler that Sonia made with the fat blueberries Ian spotted up the trail.

One night it was just Sonia and Deborah and Ian and Patience on the porch. Sonia and Deborah leaned back, their sleeves pushed up to let the sweat dry. "Edelweiss," the song playing on Patience's windup swing, ground down to its final notes.

Deborah put down her bowl with Sonia's sweet cobbler in it and looked at her. "I'm thinking about another place," she said.

Sonia leaned in a little. "What do you mean another place?"

"For Ian and me. Maybe just try it."

The cobbler was warm and the dough slightly crunchy and sweet with the berries. It was a perfect night before the cold took them over.

"What's the matter with here? We worked so hard."

"I know."

"But it's not what you want," Sonia said.

Ian was in Deborah's lap and their voices would have been his background music to fall to sleep to.

"I saw a sign on that yellow house on Main Street and I was thinking about town."

Sonia didn't answer. She got up and slipped a tape into the portable tape player. It was nearly dark. Eight o'clock and it was already dark. Beethoven's piano filled the porch softly. "Well," she said, "why don't you think about it."

"I have been thinking about it."

"If you go it'll change everything."

The night was so lovely. The children slept.

They still plotted about how to make Sonia's stomach go down. About herbs to get a woman's period regular again. But when Deborah looked at Sonia she couldn't stay. She'd spent the past months building a reality of Christy in her head, just like she was making a painting. She thought she was developing the instincts that she had mislaid in her marriage. Sonia seemed so serene and Deborah was lost.

She did go to town. She got a tiny room in one of the turn-of-the-century houses with splintered strips of latticework under the porch, full of gaps, shutters that hung cockeyed, a screen door that did not catch and blew in the wind.

Other things changed when she moved to the yellow house. She was close to the old Milk and Honey that was about to open as the Three Eves, and she worked with Val on the new store most of every day. And most nights, in the house where Ian and she slept, Christy sat outside on their derelict porch.

Her life was made up of a boy who cried for his father, whose loitering downstairs affected them. It was made up of picture books about machines and trips to the library for more picture books with yellow earthmovers. And it was made up of yards and yards of fabric, so that she dreamed textures. It was made up of confusion and poverty. All the while she collected from dead women's attics boxes of clothes that she and Valerie sorted, and sometimes Sonia brought the baby and she worked with them, too.

Christy read on the porch by a camping light. He was friends with the guys who lived in other parts of the house. Nobody would question Christy anyway. He still had his charisma. People liked him. He had conversations with the other people as they were coming and going from Deborah's house. Fucking shame about the college. No, he didn't think he'd be leaving. Expect he'd stay on. Maybe sell men's antiques. One night he wrote Deborah a note and sent it up with Bobby who lived next door to her. The note said, "Marry me." She wrote on the other side, "I married you," and sent it back.

Ian was excited that his father sat on the porch at night. He was happy. He decided his family had all moved to this house, because this place had more people as well as indoor johns. Now at night Ian and Christy sat on the porch and read by camp light. Ian was able to sleep at night again. One night Christy brought Ian up to his bed. Ian had been asleep on his father's shoulder and when he was in his bed he rolled into a ball in a deep, deep sleep.

Christy touched Deborah's neck. It was electric. She had been sitting in the chair by the window, but then she got up and moved to the wall. She could still feel his hand on her neck. They didn't talk and after a while he went down the stairs.

They had become something different to each other since Sonia's baby was born. Christy paid precise attention to Deborah, to her eyes, to her hands while she worked, and she began to relax with him slightly.

Christy made a habit of writing notes to her. He wrote small notes and left them at the screen door. For example:

> Deborah, we've got windfalls in quantity. You're
> the only one who can get the press to work. What

do you say? Wait a little. What I mean is wait a little before you say no. I'm seeing your walk in my sleep. I'm seeing your body swing the way it does. I'm walking behind you to the dismal old fellow the Buddha. All the slugs bow to that fellow. So what the hell. You might as well come home where your garden is. Christy.

On a night when fall had just come, he brought Ian upstairs. Deborah was sitting at the small table she had scrounged. This time she watched him. He came and stood by the window. When he touched her neck she didn't move. She was confused about what man he was now.

He squatted down in front of her and began slowly to unbutton her shirt. He didn't touch her. He left it unbuttoned and falling off one shoulder. She stood up and he unzipped her jeans and took them off as if she would break. He eased the sleeves down over her wrists, being careful not to brush her exposed breasts with his arm, though he looked at her. Then he was gone. She heard him down the hall. She heard him in the bathroom. She heard water from the faucet and knew that for her he would try to cover the sounds that came with his unease. When he came back Deborah said, "Why do you come to me?"

"I'm sorry," he said huskily. It was very dark and she could only make out the shape of his face and beard just covering his cheeks and chin. He began to slide off her underpants. "Stay where you are," he said. She whispered, "You bastard." He stopped and put his hand on her and sucked in his breath. He sat back and explored her. He reached up and traced the shape of her face and her cropped hair as if he were blind and needed to know her with his hands. She felt his fingers open her and he knew her body gave over to him, he knew he could have anything he wanted from her body, but he wanted to study it. She shut her eyes and felt his hand slide over her. He took loud, shallow breaths. She reached to hold him. "No," he said, "wait." She could see his eyes gleam.

She knew she would do what he said. He pulled a razor from his pocket and set it on the table. He went to the sink in the corner of the room. He lathered his hands with soap that smelled like lavender. He made a thick lather. He came back and knelt by her and she reached out to his broad shoulders.

"Wait," he said.

He caressed her between the legs with his soapy hands. He spread her sleeping bag on the floor under the window. She lay on it and he shaved the darkness from between her legs. He worked carefully, like an artist, and it took him a long time. She shut her eyes. When he dropped the razor, she heard it settle on the wood floor.

She felt his hands, hard, moving from her hipbones to her breasts. She moved to unbuckle his belt. He moved back and undid it himself. He threw his clothes down. Deborah said, "God damn you, I have to touch you." He shook his head. It was hot and she was flushed and his sweat dripped on her belly and nipples. He pulled his knee up between her legs. When he entered her they both came and coming made her cry out in fury and hunger and disgust. Christy lay back with his arm over his face.

AT the cabin, it was too cold for the muck out back that drew frogs to sing. Deborah missed the honeysuckle and dogwood and the thick, sweet smell of the woods that had come creeping on the cabin before she left.

"Sit down," Sonia said. "I bartered with Mackie," she said about the wooden table in the middle of the room. "I got the table and he gets pies. I'm making pies for him to sell at the store for the season."

Deborah ran her hands over the rough wood.

"Chairs, too," Sonia said. The chairs were dark, thick chairs with tapestry seats that together with the table took up a lot of the cabin. Deborah didn't say anything snide about the tourist season in Bethlehem not being in its prime. "I'm doing about a dozen pies a week." Sonia pulled down the cutting board and gathered zucchini and onions and garlic.

Deborah didn't want to leave Sonia's sight. It was like her to not to ask why Deborah was there. She chopped vegetables to stir in with the rice Sonia was cooking. Deborah sat on one of Sonia's chairs — worth about thirty pies — and her legs began to shake. Sonia put water on for tea. She came back and put her hands on Deborah's thighs. Deborah felt the strength of her fingers.

"Sometimes I can't remember what I'm struggling to do," Deborah said. "I can't remember who I'm supposed to be."

They sat still and let the dark come in. Sonia took her sweatshirt off the hook on the back of the door and pulled it over her smooth hair. She poured milk into red goblets and they ate on plates with gold borders and an intricate wildwood rose pattern that looked like broadside ballads and unrequited love and treacherous lovers.

A phone rang and Deborah jumped. "Did you get the phone fixed?"

"Let it ring," Sonia said.

They sat in the dark listening to the phone.

"Did you tell him you were here?"

"No," Deborah said.

The phone rang seven times and they ignored it.

Sonia had been there so much alone with the baby. The place felt sensual and earthy with the jewelweeds and foxgloves lingering in the damp night; the baby's sucking sounds mixed with a melancholy. The mood was in the trees and the way their limbs hugged the windows and doors, and threatened the light, and maybe that's why the men got rattled when they heard Sonia's piano from below when all she was doing was finessing the trees.

After dinner, Sonia picked up the light. Deborah said, "Where are you going?"

"Just to the outhouse."

"I'll walk with you."

They walked around the path to the outhouse. Sonia carried the light and Deborah walked in her footsteps. The weeds were tall on either side of the path and made their jeans cold and wet.

While they were in the grass, the phone began to ring. Sonia took the light with her and went into the outhouse.

"Where's Ian?"

Deborah bent over in the tall grass then and couldn't answer her. When Sonia came out, Deorah didn't stand up, just took in the smell of the wet grass and the night. After a while she said, simply, "Ian is at Christy's. He wanted to be with his father. After I wouldn't let Christy in anymore." She couldn't stand up.

"Deborah, why won't you ever get mad at that asshole. He took Ian?"

Then she stood up. "Don't give me advice," she said.

"No, I won't."

DEBORAH woke up sensing Sonia and Patience in the loft. Patience would have woken and wanted to nurse. The image wrenched her. She could feel her own baby nursing and thought, No, she had never meant to live her life like this, without her child. She had wanted more children. She had wanted houses full of children. She slept very little. Later in the dawn, she heard a coffeepot gurgling and soon the smell of coffee filled the cabin. It was surreal, sleeping under a medieval table and now coffee going off in a coffeepot with a timer. And Cody was there, too, the old dog with long legs like a wolfhound that Sonia took in when she was pregnant.

Deborah lay on the floor, breathing. She counted the baby's breaths, after the coffee began to drip, or imagined the breaths like she could imagine her son's. She imagined a sparrow's whistle, then a vireo, his funny call, Where am I? here I am. Where am I? here I am. It was cold and barely light. Sonia wore long johns and a ribbed shirt and she climbed down the ladder.

"Sonia," she whispered.

Sonia said, "Yeah, it's me." She wrapped her blanket around herself.

Deborah sat up in her sleeping bag, her legs folded, her knees crossed.

"She'll sleep a little longer," Sonia said.

They went to the outhouse together, tramping through the tall grass. In the cabin, Sonia poured coffee that was dark and strong. They sat on the tapestry-covered chairs and it started to rain.

"I have to go to work, " Sonia said. "I started a job last week to get some cash. I can take Patience. It's not too bad."

"Where are you going?"

"To the hotel."

"Mount Washington?"

"Yeah."

The rain was heavy. Christy's garden would have its fill, now that it didn't need it anymore.

"What do you do?" Deborah said.

"Bake bread and rolls."

Sonia had gotten Patience and was packing the baby and her duffel bag of diapers and baby things.

Deborah's hands shook slightly around her coffee cup. "I can't remember what I dreamed about but what's left I can taste, it's like fear you can taste. It's like fear unattached to anything. Do you think that's how it is for Christy?"

Sonia was at the door. She had a maroon apron in her hand and behind her was the rainy, gray chill of the woods where the trees seemed to have turned golden and orange and red in the night. Deborah was alone on the massive, dark chair.

Sonia shook her head and her hair fell over her cheek.

Deborah kept talking to her to hold her. "The rain smells like fear and like something bad's going to happen." Sonia rested her hand on Deborah's hair. Deborah put her arm around Sonia's waist and they were still for a few seconds. Her waist was solid under her red ski jacket. Sonia dropped the apron over her shoulder so that its purple tie strings mixed with her hair. Then she left with the baby who was bumping across her shoulder in her yellow sleeper, her alert, black eyes hushed in sleep.

When they had gone Deborah sat on the porch steps. They were wobbly. They had been thrown together in a rush. Deborah would rebuild them solidly from the stash of lumber behind the greenhouse. She would do this for Sonia, as soon as she could move and put some clothes on.

The phone rang. She picked it up, knowing that Sonia would have prevented her from picking it up with a glance.

"Didn't we have everything?" Christy said. "Come over and let's talk."

"Talk?" she said.

"Why don't we get away, Darling," Christy said, quoting a song. "Why don't we say, fuck it, we can do this."

She lit a cigarette and sat on the stone they had rolled to the door. She listened to him, to give herself a break from her non-stop talking to him. She took him in like a drug.

"Yeah," she said, "why do we make it so hard."

"So come back," he said.

"I can't breathe there."

"Yes you can. You can breathe."

She didn't answer.

"When can I see you?"

She could hear a car go by, someone looking at the orange trees.

"Look, I'll just cook and you come and eat and sleep here. One night at a time. Let's not fuck this up."

Today I let my son go. He's three years old.

"Well, if you want a shower, there's no shower there."

"Yes."

My little boy needs his father. I'll make a good solid home for you, Ian.

"Stop in," Christy said. "I just want to see if you still have sheep hair. All you need to do is relax. What are you running from, Deborah?"

She fell to her knees again.

Is this what it's like for you Christy? Is it always like this, how can you live in this place in your head? You don't have to marry me. Just tell me we can go on somehow. I don't think I can go on if you can't imagine it. Is Ian swimmimg? No he's spinning in the cabbage bowl. What am I now? Please imagine me. Do you want me to undress for you the way I did when you took my pictures? I would look into your eyes and not ask any questions. I would do anything you asked. I would draw your hands down to my ass and I would hold you. We are all right in the world. . . . Tell me.

Christy said, "Give me some relief, Deborah."

He wouldn't help her leave him.

EARLY in the morning Deborah came back to Sonia's in the rain. She went back to Sonia's door in a plaid shirt and long skirt, wet and cold against her, the rain still coming down like monsoon rain.

Sonia sat at the table in the shirt and leggings she had slept in. She had left the heavy door swung open. The coffee on a timer had not brewed yet. When it did she would have to get dressed for work.

Deborah said, "The road's too muddy to drive."

"It always is in the rain," she said.

Their eyes rested on each other. Deborah turned around at the doorsill and wrung out her skirt and shivered.

The air was cold and foggy and burly with the smell of cut cedars and pines, somebody making a clearing in the woods.

That, mixed with the smell of new pies. She was stuck on the doorsill. She couldn't go forward and she couldn't go back.

Sonia tossed her a dry shirt and a towel. Deborah peeled off her wet clothes, put on the shirt and the towel around her waist. They sat in the dark and listened to the hard rain while the knot grew in her stomach. After a while, Sonia got a book and began to read. Deborah unrolled her sleeping bag. She listened to Sonia turning pages. "What will you do at the hotel today?" she said.

"They put me on the braising line. I said I was a baker. I don't even eat meat," Sonia said. "But they put me on the braising line."

Deborah imagined the hotel's layout. She moved from room to room to room, down corridors, as if she had died away from Christy, and had gone to another world, into bathrooms with bathtubs on lion's paws, into the kitchen where Sonia pulled loaves from steel ovens, past the braising line, into the bar, past the ladies in silk suits, down long carpeted hallways where she didn't make a sound even in work boots. She had slept on the couch in her old cabin until 4 A.M. She didn't sleep with Christy. What if Ian woke up? He would be confused. She had explained that she and Christy were not going to be a husband and wife anymore and he had tried to understand. What would he think if he came in and saw them in bed? So she couldn't. Christy had said, come to bed. She craved the habit of it. She craved to sleep all night in the bed with him. In Sonia's cabin, the coffee began to brew.

They repeated the routine of the morning before. They went to the outhouse, Sonia with the light. They drank the coffee. Sonia explained her day. Deborah did not say if she would stay there. She didn't remember eating.

"Come to the store," she said to Sonia.

"Yes, I might."

◆   ◆   ◆

DEBORAH met Christy at the Buddha on the trail in the woods. He leaned against the ash tree. He was propped against it so that had it been a youth, a thin youthful ash, he'd have bent the tree, curved the trunk over. He was in a holey T-shirt and some baggy pants he must have picked up at the Saturday flea market on Rt. 142.

"Ian misses the coconuts."

"What coconuts?"

"The stuff you put in your hair," Christy said. "He smelled it and it made him cry, which he wasn't proud of. Why are you doing this to us?"

She looked for the wild licorice they had transplanted to this spot and watched Christy leaning against the tree, his arms folded over his chest, his hair in a ponytail. He looked just the same. His amused, boyish eyes that were full of what she saw then as Irish sorrow and drink.

He knelt down. He took out a knife and began carving on a fallen oak branch that he would make into a rabbit or a candleholder. First he bared the wood.

"Maybe you could move to Jamaica with Michael or maybe Swede."

"It's the only place nuclear fallout won't hit," Christy said, "or the Dominican Republic. We could all go."

"Nuclear fallout is not our immediate problem." At some point there by the Buddha, Deborah realized she was thinking about Sonia.

"You're not going to disappear are you?" he said.

She shook her head.

"Think about coming back."

"I feel like all I ever do is have endings. Even beginnings are endings."

Christy left off with the paring he was doing with the knife. "That's strange," he said. "I feel like nothing ever ends."

"So I get all these books from the library on war and read

them in the basement of the store and learn a lot about war, but nothing about my husband to make a beginning instead of an ending. . . ."

"Deborah. . . ."

"So I go on sleeping with you and your buddy who was going to be a chef until I can't do it anymore."

Christy got that sentimental, romantic turn to his shoulders, full of remorse over what he had not been. Deborah found this more intolerable than his being absent or nasty.

Watching him carve that day was the first time she believed that it could be true that they might not live their lives together. After all the things she had done to leave. She'd been leaving and leaving and leaving and vowing she was leaving. She watched him carve. She watched his hands and remembered them holding their son's little body when he was born. "Oh, Christy," she said. "Oh."

WHEN Sonia got home at four, Deborah had dug out dirt and rocks to build a lean-to that had the potential for being a bathroom or at least a shower room if they got pumps going. Sonia had picked up some rice and milk and coffee at Kelley's. It was already dark and they cooked, listening to Chopin's piano. If Patience cried, one or the other of them went to her.

A routine had come to them. Deborah worked in the store in the day. At night sometimes she went to Christy. It hurt so much each time she walked into her house and each time she left Ian in his bed. She stopped eating. She slept with Christy like the adulterer, not the wife. She couldn't make the move to come home to him.

She and Sonia incorporated a walk with Cody into the routine. After the outhouse, while Patience slept, they fixed tumblers of coffee — sometimes Deborah had half-and-half with hot chocolate, to which Sonia shook her head.

It awed Deborah what a person could accommodate. Ian

came to play. Sometimes he slept at Sonia and Deborah's place. Sometimes he went back to his father. When he was with them, they sat at the medieval table and Ian drew critters like the ones his father chiseled in wood and used to shingle the cabin. Deborah moved on from von Clausewitz to moral philosophy. She read the theory of Just War. It was really very satisfying, as it had nothing to do with the world for her. They were satisfying and lovely constructs, geometric shapes for the soul. Christy was the realm of emotion. The thought of him continued to take her breath. Ian drew owls. Sonia baked pies. Fall came to a climax.

THE vintage clothing store was taking shape. They would open it in late October, if only for a while, maybe till Christmas. They called it the Three Eves after Sonia left the braising line and took the baby and worked in the store sewing ribbon straps on camisoles, and airing the smell of age out of antique fabric that had been stored in mothballs. Their excitement grew. Sonia packaged individual baked goods, date-filled cookies, apple cake, and brought them to the new Three Eves the day it opened. People who hadn't seen Deborah in a while kidded her like Brer Fox kidded the waning moon, about Sister Moon being so thin and losing her light. But that day, they served cider at the cash register and Swede came in with his guitar and played his couple of songs. Deborah walked down the creaky wooden floor the length of the counter that had been the soda fountain, with evening gowns and feathery things over her arms instead of carrying thick, white plates of pancakes. They had replaced the smell of coffee and ginger cake and curry with incense and wool and the leather of the belts and high top boots.

The temperature dropped. Sonia and Deborah created a separate circle inside the circle of people in the woods and it might have gone on. Ian might have grown up moving from their circle to the whole-woods circle, and Octobers might have come around with Sonia and Deborah carrying water to this cabin and taking shifts at the store. But they didn't.

Early on the morning after Halloween, the coffee was brewing and Cody stood elklike at the door. Ian had not slept at their place. It was the morning before daylight saving time, so it was dark still at six. It was very cold and in the dawn, Sonia had slipped into Deborah's sleeping bag for warmth.

"What kind of coffee did you make?" Sonia said.

"I don't know. Just the plain, I guess."

They shivered, their bodies together, and they listened to the coffee perk.

"We have to fly out of here when it's done."

"Yes," Deborah said.

They had been together in their circle for what seemed like a very long time. Sometimes they had days in which they didn't talk. But it was not a deprivation. It was peaceful and easy. They didn't make demands on each other. They each understood what the other was thinking. When they talked to Cody they talked with the same inflections. They read to each other impromptu when a passage one of them was reading needed to be spoken. When they were hungry, they cooked. It was intellectual intimacy.

They went to the outhouse, but afterward they didn't take Cody into the woods. And then it seemed less likely that Deborah could stay. They let Cody go and Sonia and Deborah sat at the dark table and Sonia drank the coffee but Deborah couldn't. She wanted to walk but Sonia wanted to stay at the table. She had the awful sensation that here was another ending. Please, Sonia.

Sonia ran her hands over the crockery bowl on the table that held apples. Their routines were ritualized, almost sacred, like sex. Their rituals were sweet and lovely and ancient though they had just made them. Their talk was about melancholy and memory. It was deeply and intellectually satisfying. But Deborah craved Christy's tongue. In this cabin, even Ian's pictures had repose. Dogs slept. At home they rode in slamming circles in wooden bowls, splashed, overdosed, where Deborah reeked with female wetness and nipples aching.

But still, she and Sonia had gotten up at six all these mornings. Sonia had held back the dark. This talk was excruciating.

"Go," Sonia said.

Deborah looked at her. Sonia's voice was high pitched.

"Go."

Deborah was leaving and had nowhere in particular to go, although she told herself that wasn't a reason to stay.

That morning when they went to the store, Deborah was aware of the abandoned hotel building on Main Street. When the sun came up it cast an eerie, hazy light over the clapboards. It was displaced. She could read the letters on the long barn behind the hotel. They were faded but she could make out that they had proclaimed ALPINE HOTEL, GOLF OUT THE BACK DOOR. She imagined a long, green lawn and the first tee. The people who had played golf would have a clear focus on the flag stuck in the hole on the green. Deborah didn't think it was true that a new lover could come in and fill the void of another. It would be a new lover and that would be its own loss. And each vivid loss and dissolution remains. She looked at the hotel's windows which glittered with facets of broken glass.

She would go back to the seacoast, because then she would have her son, or she would not have her son, but as it was, the woods were too sad to bear, so close to what had been, and kept her always thinking, if only she would try harder, she could have it again.

13. China Doll

DEBORAH left the mountains. Sonia stayed on, so that she became one of the myths, Christy and she and a few others who were on Jenny's commune.

Ian stayed with Deborah then and he came up for a lot of the summers. Christy and Deborah got married again by a justice of the peace, an old Franconia student willing to do it at three in the morning when to marry again seemed not so much full of promise as a stoical resolve, since there seemed to be no escape, and out of a craving for sleep that marriage granted them and they slept through the day, satiated by the strength of their hard arms and legs around each other, their eyes bloodshot with exhaustion. They settled in Portsmouth for a while, but then Christy came back to the cabin. After that they both made treks back and forth, and Patience, too, because she and Ian were often together, their cabins being near each other and remote from the town.

IN many ways, the accident happened to Ian. Patience

remained in awe, probably of the knowledge that one person could do that to another person, and of what death could look like, that it could come on the song of a mockingbird or on the curve of a birch limb, how immediate it could be.

Patience was a tall, large, and ungainly five. She was clunky and awkward, and an endearing child. She loved books, and in her fifth summer she especially loved a book Christy read to her, and now she could read herself. It was called *Mommy, Buy Me a China Doll*. She read it with all her meals, forward, backward, and upside down.

The accident happened that summer when Patience was hanging out at Christy and Ian's place, which she loved to do. They kept a lamb for the season, and in the spring Ian and Christy had babied him with a bottle and kept him in the cabin. Patience didn't know the lamb was meant to be slaughtered, and she gave the lamb the bathroom behind the beaded door, until Christy built a shed with windows and a salt lick and put her out.

Patience adored Ian but her affection was unrequited. Oh, please, she would beg, can I have some of your muffin — they would have gotten enormous muffins at the bakery in Franconia. But Patience's envy of his food made him cruel, and whatever it was of his she craved, he deprived her of it. Maybe it was jealousy. Christy was more aware of Patience than he had been able to be of his son. Ian was invisible. Christy could walk in and out of a room and not see his son at the table.

"Please, Ian, please, let me hold the gun." This was a game that had started up that summer Patience read the *China Doll* book.

"It's not a gun. It's a rifle," Ian said.

"Let me hold it the way you hold it," she said, the same way she pleaded for a mouthful of his muffin.

"Look Patience, you can't touch the rifle. You're showing off."

"That's sexist, Ian. If you can hold it, I can."

Christy kept the rifle in a bench, the seat of which was a door and opened up like a deacon's bench. The bench was in the entryway between the shed where the woodpile was and the kitchen. Ian had taken the rifle from inside the bench. He liked to hold things the way his father did. He practiced placing his fingers in position. Ian was eight.

"Go away," he said to Patience.

Patience quieted down and watched him wipe the metal the way Christy had been taught to care for his weapon. Clean it. Keep the jungle slime off its chamber. Ian was drawn to soldiering. Christy never told him anything about the war. But Ian heard him wake up yelling. Two guys in the cabin, except when Patience came and wanted to make the third, this chunky kid who hid food in her pockets and went outdoors to eat alone where nobody could see her chew. Sonia's odd clunky girl joined the two males in the summer with the lamb which was now a sheep and which no one would slaughter. At night they all sat on the lawn facing the garden. Christy was unpredictable. Sometimes he told stories and sang. Often he didn't speak. The children never knew who would be with them. The summer had not been a good one for Christy, and his headaches had slowed his step and invaded his sleep. Ian was generally taciturn. Patience talked. "What if there were more moons than that one?" she said in the night, in the garden, lying on her back in the dirt. "We just only see one. There could really be five moons. What if we had twenty-two?"

She was foreign to them. They did not think of extra moons.

"It's bad luck to shoot an owl," she told them. "If you shoot an owl, they pull you by your neck into the sky and drop you."

"Patience, you are insane."

"She's not insane," Christy said. "Come here," and he pulled the girl toward him and looked into her eyes.

Trade our Daddy's featherbed?

Then where would our Daddy sleep, Eliza Lou?
He would sleep in horsey's bed.
Buy me a china doll
Do Mommy, do.

Christy was tall and lean and had broad shoulders. Gawky Patience followed him around. She told him, "I think all the dogs should be named Dennis and no matter what breed they are they'll all know they belong to this family."

Christy and Ian would look up from what they were doing and consider her. Then she would sneak slices of raisin bread, which was quiet to chew, and go sit in the chaise lounge with her book.

Patience could make Christy laugh and she had developed this talent into an art for survival. She was just a little girl, but on the days Christy withdrew, she was bereft. Already Ian had learned to blame himself, and he absorbed Christy's exits as rejection. Patience, though, fought them head to head, and it took all of her five-year-old self. And later, when Ian and Patience talked, they wondered if it would have been better if Christy had hit them, but he never hit them, he died; not all the time, not even most of the time, but repeatedly after he had seduced them into safety.

That summer, in addition to the sheep's house, they also built a tree fort. After they had nailed in various platforms, Christy made pancakes and served them in the tree, each kid on his and her own deck and Christy, himself, elongated in the curve of two limbs like it was a hammock, with a beer and pancakes, and him and the kids blaring out, "I'm a rocker, Baby I'm a rocker," Ian taking the pretend guitar solo. It was later, when Christy was in the middle of passing the hammer up to Ian to nail in the next cross board, that he did that kind of dying. He didn't have it in him to talk anymore. He went inside to his desk. He didn't pick up the phone when it rang. He was unaware of lunch- or dinnertime. Ian made the meals and spent most of the day in the oak tree where he was making the fort more and more complex. Patience stopped sneaking food and going to the chaise lounge to chew it as if nobody knew. She played beside Christy. She read her books quietly out loud and if she didn't know the words, she made up whole other stories, telling them, if not directly to Christy, then obliquely beside him, obliquely wooing him.

Although she could read well, after the summer sun set, she took the book to him and she asked him to read to her the china doll story.

"Would you please read this in French," she said.

He looked up at her and told her, distractedly, "Sorry, Patience, I don't know French."

"That's okay," she said and he would have seen that she had exactly Sonia's eyes. Patience patted his arm. "Let's see if we can figure it out." She sat with lean Christy. He was silent. Then he rested his chin across the back of her head. She coaxed him and Christy read the *China Doll* in a thick accent, as French as he could make it, ending each page with phrases such as *mon dieu!* and *tout de suite* and *beaucoup,* and *mon dieu beaucoup,* which pleased Patience immensely.

"*Beaucoup* chickens in the rocking chair, granny in the piggy pen," said Christy.

"Just for a day or *parlez vous,*" said Patience. Laugh tears came out of Christy's eyes.

Patience was impressed with his inflections. She was a self-possessed child. Now she could eat something.

THE next afternoon Ian and Patience were playing in the garden. The corn was as tall as Patience. Christy was up the road working on the barn. Patience and Ian heard a cry. It was an ugly sound, high pitched and thready.

"Coyote," Ian said.

"You don't know."

"I know. There's been a lot of mountain coyotes seen this year."

The ugly cry was close. It seemed to be not far from the edge of the woods that were just beyond Christy's sprawling garden, comprised of roses, a field of corn, a raspberry thicket, purple peonies, trailing zucchini, yellow squashes, green peppers, hot peppers, ripening tomatoes, sunflowers, lavender, Chinese mustard, red-fringed lettuce, vines of sweet peas. It was a thick maze of a garden to walk through, chicken wire enclosures here and there to ward off desperadoes, and only Christy and Ian knew the paths.

"You wait here," Ian said. "I'm going to have a look."

Patience had no intention of waiting there.

They were both bare chested in shorts. Patience was dirty to her knees and elbows in garden dirt, her round belly and cheeks sticky with the marshmallows she had been eating in the bushes. When Ian said he was going for the coyote, Patience screamed until he picked her up and took her with him to the bathtub by the van converted to a sauna, sticking to him by marshmallow and unwilling to be put down. "You don't say a word," Ian ordered, "You stay here and guard. I'm going to get the rifle."

He ran into the cabin, where the air was suddenly cool against his chest. He opened the bench, took the rifle between his two hands. He ran to the garden, carrying the rifle in his right hand, shoulder high. At the other side of the corn he slowed, and walked carefully to the trail where he and Christy had transplanted cuttings of wildflowers and where irises and columbines thrived, and Ian had wanted to miss them even now and stepped carefully. He came to the small clearing inside the woods and stopped there, listening.

Patience stopped then too. She had preceded him into the woods, not going nearly as carefully as Ian had through the new transplants. She could not see him from the distance, on the other side of the stream, but she could hear him. She walked only when he walked and played statue when he stopped. Patience was competitive, and despite the fact that Ian was lithe and she was stocky, she was faster, partly because she knew where her prey was and Ian was exploring. She was able to circle around him, moving when Ian moved, and she would surprise him just as the trees closed in and the light dimmed.

It was at this point that Ian most feared the coyote or whatever could cry that ugly way, because it was dark on the other side. But Patience made a mistake. She moved out of rhythm with Ian.

Ian heard the snap of a dried branch on the ground. He lifted the rifle and fired. It was loaded as he had known it would be, and the cry he heard he couldn't immediately identify. He walked into the woods, past a pin cherry tree, a spindly tree with red bark and very sour cherries his mother had made into jelly.

At the foot of a tall white pine he saw Patience. At first he thought it was a trick, which of course it was, but she was downed in the moss. He could see her body that he knew was sticky to the touch, but she wasn't talking. His heart raced and he walked closer. Her eyes were wide and full of something he'd seen in his father's eyes and knew as terror. His father's eyes came from his dreams in the night. Patience was downed in the moss. He forced himself to turn his eyes from her face to her body. He saw her round bare chest. He could see the little nipples. He heard a bird call. He saw her leg which might have been blown away. He couldn't tell. He couldn't see it. It was all blood below her little nipples. She looked down at her leg and she looked back at Ian. Before they had been in the corn. They were the same two people, but now they were in the woods between the cherry tree and the tall pine and Patience had so much blood on her.

"I'm going to die, aren't I," Patience said.

Ian dropped the rifle and lifted her up. The leg was in place but blood ran from Patience's thigh and thickly across Ian's arm and down his body. But they watched each other. They had created some other place that was safe, with their eyes holding on to each other. Ian carried her through the woods to the barn that Christy was building. He would remember that his father ripped his T-shirt up over his head, tore the seam open, tied Patience's leg tight, just below where it joined her hip. This slowed all that blood that was coming. Ian carried her in his arms in the car and he wouldn't let Christy have her. Ian carried her all the way while they drove to the hospital, tapping her temple with the tip of one finger, and said over and over, "Hey, hey, Patience," as if he were trying to wake her up. She nodded to him, and he memorized the blood on her hair and the way it stained her face.

At the emergency room they took Patience away from Ian. He was alone in the waiting room for a long, long time. He thought they must have let Christy in but they wouldn't let him in. After a while a doctor came out. He was in green scrubs with a stethoscope around his neck and a gold ring in his ear. He said, "Where's your father, son?"

"He's in there," he said. "Can I see her?"

The doc said he could in a while, but where was his dad? And when Christy could not be found, they called Sonia. Maybe they thought Christy was Patience's father and that's why they didn't call her right away.

They let Ian and Sonia have a cot in Patience's room, and he would not leave her.

They sat on the cot and watched Patience sleep. The doc came back in and sat with them. He used the phrase, "full metal jacket." He said that was a lucky thing. The bullet hadn't fragmented. It had stayed in the muscle of the child's thigh. Must have been fired from a distance. Had Ian been nearer, he'd have blasted her away.

Ian felt the rifle jerk up in his arms. They listened to the bullet in slow motion as it was fired, maybe slightly slowed as it nicked a branch here, a branch there, but it had still found Patience. In surgery they had plucked it out.

It was dead still in the hospital room. In the deep night, the doctor was gone. It was Deborah now by Ian's cot. She was wearing the black dress he had seen her wear on dates.

Deborah sat beside Sonia, and Ian pretended to be asleep while he saw his mother's arm go around Sonia's thin shoulders. He was glad she was there, but he was most aware of the IV dripping in Patience's arm — it looked way too large for Patience's body. Deborah and Sonia watched the tubes circling around to Patience's small hand and the emergency light on the bedside table and around them the tragic, antibacterial hospital smell. Deborah went to Patience's bed. The boy hadn't moved and one would have assumed he was asleep but he wasn't. He watched everything.

Ian watched her stiff back. With his mother had come the slight smell of coconut. She bent and kissed Patience. Then she looked around and saw Ian who lay like a dog at the window by her side. Ian had been stalwart, which was his nature, until then. His father had had to go. Ian bore the weight of what he had done and the weight of the waiting to see if Patience would breathe, her round belly moving up and down like it did when she fell asleep on the chaise lounge. He had borne that. He had listened to the doctor. He had borne the doctor's small talk with Sonia while the doc thought Ian was sleeping. *Could have blown her leg off completely had he been any nearer.* But when he saw his mother, Ian's body started to shake.

"So where's Christy?" she whispered. She went to Ian and he knew she'd see he was shaking.

"He got scared." Ian tried to talk normally and bear seeing his mother see what he had done. But Ian struggled with words. "He made her stop bleeding. But then he couldn't stay."

"He left you alone?"

Ian shook his head, "He had to go."

"The bastard," but Ian had her hand so tight. He didn't want her to do that. She didn't know how it was for him and his father. Maybe Sonia knew more than Deborah about this. Ian had talked and talked earlier that night because he could see Sonia needed all the words he could give her while they waited. He said once Christy had slept on the floor in Ian's room, after Christy had cried out in the night. Christy on the floor so that if Ian had reached down on the side of his bed he would have touched his father's face. They never talked about it. Now Sonia and Ian added this image to the language of full metal jacket and fragmentation.

PATIENCE stayed in the hospital four days. Deborah stayed in the cabin with Sonia.

On the fourth morning they drove into town to get some milk and gummi worms, which had been requested. That was the first time they saw Christy, and they hadn't seen Ian that day. Christy was at the antique shop in town where he was working with Mackie. Mackie's was slowly sinking into the earth, so rotted was the porch and the floor. Christy was sitting by the round EX-LAX sign above the rusted sled and the rabbit lawn ornaments and, on a supporting post, the skull and antlers of a deer in among the trailing vines of a dozen English ivies. He was a statue here. They pulled up in front of the store. Deborah got out. It was warm that day and she wore shorts and a blue, striped shirt. As she walked, a breeze made her shirt balloon and she zipped her fleece jacket over it. She stood in front of Christy, her hands by her sides. "I'm taking Ian home."

He didn't answer.

"Where is he?"

Christy gestured across the street where the Three Eves still was and several more stores and down the way the public library. Ian came walking, this kid who was eight, almost nine. Lightly built, the stride of his long-legged father. Maybe Deborah and Sonia both noticed for the first time that he walked like his father. Ian nodded to his mother. Then he allowed himself to wrap his arms around her and bury his face only for a second into the fleece of the shoulder of her jacket. A second more.

"You want to come?" Deborah asked Ian as she went back to the car.

Ian shook his head.

"It's you she asks for," she yelled at Christy before she slammed the door.

They made an elaborate ritual of eating caramel ice cream, which was Patience's food request in addition to the worms, but she didn't eat more than a spoonful. Patience's leg was wrapped to twice the size of the other one, and if she was in pain she wouldn't say. They all sat around the dark, round table. Then they went outside and sat on the porch, trying to find things that would make Patience the way she had been before.

"What do you want?" Sonia asked Patience.

"I want . . ." Her face got round and red. "I want to play store."

"Okay," Sonia said. "How do you play?"

"I'll show you."

Patience made signs on pieces of paper. She played clerk. She asked for the clothes in her bottom drawer. Patience found a lace shawl with fringe and wrapped it around her face. Cody came and sat beside her and Patience added pets to the stock. She sold puppies as well as evening gowns. She rang them up on a box that was a pretend cash register. She allowed Cody to be a customer. She created an entire fantasy around the table with her veil, and the pretend cash register.

"That's okay," she kept saying to Cody. "That's okay," and

she stroked her leg in circular motions. "That's okay. That's okay."

She looked at Sonia and smiled as if to tell her, too, That's okay, Mommy. She never cried. She reassured.

Deborah sat down at the table with Patience and Sonia with whom Patience was sharing the dog. Patience was enfolded in the lace shawl so that she looked like an old woman, or they were able to imagine her as an old woman. She held the lace between her fingers and stroked it back and forth. She smiled at Deborah from underneath.

They heard the sound of the car and Patience's face lit. When Christy came in, she threw herself into his arms. She wept and he held her although he was withdrawn and rigid, even on his knees.

Ian stood by the door. He swung the thick door between his bare feet, nonchalant, chewing a stick of black licorice between his left molars.

"Didn't you get any red?" Patience said to him.

He ignored her. Christy was up and striding around.

Deborah got up from the table and went to the sink. She was trying to pour a glass of juice from a green pitcher made of faceted glass. "The man's got an arsenal," she said, "and he never has to respond to the fact that he's got an arsenal." She had said this softly, but now she threw the glass pitcher out through the window, which it smashed as well as smashing itself on the rock below. Each smash was at a slightly different pitch and seemed to last a long time. "Bastard." She walked to him, her hands by her side. "Get the weapons out of the house. Do you have more? What is in the homestead? Are you crazy?"

Everyone had turned to watch her and Christy. It had always been a quiet house with only music and details, the fine trim around the plates. A tea ball left just so long. "How does a man get so many people to fall in love with him?" Deborah screamed. "How does a man get so much devotion?" she said hoarsely.

Patience sold Cody to an imaginary girl.

"That's it, Mom," Ian said. "That's the only rifle we had. I knew."

"Get it out."

"It's gone," Christy said.

"Get it out. Get it out."

PART II

We've only been fighting ten years.
Do you really have to go?

GREG BROWN

Not everything in America has to
be permanent.

LEON BOTSTEIN

14. The Soldier

CHRISTY had been talking to Sonia and when he got home, Ian was out. Now Christy would stay by the phone in case Patience called. Dennis was about to whelp. The air was thick with Jane, his neighbor.

This was Dennis's first litter and it would be her only litter because it had been too hard on Christy. He had worried about her from the time she sneaked out when she was in heat, cursing himself for not having her spayed when he should have. She came back that night, her ears flat and her white ruff soiled, and he made her fried egg on toast with milk which she ate on the sly, the beginning of her maternal testiness.

Once, between times that he followed Deborah to Portsmouth, Jane, a kindergarten teacher, had invited Christy to come and speak to her class about Asia because he had been there, and the children were reading stories about China. Jane used to live in a teepee that she built and set up on a small, flat clearing down the hill from the spring and the homestead and the arts and crafts cabin. It was okay for her there in the summer, and she survived the muddy spring, but in the winter she started bringing her sleeping bag up to Christy's. Christy didn't know how it came to be that she was telling stories about Asia to little children. But he was willing to go.

The kindergarten was in a small room with desks in a cluster and a large bean bag chair all the children clung to like it was a dirigible from which they could watch this solidly built man in a white shirt he had ironed carefully (even the collar tabs and the cuffs, though one cuff was scorched). They clung to it when Christy first walked in, though later they were tugging his hands. One of the students, a boy, asked what Christy ate there, confusing Asia with the Arctic, which they had studied previously, and suspecting he had killed Arctic moose or something. Christy said No, he hadn't shot moose. Not in Asia. In Vietnam, among other things, he shot rats, which he didn't tell the kids about. They asked him how he had traveled. He tried to explain that sometimes they were in helicopters, but mostly they walked very slowly on dirt roads.

He became one of them and while he talked, he could see himself down there in front. He could tell the children were trying to picture him in a dogsled, calling out to his dogs. They didn't have chronology down so they could hold in their heads that the Cold War followed Arctic expeditions. Christy liked that. He didn't have chronology down either. Some days he was in Vietnam, some days he was with his wife, and some days he made a fantasy with the smell of Jane's hydrangea oil that stayed in the house after she left at dawn; and some days he was with his chain saw, clearing off fallen trees and trying to let in the light, first to his house, then to the garden, trying to make the ring of light wider or sometimes just holding back the forest as best that he could from taking back the house.

It surprised him how much he liked being with the kids. He liked the urgency of everything with them — why was his dog on the roof? (Dennis used to climb out the window from the loft and nap in the sun on the overhang.) Could they come over and see him? What did Christy eat for supper? What about his dog? what time? would he come back and tell them about the Civil War?

Christy said he didn't know too much about the Civil War. A little girl slid off the ship and undid his bootlaces and redid them. Jane smiled and Christy was aware of the slight arch of Jane's lips and he wondered briefly if it was with her that he could say, Baby, it doesn't get any better than this, something he had read in a book and had never considered saying to anyone.

Jane was explaining that Christy had taught at Franconia College when it used to be here. Nothing remained of the college except some dorms in Franconia that were now office buildings. The college, to the children, could have been the ruin of a Roman villa. They had been told to look at a field off Forest Hills Road where a sign across the way offered "magnificent home sites." They had been told, here was the dining hall, at this end were the administration offices, here was the room where they held the core lectures. On the upper floors were the dorms. And some students never set foot outdoors all winter. If the children knew there had been a college here, those were the things they had heard.

The children looked at Christy and to them, maybe he was mythic. If he was from the ruins of the college, couldn't he be an Arctic explorer, a Roman king, a soldier from any war? The girl gave him double knots and he left them, this guy in a white shirt, starched and billowed and armorlike.

And now his wife was coming back. Something happened inside of him when he knew he was about to see her. It was a pain that he'd begun to savor. All torch songs were their songs. She had become a kind of fiction to him. He replayed their marriage and made it probably a lot nicer than it had been, but that was a habit now. Sometimes he pretended that they didn't marry. That she was someone he could have married for love, but he never asked her. They were tragic lovers who didn't speak at the right time and their lives moved on. He spent a lot of time in his head. This fiction was off-putting to the single women who had made mountain forays, some for years, or their whole lives, and were attracted to the man in the book-lined cabin who watched them with appreciation, his eyes quiet and attentive. It was a skill he had developed as a boy and the women had always been there, but this gave him little pleasure. So he did look at women with extreme affection, maybe re-membering lines such as, Oh, Baby, it doesn't get any better than this. But when the opportunity came, he cooked them lovely, hearty whole-grain pasta with rainbow-colored vegeta-bles and maybe made love to them, and groaned with pleasure, to give the women pleasure for which women fell in love with him on the spot, and then he went back to his desk or the gar-den and the women slipped his mind because he lived in his fic-tions, and didn't seem to notice when the women went, which the women tended to forgive him for too many times because they were creating their own fictions about themselves and Christy cooking together and making love together, two free spirits who would ease each other's lives.

He felt alive in life-or-death matters, but if life should pre-vail, he fell into a dark place of drink and listening to the night and the day. When the headaches came, he could take the edge off them with painkillers, but they never lifted completely, just as his mind never stilled.

He sat with the dog as the evening descended and poured himself a drink and let in the riot of sound that to others would have been stillness: only the owl in the spruce tree, and farther out a piano note here and there from Sonia's cabin. The sounds pulsed across his left temple.

Some people would think it naive that Christy would con-tinue to marry his wife, if not every time she came back, then at least, too often. Dennis had come closer than anybody to taking on the significance of wife to him with her careless ways since the puppies were due.

When Ian was six or seven, the school year before Patience's accident, he spent almost as much time at his father's house as his mother's house. He and Christy had lived together silently. In the silence Ian had been hyperaware of his father's hands and his manner of doing things, the way he held an ax or the way he held a kitchen knife or his shotgun. Sometimes he had been overcome with a question. Once he came in and stood by the woodstove, his face scrunched under his snow hat with flaps. He stroked an earlier Dennis but clearly had something else on his mind. Eventually he said, "Do you have a wife and she doesn't come out?"

"Well, no," Christy said.

"I thought you might have a wife and she doesn't come out."

"No."

"Do you have a wife someplace else?"

"Not a wife."

"Because Lisa's not your wife."

"No, Lisa's my friend."

Ian nodded. Christy wanted to lift his flaps so he wouldn't look so wizened.

"And Ms. Saucily isn't your wife. Mom said that," Ian said. Ms. Saucily was one of the teachers at the high school.

"No, she just lived up in a cabin for a while and we got to be friends."

Ian studied him. He said, "Mom's not married either."

Dennis dropped down on the kitchen floor, weary from standing. She dropped on the long cord of the telephone so that it lay under one leg and over another and Ian and Christy looked and foresaw the crash of the telephone, the pottery lamp that Deborah had turned on a wheel in the studio, the table the lamp sat on. The lamp was squat and creviced like the waist of a plump, solid woman. They lifted the cord free of Dennis's paws and then, because they seemed to have more to talk about, Christy invited Ian to go get groceries with him.

"Coffee?" he asked Ian when they got to the store. Customers could get a cup of coffee in the bakery department. Ian looked at the sign on the coffee stand. It said, FREE. HELP YOURSELF. The bakery man had put it there and he wore a Red Sox cap that Ian studied as well. Colombian or French Roast.

"French," Ian said.

They each got a small white styrofoam cupful, black, since Christy drank it that way. They walked through the bakery section. Both of them were wearing snow pants and walked stiff legged.

Ian said, "Do you wish you could have a wife?"

"I can't remember having one," Christy said.

"But you want one?"

"Ian, I have bad luck with women."

"Maybe you should learn to dance."

Christy looked at him. He shimmied down, his shoulders raised, and sang, "Get down low."

Ian insisted on being the straight man. "Mom likes to dance," he said. "Sometimes when I'm in bed, she puts on the radio and dances around the living room all by herself with the lights out."

Christy thought of Deborah dancing. He could see her arms in the air and her hips sway, listening to the Dead. He could see shadows on her living-room wall from her body moving, her head back. He followed the shape of her ears.

They bought the baker's bread, still warm, not sliced. After they got in the car and were driving along the Gale River, Ian and Christy passed the loaf back and forth, ripping at it with their teeth, dropping hunks of crumbs over their snowsuits and all over Christy's little, two-door Ford without any shocks that he got when the Newport died. The Newport was still there on a turn, off the dirt road, on the way to the cabin.

♦ ♦ ♦

IT was winter. One snowstorm after another had blown through the Notch. Now Ian was working on the mountain or getting ready to go, and Patience would be coming home from Rindge. The thought of Patience made Christy anxious and he didn't know if it was just a habit. Was there really trouble? The child had always made his heart race and he had gone to lengths not to be around much if she was coming home.

By the time Christmas week came, the woods were deep with snow and the trees were rimed. Christy's cabin was a sprawling wooden house with roof shingles crisscrossed to form a pattern almost Navajo-like, an A-frame section, a long deck into the trees, shingles in which he had chiseled designs into the soft wood. It was a sculpture. He had added on to it nearly every summer since he had built it.

There had been a lot of women. Christy didn't understand it so there was no way he could explain women to Ian, and that hadn't changed over the years. Now there was Jane. She was in the house sometimes. She collected wrecks of bicycles that she repaired and sold. Now a dozen rusted bicycles under snow-covered turquoise tarps leaned against the trees. Her futon draped in a throw rug was in the living room, and she'd hung curtains from birch branches resting on teacup hooks over the windows. He had let her stay there when the teepee began to leak. He said teepees were not a long-term house and she had nodded and asked if she could put some of her stuff in Christy's house until she found a place, so that's how it began. But Christy had come to be aware that she was not leaving. He wasn't a man with a wide focus and a lot of people had come and gone from his place, so it took him a while to notice the curtains on birch branches. The paperbacks on his coffee table.

He opened the back door and went in to his kitchen in which Deborah and he had hung everything from bunches of onions to asters to skillets. The same dead asters were still hanging there, or at least they seemed to be the same to Christy. He disliked change.

Jane came racing down the stairs into the kitchen. She said, "Oh, Christ."

She had the longest hair in New Hampshire and a lot of people had long hair there. It was pale yellow, almost white.

"Packing, Jane?" he said. "What is that smell?"

"Damn," she said, "I forgot." She had stopped short at the sight of him. She was wearing little flats over short crew socks that came just to her ankles, a jean skirt and a navy ribbed sweater. "Bend to Me," she said.

"What?" he said.

"It's called Bend to Me." She showed him a little vial she had left on the counter. "It's oil made from hydrangeas. You can get it at the incense store."

It did indeed have the strong and heavy scent of hydrangeas.

He said, "Moving's not something you forget. You forgot to move?"

She pulled on a flannel shirt over her sweater and the strap of a cotton bag over her shoulder. Dennis adored her and came and laid her face against Jane's thigh.

"Maybe I'll be a model," Jane said. "Maybe I'll be in the Three Eve's Shopping Night." She walked lightly across the floor into the living room with the picture window. Both Christy's and Dennis's eyes followed her.

Deborah had liked to work in the pottery studio. Looking at Jane, her hand on her waist with a corner of her jean skirt hiked up, Christy remembered sometimes when he put his arms around his wife, her hands were wet with clay and she held them in the air until their legs were starting to give way and there was nothing for them to do but lie down on their mattress by the window.

"Did you ever read *The Stranger*?" he asked Jane who was standing, her hands on her hips, her legs squared.

Jane shook her head.

"The guy is tried for not loving enough. He didn't love his mother. He drank latte at her wake. And when his girlfriend asks him, Do you want to get married? he says, I don't care, if you want to. Not, I love you Baby, it doesn't get any better than this."

Jane listened to this, her head to one side.

He always wanted to talk about *The Stranger* and there weren't too many people around who would take it.

Jane sat down, catlike, on the couch Christy had built into the wall under his picture window. She said, "Oh, Christy, why is it we're never happy with what we've got? Why are we always looking around the corner? Why are we so tragic? You know. What if, what if everything we have ever done was the right thing? Maybe the stranger was right not to love his mother. Do you know the kind I mean? The woman who has never been wrong and if you don't agree with her she doesn't love you anymore. Why should he love her?" She shrugged and he thought of her bumper sticker, something about national health insurance. She was the only person he knew with a bumper sticker about health insurance, and that touched him.

He remembered going to see Deborah in her office in Portsmouth, after he tracked her to the city the second time. She was wearing her suit and held her hands as if she were holding something fragile and she said, "It's so frustrating because it has to unfold." She had said it as tears streamed down her cheeks, messing up the eyeliner she also wore in the city.

That day in her office, she had shut the door. "I never thought you'd come here. Why can't you ever have things when you want them so bad? Why do you always have to wait and lose hope? What does that mean?"

She'd had the radio on. It was winter then too. It was 1986 and on the radio they had been covering the liftoff of the

Challenger and then, while Deborah's hands were extended, they said on the radio that the Challenger had exploded. Christy always had an image of that day, of the two of them, he at the door, Deborah standing over a pile of books at her desk, both of them with their arms a little away from their bodies as if to catch the astronauts who would float into their arms. Deborah would never understand that. She would say he was crazy.

Jane had gotten up from the couch to make tea.

"Deborah said my problem was that people were interchangeable to me. I don't see it that way. Maybe a person has the capacity only to hold in their imagination a few types of people. It doesn't mean you don't love them. You just can't conceive of them. So you make a person what you can conceive."

"Do I do that?" she said.

He shrugged. "I don't know."

"I can conceive of me not as a teacher."

"What else is there to do?" Christy said. "It's kind of late to be something else."

"I could work in the bakery where a friend of mine works. The one by the mill where they bake bread for the hotels? She said last summer they worked in cutoffs and halter tops and when it got hotter than they could stand, they took off their clothes and dove into the falls."

Christy got up in a waft of hot summer air and the smell of bread. He felt old and disoriented and his head throbbed. Another woman going to a bakery. His hair was heavily gray and still slightly long, past his collar. He had a son who was twenty and a girl like a daughter who was seventeen and no one really knew where she was. He was aware the phone had not rung. He could go in and out of conversations with people, not aware he was doing it, but Jane would have felt it. He thought maybe she had asked him something. It had been important, and he hadn't answered and the time had passed in which for him to answer it.

He was aware of her standing in the doorway. Her coat was on. She wore boots and not the little shoes she had come down in. Her hair streamed down her back. He had taken her in slowly from the boots and up to her hair and, feeling some embarrassment, to her blue, and now still eyes that were so animated with the children.

"Don't worry," she said. "I'm out of here."

His mind went off to a restaurant Michael had opened in town. A Jamaican restaurant. It offered Jamaican food and beer and it was fine. Michael had been collecting ideas all the times he'd gone there.

Jane said, "Maybe it doesn't matter, like the stranger says."

Christy was vaguely aware that the door slammed and Jane had left, and he was full of despair for the dissolution of things and the people he had failed and middle-aged Jane jumping into the falls at the bakery and him maybe working the bar in the Jamaican place in the Notch where there used to be hotels and then a college where he had come and then he married, vowing never to look back. How had he let it all slip?

Bend to Me lingered in the air.

The solstice had already come. If the dog would just hold off on the pups. But now Christy shoveled some of the path from the back door to his truck. Dennis came. It had been snowing all day. Now it was dusk and about fourteen inches had fallen. Dennis yelped, glad to be outdoors, and lumbered through the high snow. Christy worked for a while, then took his gloves off to curl and uncurl his fingers. He ran his hand over Dennis's cold, tawny fur, then against his cheek with four days worth of beard, wondering when Patience and Deborah would appear and if it would seem like mostly indigestion, the chronic pain that would come in his gut. The dog leaned into him.

15. Runaway

It was Sunday before Christmas, the night Deborah and Phuong baked at the Ceres in Portsmouth and she gave him the bird made of wood.

In the town of Rindge, two girls sat in rickety captain's chairs in a kitchen in a farmhouse with sloping floors and ceilings so low they cut a right angle with the door frames. On a third chair was a doll of sorts, a limp doll with yellow yarn hair, its arms and legs stuffed with cotton, in a child's vivid green long underwear. It sat nonchalantly in the chair with one green leg draped over the other.

This was a house where Ian and Christy, both over six feet, could be injured in a moment of inattention, a downtrodden eighteenth-century farmhouse Patience and Molly, the girls, shared with four other students. Patience sat, her chin propped on her hands, her thick pale brown hair the color of a sand dollar, Deborah had always said. Now it was divided in sections and wrapped in silver electrical wire, hanging decoratively from the crown of her head and on the sides to her temples.

They were learning to bake bagels. They had worked stiff dough into rings and rubbed the tops with garlic and now waited for them to come out of the oven.

"Do you think he'll like it?" Patience said.

They both eyed the doll. Then they burst out laughing, imagining Christy, whom Molly had met safely in the garden one late summer day when he and Ian came with Patience's trunk.

"Will he notice it's a Raggedy Ann and not a china doll?"

Molly couldn't stop laughing. "It doesn't look like either. It looks like the Grinch."

"How can we make it look like a china doll?"

Molly pushed up the sleeves on her baggy sweater and considered the doll's face. Then she went away and came back with a paintbrush and paint. She went to work and painted perfect, red, china-doll lips and then blue, liquid eyes but, of course, it still had the ability to throw one limp Grinch leg nonchalantly across the other.

"Okay, that's better," said Patience who had sewn the doll, a skill she had gotten at the Meeting School, and she pulled down the cuff of its long underwear so its pale, muslin legs were not exposed. "I can't find the book but I remember every word of it. I made him read it five million times. *Buy me a china doll, do Daddy do.* We changed the words. Christy always does that."

Patience and Molly left the doll on the chair, looking surprised at its own transformation.

At the Meeting School, Andrew, the head teacher, sat with students in these captain's chairs around the dining-room table and they wrote small stories and sometimes read them out loud. Patience discovered Sarah Orne Jewett in a book on the shelves of the living-room library. She tended to read one book over and over and over.

Molly said, "I wish I didn't have to go home anymore." She pulled her thick blond hair back and held it loosely in both of her hands.

Patience wore a bulky gray sweater over a round-necked pink shirt and had wiped flour on the gray wool. She pushed up the wool sleeves and set back to work on more bagels. She thought she would be either a baker or a ranger.

Before vacation began, they were making confessions to each other.

"What do you talk about? You and Ian." They wound together five more bagels. They worked, both with silver rings on each of their fingers.

"Nothing. We just look at stuff together."

They brewed raspberry herb tea in a pot. They got out the fancy set of cups with saucers. Molly poured milk in each cup. She put the hood up on her sweater against the chill of the house.

"See, there was an accident when we were little," Patience said. "I think that's why he lets me hang out with him."

"What happened?" They had started this tea idea after they got back at Thanksgiving. Every parting, now, they confessed something to each other. It had something to do with the ritual of the milk and the tea strainer, and the honey, that there were necessary steps to making the tea. At Thanksgiving, Molly told Patience about being touched in her private places and that it had not been by her choice, and that she dreaded going home.

Patience laid the tea strainer over Molly's cup and poured the tea, then she laid the strainer over her own cup and poured.

"With a rifle," Patience explained. "Ian thought I was a coyote. Maybe I was a coyote."

In the milky mixture they each put two spoonfuls of turbinado sugar from a silver sugar bowl shaped like an apple and stirred, the clink, clink of the spoons making them feel innocent, like they hadn't done every drug and experienced life at its most fragile. Molly looked up at Patience from under her hood, her eyes dark and without emotion. That's why Patience could talk to her.

"Do you mean you got shot?"

"Yeah, but he wasn't a very good aim. That's what they were saying in the emergency room. We were just kids. It was just something that happened."

"I don't understand," Molly said. "How old was he? Why did he think you were a coyote?"

"He was eight. I don't know. It was dark, I guess."

They took the first bagels out of the oven, put in the last ones, and each put a bagel on a china plate. They sat down with the doll. They tried to split the bagels with dinner knives. They finally just smeared them with soft butter and raspberry jam.

"Things just happen to you. Bullets happen to you. Why is that?"

Patience leaned forward and Molly leaned forward and they looked at each other in the light of their candle. "It wasn't dark, really," Patience said. "I remember the sun shining through the pine trees. You know how the sun can be blocked but you can see all the rays splayed between a row of pine trees."

"I wish I could go with you," Molly said. She had gotten jam in her blond hair and on the little hairs around the corner of her finely shaped mouth.

"Me, too." She sighed. "I'd give anything."

They went back to chewing the rugged, garlicky bagels.

"You're gonna come back?" Molly said.

"Oh, yeah."

"We promised we'd finish the year."

"Yeah, we will. Are you scared to go home?" Patience said.

"No."

"Take this." Patience slid a knife toward Molly. It was the sharp one they used to slice vegetables.

"You are tough," Molly said. "But he wouldn't dare anymore. That's when I was little."

"This one gives you permission," Patience said about the knife.

"Did you ever sleep with Ian?"

Patience shook her head and the coils moved from side to side. "Oh no. Not Ian."

Molly shoved the knife back. "Don't let anybody hurt you."

They went to their room. Someone had left a letter underneath the door. Patience had not been picking up her mail so this one had been sitting in her box since yesterday. It was from Ian. She opened it. It was only a few lines. He was worried. Ian was the worrier and the planner. He said, Where would she go if she didn't come home? Was she crazy? He'd keep trying to call and then he would just come down.

Patience put the letter on her dresser and got into bed with all her clothes still on. She and Molly reached out and held hands from their beds which were close to each other in the small room.

"You better come back," Molly said.

"Yes," Patience said.

"And when we graduate we can get a house in Peterborough and we can stay together."

"Yeah, we can do that." But Christmas lay heavy on her.

In the early, early morning the girls hugged each other good-bye.

Patience strapped her sleeping bag on her back. She put on white evening gloves, the kind a great-grandmother would have worn to church, and over them her winter gloves. She had a supply of bagels, wrapped in thin tinfoil, and a book, and the homemade, muslin china doll, whose lips and eyes had by then dried, wrapped in a piece of weaving she had made for her mother, tucked in the sleeping bag straps.

"What do I say when they think you're missing."

"Just say I wanted to get home by myself. I love you, Moll."

Molly buttoned her heavy sweater over her nightgown and sat cross-legged on the bed. She let her long hair fall over her face and didn't look up even after the sound of the door latching. "I love you, too."

So that is what Molly told Andrew and that is what Andrew told Sonia when Sonia called again, and what Molly explained in more detail to Ian when he got her to talk to him Monday night, so in the end he didn't drive down because Patience was no longer there.

IAN was a ragtag kid. He could ski anything. He grew up skiing the long, racy trails from top to bottom of Cannon. In the summer he and his friends cleared the ski trail down Mittersill, a lost trail. In the winter no grooming machine would touch it, but he could take the Cannon tram almost to the top of it. It was a straight shot down, then high speed turns into a tuck. Ian was a mountain animal with a wide chest and strong legs. He was dogged and a loner.

He hated when the dark came and the tram stopped running, and that was when he hung out with the guys who did rescue and in this way spent little time at home.

Ian always wanted to be insouciant and sometimes, walking down the street in town when he wasn't talking to anybody, just walking alone, he took his easygoing smile off his face and attempted an attitude. He tried to put it in his walk. He pictured a man unaware of other people unless they could be of use to him, as he was occasionally to his father. A man with important things on his mind that weren't anybody else's business.

The women who came to his father's Wednesday night sauna took the insouciance out of him, because everyone was nude and he found women beautiful. He got hard on Wednesdays from about four o'clock, before anyone came over with the potluck dishes.

He'd told the crew at the fire station he'd come down and hang out that night, listen to the scanner. He was on the rescue crew and people did more unusual things over the holidays than other weeks. He was also expecting Patience to call. She'd show up out of nowhere. She had done that other weekends. Everybody was worried. Sonia and Christy had stood in the road talking for a long time. His mother was coming soon. She might be here already. He didn't like it when Patience hitched. He would tell her this time. It would make her furious.

He and Patience had talked often on the phone since she got sent to the Meeting School. They had short conversations in which there was a lot of silence. Once he had called her at midnight and a mockingbird had been singing. The conversation was composed of the mockingbird singing — a mockingbird at midnight. They had been the only two people in the world and later they didn't know at which end of the phone in real life the mockingbird had been, though they'd had the same moon.

One time she called him and said, "I dreamt I was in Bethlehem. I knew I was because it was minus ten and Hasidic Jews with ear curls were walking down Main Street."

"You got it," he said.

"You know my favorite place in the world, Ian?"

"No."

"The stupid store. I miss the way it smells. Yesterday somebody dug up a coat from out of mothballs, and now even mothballs make me homesick. And I miss the restaurant, too."

"I don't even remember the restaurant so how could you?"

"Yeah, well, I miss the midnight feasts Mom said they served when the bands stopped playing and they went back to Boston. Ian, how come we never had any bands?"

"'Cause we lost out. 'Cause we're crackheads," he said. "'Cause you're crazy."

"You know nothing," she said. And they went on in this way and tonight he missed it.

On Monday around midafternoon, he was in his room in the loft, playing his guitar. He was playing the single notes of the

Doors' song, "Hello, I love you, won't you tell me your name?" He played this repeatedly, listening for the door to open and slam and for Patience to call his name.

The snow was packed in around the small porch on the front as it had been on all the other Christmases. He could see it in the spotlight they had over the area that was their garden. The snow had blown deep by the greenhouse and by the arbor they had built going into the garden. The chicken-wire fences were buried. A cat, Jane's, lay tapered like a violin across his bureau. The cat was silver gray.

He thought he heard something on the road. Ian, bare-faced with brown hair in a ponytail, thundered down the open, wooden staircase. He wore heavy olive drab boots, open and loose, and eased his head back at the top of the landing to keep from hitting his forehead, a motion so smooth, it made it seem he always descended the stairs this way.

Nothing was there. Only his father up the driveway, shoveling. He saw the dog's tracks in the snow.

Still he imagined her. She was eerily like her mother, except for the metal cylinders in her hair that shook while she talked. "Nice," Ian would say about them. He would grin and shake his head at her, then hug her, then pick her up and walk around with her.

He would say, Damn you, girl, do you know he's called every cop in the state?

The cat had followed him down. A memory filled his brain: a flash of the pin cherry tree and the sound of his rifle.

He got a beer from the fridge. He was nothing but a shit-faced ski bum. Shit. He paced with the beer, and the cat watched him. He wanted to move far away or at least out of the house, but he didn't have the money. He loved the rescue team, but it was volunteer time. They were all volunteers. Besides that, he liked to drink. He was an easygoing guy. Everybody liked him. It was just this lazy streak.

The cat got up and stretched out — a thin elongated creature. Ian heated up some chili that was in a skillet, knowing he was a son that didn't measure up.

He wanted to put on his parka and his stocking cap and get out of there, but he knew Patience would try to reach him. Time was on hold. He watched his father and the dog and ate chili from the pot with a wooden spoon as he and Patience would have done, the skillet between them on the table.

PATIENCE hitched a ride from Rindge as far as Peterborough with a locksmith named Maurice. He let her out at Nonie's Café in the early morning where she could hear the crash of the falls across the road.

She walked up the street, like a lot of kids with packs who have nowhere to go, but Maurice would have thought the girl had somewhere to go. She felt him watch her until she was out of sight. She hoped he wouldn't call the cops. She walked around the corner, past the jeweler's shop, the stationers, a gift shop, all of which were quiet. She stopped at the pay phone down from the restaurant from which she knew piano music would come in the night. She called her mother. Nobody was home. Her mother's soft voice on the machine almost made her cry. She wasn't sure what her plans were. But she tried to push away that voice. She left a message saying she was on her way. Don't worry about her. Ian didn't have to take time off work to drive down.

In the town, Roy's market was open, and beside it was the diner where four cars were pulled up in front. The marquee on the cinema across the street said THE PASSION OF SAINT JOAN. What if she stayed? She'd find a ride north later. She was attracted to the name, *The Passion of Saint Joan*. She wanted to be able to tell Ian about it. Patience hung around the town. She sat on the curb by the pet store, smoking Marlboros in the white gloves over which she had pulled woolen fingerless gloves. She was wearing a long dress and she pulled the skirt of it over her knees and ankles in gray woolen tights.

She was a child of the woods. What if she couldn't go back? What if she stayed in the town with art cinemas and cafés where they sold cinnamon coffee and croissants? She thought of Deborah, speckled with paint across her baggy sweater from one of her projects and her thick black hair with strands of gray around her face and her hair caught under the collar of her flannel.

She sat with her pack against her knees and the china doll, too, who looked alert, and, with Molly's painted-on eyes and plum-colored mouth, looked startled and self-satisfied at the same time, if already a little beat up.

16. Consigned to the Moon

AT seven o'clock that night, since she had not yet left the dark little town with the falls, Patience went into the theater. It was a small, refurbished theater with red carpet runners and a velvet drape across the stage. She had been here once with Molly and Daniel from the Meeting School when they had seen *Black Orpheus*.

Patience walked down to the front of the theater and sat down in the soft-piled seats. The film would begin soon. A few people came in and Patience remembered the community she had left at school. She thought of the meeting time when no one would be talking. She had hated that when Andrew said it was time to worship, she did not know what to worship. They sat in the main room of the old, sprawling farmhouse with the quilt tacked over the drafty fireplace. What should she worship, the dirt? or the rug? But she missed worship and knew they would worry about her.

The floors creaked as people entered the theater and walked

down the red carpet runners toward the red velvet stage curtain. She took off her coat. Her gloves made her wrist bones stand out. Under her sweater was revealed a polka-dot dress. In the heated theater, she took off the sweater. She felt appropriately dressed, and she was in a way for Peterborough, a town with a 1930s feel. She did have the addition of the silver wire in coils around bunches of her hair.

When the movie began, she was transfixed. She thought Joan of Arc's eyes were the most beautiful eyes she had ever seen. She saw them in the cinema in a haze. She was unaware of anyone else in the theater, though there were small pockets of people around her. She sat motionless and watched the screen and her eyes became more and more spellbound by Joan's face, which was almost always in close-up, her eyes swimming, always in ecstasy or anguish. Patience took in every stab of emotion, so that when the movie was over, she couldn't move. She sat there, her gloved hands clasping her left thigh over the gunshot wound, her shoulders forward, her polka dots enhanced with dark tearstains, her lips, which were round with a distinct and chiseled notch above, open and lax.

Finally the guy who had sold muffins and springwater in the small lobby came through. "All right," he said. He was young, a prep school type, she thought, skinny, in a greatcoat with the belt looped in the back, pushing a broom. He pushed the broom by her.

She held her thighs tighter.

"Hey, they're locking up," he said. He went down the center, up the far side with the broom. Patience started to come back, in her head, to the theater.

The young man said, "You need a ride? If you need a ride or something, I can help you out."

She said, "How much time do you have?"

He shrugged.

She was unsmiling. She came and stood by him where he worked. He said, "You know, that actress never made another movie."

Patience didn't answer. She watched him moving up and down the aisles but she kept seeing the actress's swimming eyes.

He said his name was Jamie. He said he was studying film-making in Boston and he could tell her a lot of things about films. He said this was a job for over the holidays, but he liked it because now he could almost recite the lines, watching these movies over and over every night. Patience continued to watch him. He was slightly flustered talking to her and then told her his family had summered here and finally stayed on because, more and more, coming to Peterborough was like coming home. She listened and then asked if he'd drive her north, up to Franconia Notch.

17. The Thrush's Call: Come In

DEBORAH left the town, its white Christmas lights muted by a light snow, and headed out Mount Cleveland Road toward what had been the commune. It was cold. The temperature had dropped, the sky was overcast but still bigger than Deborah was accustomed to it being. A stack of empty plastic pots on a porch, like she had used for starting tomato plants inside, brought her a flash of spring. She had the memory of lushness and a curtain billowing in a temperate breeze. Sometimes she thought she could imagine spring better than she could experience it. She wanted to think nothing bad could happen to a girl in this muted, lighted winter. She remembered the time she and Ian and Patience put the canoe in at dusk on the Piscataqua, and by the time they came back toward home under the bridge, how the water under their paddles fell like fireworks of light — emitting showers of sparks like those from the firecrackers Ian set up on the grass on the Fourth of July.

Patience wasn't like Deborah's family of women, thin-skinned as poppies, all showy with lips too full, black hair coiled, and earrings made of papier-mâché and clay bought in seaside shops. Her mother recounted failures years before anyone lived them. What if you are sick, honey? You have to think of these things. Or lose your legs, like Christy — Helen had always viewed Christy as somebody without legs, in her opinion he was that equivalently impaired. Don't you ever set foot in my house again, was what Helen said after one Christmas when Christy and Deborah came, ragged hippies, having driven all night on a lark to get there Christmas Day.

Deborah continued down Mount Cleveland Road. The snow was deep but she followed in another car's tracks and drove the road that, under the snow, would have turned from paved to dirt. She left the car by the homestead house where the snow had accumulated in drifts. There were roads now, not just the paths. Christy had been working on the barn. It loomed over the outhouse below and below that the garden where they had grown marijuana until the whole area became more accessible. Then they farmed deeper in the woods and in late June even the paths were overgrown with wild roses.

Deborah took out her pack and walked up the road that forked right, to Sonia's. Looking back at the times she had lived here, she felt the old weariness of pot, and of waking up in so many different people's sleeping bags; she used to dream of celibacy and hot inside water, not the shower where she stood on some plywood in the snow. But she hadn't been celibate at all. And she kept coming back to the woods, as if, if she hung out with the Buddha enough times, finally she would understand.

She walked up the path in high snow. She could imagine Patience talking. She'd look up from her book and smile her aw shucks smile, It's just me, Cool, so you came, So what's new in the land of good hair — she'd always made fun of

Portsmouth as the place of portobello mushrooms and good hair.

Deborah looked for light in the window.

"*Hey* you," she yelled. "*Hey* girl." Her picture of Sonia slipped back to the girl she had known the summer after the college closed. The summer when Christy had said Deborah had used up three of her lives and she'd better not count on any more since he wasn't going to be around so maybe she'd better get a flack vest.

"Hey," she yelled.

She opened the door and stood in the middle of the room. The smell of solitude hit her. She stirred the embers in the stove and added wood to make the place ready for Sonia. Where are you? The room was orderly, and the loneliness came like a heavy, heavy coat that made her breath shallow.

"Hey you," she whispered.

It was not safe there. And there was a sureness in the sky that a storm was coming.

Sonia had gotten a guitar. It leaned against the McPhail. It was an old folk Gibson she had eyed at Mackie's for months before she made an offer. She had taught Patience to play. A ten-pound bag of rice filled an open shelf. And there were the green, flea market glasses they had used, and the plates rimmed with pink roses. They had bought them like destitute newly-weds, two of this, two of that. She scribbled a note on a cardboard box with a fat marker.

"Where are you? I'll be back tonight. Are you at the . . ." She drew a cartoon sketch of the Three Eves' storefront, garlands around its door, music coming through its windows. "Patience, you too. Get home. See you soon my Sister Friend, D"

SHE crossed the road to the sunken homestead and followed the wooded trail between the homestead and the cabin, past where the know-it-all Buddha rested, glazed in ice. She walked through the garden, making long, deep footsteps in the crusty snow. The cabin had grown. Christy had closed in the porch. She could make it out in the spotlights he had mounted. The place had wings. Christy and Ian had put in a larger front window. Deborah went through the shed where she used to imagine snakes skulking under the woodpile, and in through the back door.

"Hello," she called. "Hello."

Nothing.

The smell of licorice. Ian was around. She smiled. Some other smell, very sweet and unfamiliar. She walked into the front room of the cabin, which was the room where Christy had first asked her to stay with him, just for a while in the dark. She walked over to his desk where she had discovered his books and been impressed with his absolute absorption in them and where she had sat as a girl and read *Testament of Youth* and begun to be a treasure trove on war.

She didn't turn on a light. The spotlight lit up the iced-over snow on the garden so that it glittered. The light shone over Christy's desk so brightly that she could read the titles of his books. The cabin was still. She felt caught in time. The baby could be in the loft sleeping. She sat down at the desk and slid her fingers into the grooves on the arms of the chair, warm from the heat of the stove. The desk had a lot of cubbyholes, like the desk some students had built for the Frost place, a replica of Frost's own. She looked in the cubbyholes in the same way that she would pose questions to a stranger she wanted to know. She came upon a family picture of Ian and her, her kid who slept next to her in a sleeping bag across from the navy yard. He watched the subs come in, in the night, peering over the windowsill. Later Ian had made dragons on the windows of the top floor of the house where no mines would get them (but there were nuclear subs across the way and thousands of men in protective pants, jacket, gloves, working on nuclear reactors, climbing down into the innards, allowed in there twenty minutes — out — that's it). She put that picture back, and now here was another picture. A young girl, when she had long hair and it fell over her shoulders. She looked about sixteen years old, though she would have been twenty-one and here her hair highlighted her childish, grinning face. She faced the camera, naked, standing squarely in front of the skinny mirror they had had beside the kitchen sink before they had running water, the girl's fingers spread on her fat, round, pregnant belly.

Christy came in the back door. She looked up at him, startled, because he didn't have a beard. She had never seen him without a beard. His face was long. She was fascinated with his jawbone. It was sharp and angular. He was gnarled. He seemed to have evolved into an older man without his beard. She spent a while identifying him and for some reason thought of Vincent who had been her lover; but too many people had been her lover, and men made her feel alone. That kind of intimacy was such a ruse. She looked at this man and craved permanence, steady steady steady as she goes. Now Christy was suddenly older. She slipped the picture into the cubby.

He came and put his arms around her. He was taller than she had become accustomed to men being. Here was the height of men, to her. He smelled like wood smoke and gasoline, maybe from the chain saw.

They held each other. It was curious and natural and as familiar as sunrise. He was hard and lean.

"I was down below splitting the wood," he said.

She exhaled silently. He had been splitting the wood.

"Anything from Patience?"

"No," he said. They stepped back from each other. His mouth had the look of concentration that showed his fatigue and worry.

The dog cried out.

He said, "The dog's in a bad way." Deborah was distracted

by the shape of Christy's mouth when he talked. This Dennis lay under the table. She got up repeatedly, made a circle, lay down, stood up, circled. She yelped.

"Hey, Ma." She turned around, and Ian had come in the back door that led down to the outhouse and past that to the pond.

"Ian!" she said. She hugged him. He had a plastic pack of black string licorice in the inside pocket of his big, open parka.

"Thought I saw your little shit of a car flying through town. It's about time. So where ya been?"

Ian always treated her in this offhand, kidding way.

"It's not a shit," she said, hugging this tall boy.

"Ma," he said, "this isn't gonna do," and he untied the scarf she wore over her hair. He dropped it on the couch and pulled a thick, woolen stocking cap over her ears and low on her forehead so that her eyes looked enormous.

"He doesn't like my car, he doesn't like my hat." She grinned at Christy and the dimple in her cheek showed and they both watched her.

"You're home, Ma." Then he gave her a cup of Christy's coffee that he cut with milk. He was six foot like his father. He had a light brown ponytail and an open face. He wore jeans slung low, a baggy, dull green sweater with holes, a new beard so that she could still make out the line of his cheek.

She put her arms around his neck. She still saw the little boy in his face. The boy who said about the café down from their place with a sign listing all the things they wouldn't have (no strollers, no dogs, no parking, no barefeet, no breakfast after ten), Well, it doesn't say no horses. When they left Christy it was Ian who laid his hand on her back when she fell at odd times to her knees, unable to stop crying, and he told her that she could go on.

The gangly boy brushed wood chips off a stool and gestured for Deborah to sit down and she did.

"Have you called the sheriff about Patience?" Deborah said. "Just to tell them what we know?"

No one answered her.

Christy knelt beside the dog and felt her belly, he moved his hand high on the dog's ribs. "I think that's a pup," Christy said.

"It's Little Crapper," Ian said.

Dennis's ribs were covered with white, feathery and silky hair. Christy's was gray-streaked, long, coarse, disheveled. He stroked the dog's nose with both his hands to muffle her cries.

Ian ran water from the faucet with lavender handles and the spout that curved like a rainbow.

The dog clearly was in pain. Ian went to the woodstove, knocking over a bench and a chair on the way. Both men knelt with the dog.

"What's that smell in here?" Deborah said.

"Bend to Me," Christy said.

"What?"

"Bend to Me oil," Christy said again. "You get it at the incense shop."

"You do?" she said.

Christy circled, as agitated as the dog. "Come on. Let's get her to the vet." She followed Christy's fumblings with the phone, cursing when he couldn't find the number of the vet, Travis, to tell him they were coming. He pulled a ratty insulated jacket from the bathroom to wrap the dog in and went to the phone and recorded a rambling and disjointed message. Deborah realized it was to Patience. "I'll wait here," she said. "I'll call around."

Christy said, "Deborah, do what I say, just this once."

He put the bundled dog in her arms.

"You're scary, Ma. A real loser." Ian grinned at her. "I'm hanging out with Mark — you know, the rescue team." He put his coat on, as well. "Have a few beers. Listen to the scanner."

"You loser," Deborah said, their kidding. But she was

realizing something was going on between Ian and Christy that had been going on but she hadn't understood it. Her son was looking out for Christy. Christy wasn't aware of Ian's presence but Ian had the thing worked out. She shook her head at the lengths a man would go for a dog. Ian knew the place of the dog.

Christy went out and she heard him work the old Ford's accelerator.

She looked around the cabin where some other woman's red and yellow shawl was dropped over the couch with a cat on top — was that the woman's cat? — where another woman's bicycles littered the shed.

Ian narrowed his eyes on her, knowing what she saw.

"You two are fucked up. I swear to God."

"I like you," she said. "If I was a guy I'd want to be you. But, Honey, you ski more easily than you walk."

"He's called every hospital between here and Rindge," Ian said. "Every little crapper town police station. With Dad, I've spent years trying not to have a conversation with a cop, but today we made up for them all."

She turned around and stood for a second with the exhausted dog.

"So long, loser," Ian said.

"Hey, you too, Sweetie," she said softly.

At the car Christy said, "You drive."

He held Dennis in his lap while she cried small high-pitched notes that blasted in the dark. He looked at the black road, leaning forward, while she drove to the veterinarian's farm in the black and very cold night.

Travis was an ancient man with a face so deeply lined it was tempting to touch it, to understand the texture. Christy laid the dog on the table. Deborah looked at the old man's face and then pictured Christy becoming this wizened.

Travis examined the dog and said, "We're gonna have to do a C-section." Without changing rooms or his long johns, he put Dennis out with a quick injection and the cries stopped. "The pup's way up there. It'd have died up there." He put his hand up on Dennis's ribs where Christy had felt it.

Deborah felt a disorientation — was this the dog who was dying or was this the dog who was coming to them. Travis looked at her and Christy as if he were trying to place them. Which couple was this? Night did funny things. A man and a woman's face can transform in the night and he maybe thought he must know them. Travis would assume they had always been together. He couldn't know that she was not the one Christy slept with, that he lived in the cabin without her. The veterinarian would only see the faces tonight and wonder what they had come from, had they been fighting, had they been lying together before the dog's yelps called them back.

Deborah watched the dog's long nose and the doctor's hands as he made another injection into her rump. Why did the puppy hide up there? Why didn't it want to come out? Taking a birthing dog to the vet in the night was an intimate thing to do with a man and she couldn't completely place Christy's face. But the vet would place them together forever when he saw Christy at Kelley's or the True Value.

"You stay," the vet told them. "Somebody's going to have to take this pup." He took Dennis back to his surgery and he was washing up, chatting to them gruffly now and then.

Christy and Deborah sat on the plastic-covered couch in the waiting room and stared at fish in an aquarium.

Before long, Travis would have opened Dennis's belly and pulled out the sack with the puppy in it, then split the sack and taken out a tiny slick rat of a dog. They read the chart that showed the cycle of a heartworm in a dog's heart and Deborah tried not to look at Christy's exposed face.

Travis came out with a pup the size of his fist. The puppy

was wrapped in a padded blanket. He said gruffly, handing the bundle to Christy, "More pups die from chills than from starvation." He looked at them as if to dare them to chill this dog.

"Oh, it's Cody," Deborah said, knowing Patience would approve of this transfiguration of her beloved, elderly, long-legged dog, and laughed and it was as if they all agreed, of course it was Cody. They'd have known him anywhere. Christy wiped him down.

"If he stops breathing, massage him here," Travis said, rubbing the pup roughly on his underside behind his front legs.

"Why would he stop breathing?" Deborah said.

"Why would he keep going? They don't come weaker than that." He gave them a box of formula and a bottle and gruff instructions and Deborah followed the lines down his neck and into his scrub shirt. "I'll keep the bitch," Travis said. "Keep an IV going. Now let me get back to bed."

At the door, Christy pushed up the ribbing on Deborah's cap. He exposed her eyes and eyebrows and searched them and it seemed as if he were trying to imprint the look of her on him.

In the car, he rubbed his eyes with the heel of his hand. They bounced over the road, now with a puppy in his lap and Deborah, his wife, once, beside him, but Dennis was sleeping over, and an IV was dripping into her vein in her slender white foreleg and she wasn't with him anymore.

"Still drive thirty miles over any speed limit," Christy remarked.

"What's the speed limit?" she said.

His hand had come to her shoulder. The dog was quiet. They drove in silence. Travis had handed Christy a blue surgical towel, too, and that hung over Christy's shoulder.

18. Made Simple by the Loss

DEBORAH drove the old Ford down the road, which was becoming progressively harder to drive down in the heavy snow. She imagined Patience bundled in her sweater and parka over the long dresses she liked to wear. She let the car die in the field by the homestead.

Christy got out of the car with the wrapped dog against his chest. She watched him for a few seconds through the glass until it had a thin layer of snow. Then she watched his shape.

"You want to come down?" Christy shouted through the windy dark. "Ian should be back."

"Not now," she called. She went to him and saw his mouth in that stressed concentration which is what he and Ian did to each other.

"No, I'll go to see Sonia. I'm imagining music pounding out of the cabin. And Patience and Sonia are singing 'Babe, I'm Gonna Leave You.' Remember how they used to howl that song with their arms wrapped around each other."

"'When ol' summertime comes a'rollin',' " Christy said.

They could both see Sonia and Patience dancing across the cabin floor. Crazy Patience on a cigarette and ginger ale diet. Then Sonia cradling her to her lap, running her hands through Patience's hair.

Christy said, "They were always playing bluesy laments. You could hear them from the dirt road, Patience on the McPhail, Sonia pounding the guitar."

Deborah could hear it, and had a taste of his life in the woods.

"You gonna to stay up all night?" she said.

"Could happen."

They were a family always threatening, even while they were in each other's arms with their hands running hard through each other's hair.

"Did you say Ian was working?" she said.

"Working or lazing in his room. He hangs around with the rescue guys. Any reason to get back on the mountain."

Deborah thought he was not at the fire station or at Mark's now. The idea had come to her that maybe, wherever Patience was, Ian was there, too.

Christy and Deborah took opposite paths. She went to Sonia's and listened hard to hear Patience beating out "I'm gonna leave you."

Sonia sat cross-legged on her couch, her pink sweatshirt hood playfully up over her hair that was still blond though now dusky, the kind of blond that does not gray. For only a second her face looked vulnerable, even fearful, which Deborah had almost never seen. The sweatshirt hood was a shield to protect her. She was not quite there, some of the clarity was missing, like a layer of detail had worn off, the features, the eyes, less sharp.

They had known each other almost since the age Patience was now. She had quartered an apple. Three sections were splayed on a plate on the table. Maybe she had eaten one and been taken away by its taste.

"Where's that girl?" Deborah said.

"She does this," Sonia said. "She takes chances."

"Yes, she does." Deborah put her arms around her and felt her narrow shoulders and the softness and wornness of the fabric of the oversized sweatshirt.

Sonia sat with her knees pulled up, hugging them to her chest. It was Christmastime. They had sat in this way all the Christmases, with their children at various ages.

Sonia said, "I was remembering the college time, and I can't remember when Patience wasn't born yet. It seems like she was always around." Sonia turned and picked out the notes of a carol softly on the piano. "I was remembering when we were models. Do you remember?"

"I wasn't born," Deborah teased.

"You had a braid down your back," Sonia said.

"But I cut it off in a fury."

"A good model is hard to come by," Sonia said. "I found out we weren't good models."

"No, we were broke."

"And remember the bomb?"

"Dad's bomb, Ian called it. That was so long ago. I thought I dreamt it," Deborah said.

"No, there was a bomb," Sonia said. "You threw it and it didn't go off. Patience would say she remembered it. She says she remembers everything, even if someone just tells her the story."

"Patience is a shaman," Deborah said.

"Oh, good, we've needed one."

They laughed and Sonia brewed some ginseng tea which she poured in small cups with delicate handles that said Forest Hills around the rim. "Not cheap," Sonia said. "But I bartered."

"What'd you give him this time?"

"Deborah," Sonia said. She said her name matter-of-factly and she had let the cups slip from her mind. "Every time there's an accident. Every time she's missing. I think this is the time. She held on as long as she could."

Deborah didn't ask her what she meant.

"Sometimes I think, what if, when Patience was born, something happened to her. Christy loved her so much." Sonia shrugged and the hood fell down off her hair. "But he was so good to us."

"Yeah, he was."

Deborah remembered Patience's eyes that had been so large and black, taking in Christy. She understood what Sonia meant, since they had both seen the melancholy transpire in the girl.

"Remember those mornings Patience and I went to the hotel?" Sonia said. "Maybe I took her into another era, with all this hotel stuff — these artifacts — she grew up eating on, and the fancy clothes for dress up. And then we opened a vintage store, celebrating the grand hotels that went away or rotted. "

"Stop it. You didn't do anything wrong."

"We're all here because of a college in an old hotel. That they razed. What lasts? she must wonder."

"Or everything lasts forever. Like, to Patience, these cups are her family cups, it's her life. She has her own version of the Forest Hills, which she would have had anyway, even if it was still here." They were very tired and still knew nothing of where the girl was. The phone's silence continued to wear away on the detail of Sonia's face. "Why'd they make them all white, the hotels," Deborah said.

"Probably so they'd just be a spot, another shade of white, on the mountain. So they wouldn't stick out. You could pretend it was a door in the mountain. There's my reason."

They listened.

"That's what Christy called Ian before he was born," Deborah said.

"What?"

"Spot."

Sonia said, "Oh, yes."

Deborah said, "We came up here to go to school in a door in the mountain."

"When we wake up, she's gonna be right here. She's gonna be stretching, and lazy and groggy-eyed like she is when she sleeps a long time."

They listened.

19. Like the Ladies

AT seventeen, Patience had developed elaborate rituals in her life at school, but even in the rituals she missed Sonia. She missed Sonia's hands, how deft they were, hands that could produce pies or refurbish dresses to get married in. In her imagination, though, it was Ian she began to bring with her to milk the cow or to sit in Meeting. It was Ian she talked to. She worked away silently and interpreted for him everything she saw.

But throughout the long day since she had been with Molly in their bedroom, and especially now driving north with Jamie, the routine of school through which she functioned and talked, if mostly in her head, was melting away, and nothing came in its place. She felt a malaise deepen and take her over as they drove. It was like a dream in which Patience was struggling to do something, but she couldn't do it. The opponent — who this was she didn't know — could outrun her, or it had more strength in Indian wrestling, it overpowered her in every way, she could not beat it. And the temptation was to lie down and let it roll over her, let it just suck up her breath, because she knew she didn't have the strength to fight it. Whatever it was. She couldn't tell this to Molly. She hardly had words for the feeling itself. But as she and Jamie drove, the helplessness washed over her. She was going home to Ian whom she loved most in the world. She wanted to see him. She imagined holding his face between her hands the way she had seen Deborah hold Christy's face and when Deborah wasn't looking Christy had been washed in a peace just by her hanging around. She wanted this, but with the idea of holding Ian's face that same way, she still felt the hopelessness of fighting and the desire to succumb. Was this a dangerous desire? Is that why Molly had her worried face? She wondered if this were something that people who were suicidal felt. It didn't hurt. It was the opposite of hurt, it was easy and not something she plotted or even knew what it was, beyond a seduction. It wasn't a new feeling. It was as familiar as the walls of the mountains that made up her sweet landscape.

So when they were driving and Jamie said, Do you want to get some beer, Patience said, Sure, because that was an easy, old habit. Boys and drinking and disappearing had been easy, old habits for a long while, which was one reason they were trying the Meeting School, and it had been okay and she and Molly had made a den. But now going home, that world was coming down on her again. She didn't understand, how she could drag Ian with her everywhere in her imagination and sit on him and make him listen to her ramblings and constantly check out his heart to see that it was beating, and still it was easier to get drunk with a prep kid she found in the movies than it was to go home.

They stopped at the exit for Meredith where Patience knew there was a store that should be open. They pulled up under the lights and Jamie took her hand and he talked about camera angles in filmmaking and the idea behind all those close-up shots in the *Passion of Saint Joan*. He said the film they saw had changed the rules on making films.

They had picked up a case of beer and after midnight they pulled into Lafayette Place just beyond the face of the Old Man in the Mountain in the Notch. Jamie had drunk a great deal, Patience not so much. They had a few beers to go and they got out of Jamie's Camry in the parking lot where there were no other cars and where plows had shoved a part of the snow to one side, leaving a third of the lot cleared. The trail had been packed down by snowmobiles. They each had a beer and began the first couple of hundred yards of ascent. They couldn't see the moon, and Patience imagined the clouds lying low, although she couldn't see them. They were in a cushion of clouds right there on the mountainside. The temperature was about thirty degrees at the base of Lafayette. Jamie reached his hand to Patience's thigh.

Patience was accustomed to playing guys. She was tough and didn't put up with anything from them she didn't want. She had no use for what she called whiny girls who lost control.

"Let's go back. I want another beer," Patience said.

Jamie had been brilliant, talking about films. He, himself, was an actor.

He said, "Do you want to go down to Cambridge with me?"

"No, I don't want to go to Cambridge."

He said he would take her to the Brattle to see Chekhov. He said she reminded him of the actress who played in *Uncle Vanya,* that standoffish and sexy.

She started down the trail. What had she done? Why had she let this happen, this drinking and he was too drunk and his body had become close, hard, and insistent beside her? She had let it happen.

On the trail, he caught her and put his hands around her stomach. "In a minute, we'll go back," he said.

The cold and the beer and the dark numbed Patience. She

didn't want to feel Jamie's hands on her body. She disliked the feel of him and he had put his hands inside her coat and then inside her red dress. She tried to pull away but Jamie said, "Sweetheart," and held her tight and they both fell to the snow-packed ground. "Ahhhh." He was drunk and she felt his mouth on her ear. "Sweetheart, be my little cunt for a minute. I am so cold."

Patience didn't fight him. She looked at him and found him very stupid — that's what she began to say to Ian — he was so stupid — but there was the lethargy that had taken over her body. Maybe she said, "Jamie, I want to go down to the car."

Her mind went to when she was a little girl and she and Ian played in their mothers' store. She could see the silver shoe buckles in the glass case. She could see the bracelets, the belt buckles, the tortoiseshell hair combs. She could smell the old crocheted shawls.

"In a minute, Sweetheart. God, you are beautiful. Look at you," and he ran his hands down her hips. "Christ it is cold." He pressed her down and her jaw banged against a rock of snow. She could taste blood in her mouth. He had her hard pressed to him. Her head spun and she could also feel the softness of the black feathers they had played with while she wore a kimono and high heels and Ian wore a sailor shirt made of very thick, rough cotton. She could feel the coarseness and sturdiness of the fabric between her fingers and she could see her mother's fingers whizzing at the sewing machine while she sang.

This was Jamie who pushed the broom up and down the theater aisles. His fingers. The reality of these strange fingers shook some of the stupor off.

"I'm going down," she said. But she couldn't get away. Then she felt his hand between her legs. "Let's do it in the car," she whispered in his ear. "We'll put the heat on in the car." She began to describe to him what they would do.

"Oh, yeah," he said and his mouth was on hers and his saliva froze on her cheek. She put her hand to her mouth where blood had pooled and she slipped away from him while he held her.

She was wearing an aqua cocktail dress with shoulder pads, a felt hat with a veil that made a crosshatched shadow over her face, like the ladies on the porches of the grand hotels on Main Street.

20. Lafayette Place

Patience led Jamie to the car. She promised him what she would do to him, but by then the cold was established. When they got to the car, she reached into his jacket and got the keys out. She opened the driver's side door. "Hurry," she said, "get in, get the heat going."

He was very strong and he slid down into the seat and pulled Patience with him. "Go ahead," she said. She kissed him until he let go his grip of her arm behind her back and explained to her drunkenly, "I need someone like you." He leaned against the gearshift and narrowed his eyes on her face. He reached under her clothes and she could feel his freezing hands encircle her breast and she let him. She let him bring his other hand inside. She let him put his wet mouth on her and lay her over the gearshift and then he took the keys from her balled fist before he unzipped himself and pressed his hardness against her skin.

"I'm going to get in the back," she said to him. "Start the engine, Jamie. The heat will feel good."

He was trying to fuck her and start the engine at the same time.

She said, "Hurry, Jamie."

"You stay there," he said. He sat up to press his foot down on the clutch and then she heard the engine turn over once, slowly, and again. He pumped the accelerator and she heard the engine rev. She moved to slide toward her door but then she felt his hand hard on her hip.

"Where you going?" he said. "I need you right here." He rolled back over on top of her and she felt his insistent tongue and his hands working down her neck to her chest, and the weight of his body over her, now in the tight space of the car seat, made her start to breathe short, gasping breaths. The malaise shifted like a weight, so that it held her less solidly. He had stopped talking and he was trying to remove her clothes when they both realized the engine had stopped and the cold was a hard cold. "We need more heat," she whispered.

"Shit," he said, "shit," and he sat up and she got over in the driver's seat and started the engine and he rubbed his hands in front of the vent where the air was barely warm. "I'll run it for a while," she said, "Then let's get in the back seat." He looked at her while his hands began to warm. She nodded to him. The engine stuttered. She was afraid he would grab her. She did not know if he could turn vicious. She could not be certain who he was inside, so she didn't rush. "Just wait," she said, "now it's going. Okay?"

He exhaled watching her, and she opened the door and stepped out. But then she slammed it fast and that's when she walked away from him. It had come back to her to think of running. She knew this mountain very well. She and Ian had grown up on this mountain. She knew that if she began to ascend it, maybe the man would not follow her. She would lose him and not even have to outrun him. He got out and yelled at her and maybe it was that yell that caught the attention of the couple in the car who had come to the mountains for Christmas. The couple had come to set up a winter camp and avoid the glitz of a city Christmas and to be alone together and let go of things that would go on without them like the wife's office party. So they had packed applejack, which they never drank in the world, in canteens and ham to fry over the fire and biscuits and sleeping bags they would zip together. The wife called it a spa day, he was glad for a day not to shave. But when they had gone through the Notch and pulled off at Lafayette Place to see if this was where they wanted to be, they saw the man in the middle of the parking lot hollering out a woman's name. When Jamie saw the couple who had come for an overnight spa Christmas, free of mistletoe and high heels and aftershave and recriminations, he got into the Camry with Massachusetts plates, the only other car there, and spun the car around in the snow-packed lot and squealed up Rt. 93.

The wife happened to spot the blue Bell Atlantic box and thought, it's Christmas, and called the emergency number and reported what she and her husband had seen and the idea that someone might have been left. She didn't know. Just for the record.

"The man was yelling," she told the 911 person on the phone. "It was ironic. He was yelling 'Patience! Patience!'"

21. Climbing

MARK said to Ian. "You're not going on this one, buddy."

Mark was always slightly stooped, his knees slightly bent in concentration, with shaggy, graying hair, baggy trousers, a disturbed, concerned countenance, he talked to people face-on, peering into their eyes, which was the way he was talking to Ian now.

They had been drinking beer in Mark's barn. They had raised it last summer and it still smelled of newly cut timbers. The static and voices of the radio broke in now and then on their lassitude. Ian could handle a lot of beer, but tonight he'd also been drinking whiskey. Mark had listened to the call when it came in. Jan, the operator who also took telephone orders for the catalog store in Franconia, quoted the woman exactly. The woman had heard the guy call, Patience. Mark and Ian listened, though they remained seated. They had gotten in Mark's truck and they sat looking straight ahead. Ian put his beer on his knee, licked his lips.

Mark said, "I knew Patience was AWOL from some school, but what the story is with this guy with Mass plates, I don't know. Maybe you know." Now he looked at Ian in that concerned way.

"Well," Mark said. Ian finished the beer. "I know there's something about the girl and you. You shouldn't go on this one. I'll find some dude, we'll go check this out."

Finally Ian said, "It's not a rescue."

"What do you mean?"

Ian got out of the truck.

Ian was a natural for the squad, Mark had always said. He was an EMT, something rescuers didn't need to be, but he'd learned, memorizing the manuals the doctor used who taught cardiopulmonary resuscitation and other emergency procedures. He'd done more than his share of rescues on the mountain. He had hands that appeared too large, but they were finely skilled.

"Nothing," he said, "it's just not a rescue. I'm gonna just go." His strides were long and in only a few he was out of the barn and climbing in his own truck.

"Ian, you're not going anywhere alone." Mark followed him, calling out.

Ian leaned out of the window. "Look," he said, "it's not a rescue. I'm just going to go and talk to her. I know where she'd go. It's not gonna take two of us."

"Christ, Ian. You got a radio?"

"Yeah, I got a radio. It's good, Mark." He looked up at the cold, calm sky. "No sign of weather," he said, although it was still snowing lightly. Ian squealed onto the road, leaving Mark leaning forward, as if he were still trying to find words to keep the kid out of this one.

IAN made part of the ascent in the muted moonlight. The trail was clear enough but icy, and he stopped and strapped his crampons to his boots so the ice wouldn't slow him, as he knew it would be slowing Patience.

He wore a light strapped to his forehead and had two pairs of snowshoes lashed to his pack, though now that he was only walking and giving in to the rhythm of his crampons cutting into ice and snow, he realized he was dizzy from the mix of drinking. The moon was fuzzy. The trail was one he and Patience had hiked summer after summer. It was their back-yard. He was on the Greenleaf Trail that headed toward the Eagle Lakes. He let the cold exhilarate him. He could breathe on the mountain and he knew he would catch up with Patience soon. He climbed from 2000 feet to 2500 feet and found the track of someone. Female, he thought. Maybe five eight. Tall girl.

He found her on the trail taking a rest. He didn't want to scare her and called out from a distance.

She turned and would have watched the light of his lantern as it bounced along the trail and made a line across the bare trees.

She didn't move. She shook her head and said, "All I had to do was climb a mountain."

"What are you doing? What was that call about? Patience." He had shouted her name.

"Ian, I don't need rescuing."

"I know. That's what I told Mark." He stood over her now, with his hands slung low on his hips as his father's would have been.

"Christ, girl, would you tell me what happened? Let's get out of here." But he hunched down on the trail beside her. He pulled the radio out of the pouch where it was strapped to his pack. "Mark," he said. The sky was so close up at this level. He lay back in the snow beside her. Mark came on. "Found her," he said. He couldn't think of another thing to say. "Found her. Don't worry about us." He listened. Patience wore a black headband over her ears. He threw a wool cap at her. She had lost her coils and she pulled the cap over the headband. "Yeah," Ian said into the mike. He looked at the clouds. "Yup. On our way." He packed the radio away.

The air hovered at around fifteen or twenty degrees, Ian thought. Patience was wearing a leather jacket over her own coat and a flannel showed out the bottom. She must have taken the guy's, he thought. Her boots weren't that good anymore. He knew she'd had those boots for years. He knew what could easily happen to toes. Ian looked at the sky. He took her hand. "Come on."

"Your clothes are wet," he said to her. "You'll freeze up here in wet clothes. I've got dry clothes."

Patience said, "There's about zero chance I'm taking off my clothes."

Patience was rugged enough. She had skied Cannon with Ian. They'd skied all day long. They ate and skied. They'd come in the cabin ruddy with cold. Eat a couple loaves of bread, leftover fried chicken, burritos with peppers and sly stuff of their own concoction, then back to the mountain, to the tram to climb to the upper reaches of the mountain, Upper Cannon and Profile and Taft Slalom Trails.

But now it was time to turn back. Patience moved on up the trail. She called to him, "Ian, I don't know what's wrong with me. I just want to walk. I'll come home later."

He had an image of Mark slipping a roller paper out of an orange box and opening a small plastic box where he kept his grass. Ian had that in his pocket. He thought maybe that would calm her. He pulled out the packet. They could make a fire and sit and lick the edge of a paper and roll the grass in it. She had stopped and was watching him. He offered her the box.

Nothing doing. He pulled out two canteens. He and Patience used to use these camouflage canteens when they were kids. Christy had a stash of military gear he kept around the house the way he kept bags of hash and bottles of beer. He had a fatigue shirt, a Silver Star he put in a baggie, rank he kept in a cloth bag with other loose things so that it rattled like bones and stones, an artillery shell, a nest of grenades maybe his mother never knew about.

Ian knew his weather. He watched clouds that filled the sky here in a way they hadn't from the town. In the daylight and less dizzy, he would have been aware of how their shape changed. In a few hours, it would be Christmas Eve, very early on the dawn of Christmas Eve.

Ian's imagination turned to Patience sitting in their tattered lawn chair, her hands resting on the arms in a five-year-old, imperial way. He had basic gear. He had stashed trail mix, Hershey Bars. He unscrewed the top of the canteen and offered it to Patience. "Coffee," he said. She came closer. She wrapped her mittened hands around it and slowly took some down. He watched her Adam's apple move up and down. The temperature seemed to be dropping. Patience's neck was narrow. She turned and continued climbing.

Ian was getting used to her turning and checking on him, but she kept going. He hoped she had on long underwear under her leggings. She would not turn back. He followed her, in the beginning to try to reason with her.

The beginning of the climb had been through fairly flat hardwood forest, but they had moved out of the hardwood and into the spruce and the fir trees. By the time they got to Greenleaf Hut, it was nearly midnight. They were up to over 4000 feet. It was here that it began to snow steadily.

It was no weather to climb in and he had a sense of exhilaration now, mixed with doom. It was because Patience was so determined that he felt doom.

He yelled, "Do you know the trail?"

"Of course I know the trail."

"Let's stay together," he yelled.

He was afraid she would disappear if she took another step. As it was, he could only see the vague shape. He followed her. He could tell she wasn't going to follow him.

When he was small, he and Christy had walked up the edge of Tuckerman's. They climbed up in their ski boots, making steps, pressing their boots into the packed snow. He thought about this as he walked and wanted to tell her. But he was still booze-dizzy — the altitude and the wet snow working together — and he couldn't get to her, although he liked being her companion.

Ian thought about not coming out of the woods. What if he became a feral man who tracked his prey. What if he lived like the animals, aware of the clouds and the winds and the angle of the moon. He imagined a silent race through the snow and instant, clean, and fair death of one and dinner for the other. What if he didn't go back? What if he didn't have to see his father's eyes? The farther he walked with Patience, the more it felt like they were together, going off to be coyote and deer. He sucked air deeply into his chest, filtered by the wool mask over his mouth and cheeks. He didn't want them to turn around. He didn't care that they had passed a lean-to that would have offered them a barrier against the wind. He liked being a ski bum. He liked the rhythm of his body, which obliterated his father's eyes. He was a coyote running silently in the snow under the nimbus clouds, after the storm that must have happened in the mountains, low and shrouding the peaks.

He was aware of the scarf Patience wore, which was wet from the wet snow. She was wet through, and he knew he had to get her out of her wet clothes and make her drink some of the coffee he carried. With the light from his headlamp he saw tracks in two thin troughs — a deer's tracks. But they didn't go on for long. Maybe the deer had found cover deep inside a ravine.

He studied the deer's tracks. As he did, sharp needles began to prick the parts of his face that were exposed. It was as if an ice pick had been taken to the clouds, because they suddenly released a whiteout of snow. It descended on them, so much snow. They had been able to see the shrouded low sky one second, and while Ian was studying the deer tracks, the tracks themselves disappeared. A slight headache had been climbing with him, but now he had a headache that was more intense. He couldn't even see Patience. He took a step forward. She was there. She had stopped. She had sat down on a rock. He knelt beside her. She had trouble keeping her balance, swaying forward, then to the right, until he steadied her, or was it that she steadied him. He put his arms on her shoulders and tried to get her to look at him and see if she could talk.

They couldn't see anything, but they were on the trail. He wouldn't let them lose the trail. They had passed a cairn. There would be another. The snow bit like tiny razors into the flesh around his eyes. They would be on an exposed ridge. He tried to picture it in his mind, its distance from the summit and from the trailhead, but his mind wouldn't focus. Standing, Patience came to his shoulder. He braced his hip against hers, and together they took a step, although they couldn't see where it would take them. He couldn't see the next cairn. Now he held her by the shoulder, because as reluctant as she had been for them to walk together, he knew she wouldn't be the one to fight not to get separated. Now the wind came and made them stagger sideways, and tried to rip them apart and send them skittering. Storm force, thirty miles per hour, maybe more, but he thought it had to be a gust that came out of the unstable weather following the northeaster. The low nimbus clouds had not forewarned him of this. Maybe they hadn't been nimbus clouds at all — he'd let the weather be a wild card.

22. Locked Out

AFTER the call from the life squad, Deborah went to Christy's. It was snowing, leaving new soft snow over the old crust, avalanche conditions, and skiers around Tuckerman's and the Gulf would be at risk tomorrow. The extreme temperatures of earlier had held and by the time she got to Christy's her face burned with cold.

They stayed awake. Mark said he would call as he got more information. He said maybe they couldn't get down that fast. He said Ian was a prepared kid. At 2 A.M. Christy lost power. The lights went out on his tiny Christmas tree in the corner by the door to the greenhouse. They sat on the sofa, huddled from the wind, Deborah's chin touching Christy's collarbone. The smell of the pine needles was distinct in the compact, solidly built cabin, almost overheated by the woodstove.

Deborah talked into the soft, threadbare flannel of Christy's shirt. "Do you know how many nights I've listened for a sign of Ian? Going to the window at twelve, one, two and I'm listening for a sound that would grow and come nearer."

Christy moved away and put his arms behind his head.

She listened to the wind bang the cabin and smelled the scent of Bend to Me.

"Remember the night I took the Seconal?"

"No, that slipped my mind."

"Whatever happened to my journal?"

"Still there, I guess. The place is a mausoleum. Every dumb thing we ever did — there's traces of it in that house."

"The antique acid."

"All that shit."

The wind was violent. It shook the window over the kitchen sink. Deborah tried to picture her son like a rabbit, like a fox, winter animals in the wild who made nests in order to get out of the wind.

"I remember that night you came back in a fatigue shirt. I remember when I was waking up after that night, how funny it looked, you in a fatigue shirt with your jeans."

Cody heaved a large sigh.

"What else do we have in the homestead?" she said. "Is that where you put memories?"

"Ears," he said.

It was all soft and secret because the wind covered them and their stories. It was dream talk.

"Ian isn't safe," Deborah said.

Christy didn't answer.

Deborah got up and stood away from him. "What do you mean, ears?" she said.

"When Ian was sick I had to get them out of the house."

What Deborah remembered about Ian being sick was that Christy had gone away. He and Swede had some acid that they kept in a baby food jar and they took it and roamed the woods by Lonesome Lake.

"I don't understand," Deborah said.

"Mementos," Christy said. "War booty. You could get them from the infantry."

"From a patrol?" she said. She had stood up and was beside the picture window. She had put on her old red kimono that she had gotten at the Three Eves years ago. It was worn now and light against her body and she wore it over leggings.

Christy didn't answer.

"Me too," she said. "I'd want to get ears out of the house."

Christy looked up at her. Their faces held no emotion.

Other images came back. Ian hadn't been all that sick, a fever of about a hundred and one. He was flushed and whiny, but he was almost never sick and it scared them. He had dragged a ragged stuffed lamb over to Christy and he wouldn't go away. Christy had not wanted to deal with him. He had put jeans on the kid. Now Ian was on his own. But he wouldn't go away with the lamb. It had really been kind of funny, Deborah remembered. Ian was two and a half by then. Christy was at his desk, working through tomes, as he did, in his lavender baggy pants or whatever crazy clothes he chose to wear, loose-limbed, shrugging off things he didn't want to deal with, his son among them, charming with students in phone calls, a low gravelly, charismatic voice. Students would do anything, even be his lover.

That day Ian was whiny and Christy was on the phone. Christy would have spanked him, she thought, but Ian could see this coming on. He stopped crying and Christy took him up in his wooden chair, looking frail himself, his blue eyes exposed and in pain. The lamb fell and Ian wrapped his arms around Christy's neck and instantly fell asleep. This immobilized Christy. He wasn't one to hold the child or cuddle him. But Ian was sound asleep, finally, and breathing in and out with his rattly breath. In the end Christy put his feet up on the desk. He stretched back. He put his arms around his child and shut his eyes as well. But when Ian woke up, Christy put him down and went out the door and didn't come back for a long time.

"After that I had to get the ears out of the house."

Deborah wrapped the kimono around her tighter.

"Come here," he said. She did. He smelled like wood smoke and pine tree.

"I'm so tired," Deborah said.

She felt confused. There wasn't any rage in her. The wind blew. She talked softly and with every word she spoke she listened for the end of the wind, Okay now, okay now wind, so they could enter the mountain, so the mountain would let them in. But the wind always won. Deborah spoke, and it still screamed. She faced Christy, her knees bent, and not obliquely or slyly like a love dance, just bare and exposed, the kimono crooked on her shoulders, her feet bare where the black tights stopped.

She shook with cold and feeling in the power of the mountain that held them.

She said, "All my life I've been scared I was going to end up back here with you. And all my life I've known I'd die if I didn't."

Christy had been sitting on the edge of the couch, his knees bent, his elbows on his bent knees, his head down, and he looked up at her but not seeing, except for a flash of his eyes terribly exposed so that it hurt her to see them. But she didn't believe it, being accustomed to deprivation.

"This is my life," she said.

"You mean here?"

"No, I mean nowhere."

"You can come here."

"I can't."

"You asked me to tell you what else was in the homestead, so I told you. You get everything you ask me for."

"I always believe. You went to war and I believe that made

you understand things I couldn't understand. You've got those ears so you hear all kinds of things, don't you?"

She touched his face, his bare skin, placed her palm over his ear and then she placed it over her own and she could hear the ocean in her ear so that she knew he had been able to hear the sound of the ocean too. "Giving you the right to hold the rest of us hostage."

He didn't answer.

She put both hands to his ears, touching the flesh, tracing the intricate curve of the cartilage, down the fleshy part of the lobe.

Christy said, "It's late.

"It's so late."

She lay down with him, with the wood smoke and the forest. She inhaled his smell, as if they could will things to be different, and she drifted between awake and asleep and was in a white tent where the wind blew violently and she was lost and didn't know where the tent was and Ian and she were refugees and she was trying to save his life. In her dream they had not eaten for days.

Then she was wide awake and thinking of her mother and the wind blew. It had been her mother's story about Robert Frost in the inn in Vermont that made Robert Frost her family. It was her mother who had given her something to hold on to in the mountains when she was a pregnant girl and had gone to Frost's house. In the way that daughters confuse themselves with mothers and mothers confuse themselves with daughters, she believed, nearly, that it was she herself — the story grew — who ate with Robert Frost in the Vermont inn when she was eight. She had combed his wild, white hair before he put on his brimmed hat. She had felt his whiskers. She had been the child to whom he told "Locked Out" about the bitten nasturtium found in the morning on the stoop where he had played with it, waiting for the moon to set. And Deborah played on that stoop. Her mother would have been inside putting the coarse white sheets on the metal frame beds, and when Deborah came in, sleepy like Fran on the first night they had explored the Bethlehem woods together, Deborah would have been innocent and would have lain down and felt the rough cotton that smelled like lilacs and columbine against her cheek and fallen asleep to the sound of Helen's footsteps and the flinging and tucking of her own sheets just remembered and captured from the dusk.

23. On the Mountain

PATIENCE had stamina but she was clearly exhausted. As they walked sideways into the wind, Ian had to imagine what she looked like. They were vague shapes to each other but becoming more and more significant. They were forced to make up what each other was capable of.

He couldn't see her eyes. He wanted very badly to see her face. She should not be so exposed to the wind. Her boots were too worn. He thought they must be so near where they needed to be, but they'd been climbing and climbing. He imagined the white spots he'd seen on other people forming on Patience's cheeks and toes and fingers and that she might not know until the frostbite had killed her tissue. But he couldn't do anything. The cold was taking over his body. Not his fingers and his toes, more like his heart and groin.

The wind must have been up to forty miles per hour. He had been in wind like this once before, up at the Lakes of the Clouds in the Presidentials where weather was violent. He knew there wasn't a lean-to on this side of Lafayette.

He shouted to Patience, "This is only a squall. We'll walk out of it."

Still, there had been no cairn. He had pulled his balaclava down while he talked to her and now put it back up to protect his face. He packed the snow down with his snowshoes for her and she didn't falter behind him. They would walk out of this and be back at the trailhead and then go out for supper, maybe they would sit across a table from each other and have a pizza and a pitcher of beer. No big shit. But he was too cold and he couldn't remember if they were off the trail. And Christ, he wished he hadn't drunk so much. He heard Patience shout something through the wind. He stopped and turned and put both hands on her shoulders. He couldn't hear a thing she said. But he said to her. "I am cold." He could barely make it out himself. "I am so cold." And then he couldn't move. Ian sat down in the snow.

Patience took his pack off his back. He was aware that she was stomping down the snow and he wanted very much to do this too. He imagined himself doing this but then he realized he hadn't moved. He was aware she was pulling out the poles and the tent. She had found a spot, with a rock on one side, a piney scrub bush on the other. Ian's body was encased in cold. It was the most awful and helpless cold. He couldn't fend it off. His feet could not lift off the ground to stomp. He wasn't shivering. He understood that hypothermia worked from inside you. It worked from your heart and your organs out. Hypothermic cold took away your will and all the years of practice with ropes, knives, fire building. Christy always said it made you a girl.

He had packed his one-man pup tent that had saved him more than one time. Patience had sorted through the parts. He was aware of the taut orange nylon taking shape. He could hear the wind rip into it. She handed him the stuff bag of stove parts, which he dropped, and then looked down to study it in the snow. "Never mind," she yelled. "Never mind, get in." Ian crawled in the tent, then remembered his crampons which would not fit and would drag moisture into this one space that needed to be dry. He struggled to unstrap them. "Just get in the sleeping bag." He was sure he would die now and he was grateful to Patience to be out of the wind to die. A body could not be this cold. He wanted to sleep.

"Come on," she yelled. "Get in." She was searching through his bag and came up with a shirt. She was talking. He didn't know what she was saying. But he was aware of a rhythm, and when her voice rose or fell. It was as if she were telling a story, but not in words, it was in cadence and inflection. She leaned into him and held his focus when he would have slipped naturally into unconsciousness. Patience unzipped his parka, shrugged his arms out of the sleeves and then peeled off his clothes, which had been drenched with sweat and then zipped the sleeping bag around him. She found the thermos he had brought and held his head and made him take a sip of the coffee that was sweet and milky. Did they have chocolate? He did not remember. His body was too cold to desire. He was a coyote. He didn't want her to worry about him. He was aware of Patience and forced his mind back again and again to the protection inside the tent. The wind blew and he hoped, for her sake, it wouldn't rip the orange tent and toss it over the lip of the ravine. Around them were low, gnarled, wind-flattened pines, and he knew the rock would have lichen in yellow patches like the shape of the islands and continents on his father's wall.

Patience must have peeled off her wet clothes because now she was getting into the sleeping bag beside him. She gave him the warmth of her body. She put her arms tight around him and held him, leg to leg, chest to chest. She took a drink from the thermos cup and passed it across to Ian. "Why don't you not die," she said, "and not leave me here alone." Her way of instructing him to drink.

The coffee was still warm. It was pale brown and very sweet the way Ian drank it.

He thought about Mark and what Mark would say to do. Did he tell her he was thinking about Mark? He didn't think so. He hadn't spoken, but he had maintained consciousness.

Now she lay behind him and wrapped her arms around his and massaged his chest. Slowly he began to shake.

He didn't remember the next few hours. Patience had pumped up the stove at the edge of the tent so that steam filled the air. Then she brought him a spoon and a cup and in it was oatmeal. He ate the oatmeal. He swallowed the steam, his teeth coming down hard on the metal camping spoon.

They huddled together and he didn't know how long he shook or how cold she had been, trying to warm him. They slept on and off. Later he began to understand words she was saying. She was worried about dying.

"I read in the paper about a mother and her little girl and they were driving home in a snowstorm and a bridge was out. They didn't know and their car went in a river." She spoke in a soft voice into his ear. The voice had become a part of his own body. "She managed to carry her little girl out of the river and she walked as long as she could. They found her and her daughter in the morning, frozen. And she was just a few hundred yards from the light of somebody's window."

He thought that was the story she told. His thoughts were distorted the way rime ice distorts the shape of the landscape.

"I saw their picture in the paper," Patience said.

Another time he woke, he thought the wind had lessened. He hoped it was true.

"Are you awake?" he whispered.

"Yes."

"I can't hear the wind so much."

This time he slept a slightly deeper sleep.

When he woke, Patience was shivering. He took her hands

and arms that were around him and began to massage them. Her hands were small and on her left hand she wore a cheap, bendable ring like the kind you could get at K-Mart in the gum machine or in Cracker Jacks. He tried to slide the ring off so it wouldn't dig into her skin, but she made a fist. He left it and kept massaging. She had not spoken for some time and her hands weren't getting any warmer. He stopped massaging and pressed his fingers over the artery at her wrist. He didn't think a bird's heart would be faster. He turned around to check her. Her eyes were squeezed shut. "What's the matter?" he said. "Where do you hurt?"

She kept her eyes scrunched up. "I keep thinking about the woman and the little girl."

"Look at me. Let me see you."

She kept her eyes shut. "I'm not here," she said, "I'm not anyplace. Leave me alone."

"All right," he said.

She kept her eyes closed.

"When it's light, I'll check out the trail."

She didn't answer.

She had long, thick eyebrows. He rubbed his face on them and against her wet cheek.

They were damp and warm inside the sleeping bag. Her breath was stale and familiar and the smell of the cocoon that took the ice out of his body. She was extremely familiar although they had never lain together before.

"What are we doing here, Patience? Were you just going for a walk or were you listening to too much Pantera?"

"Pantera," she said. "Too much Pantera." They went into a Pantera sleep.

24. In the Valley

At five o'clock Deborah woke, sick in her stomach. They were alone in a silent world. The wind had stepped away to another part of the globe. Since the mountains make their own weather, the storm could have passed up there or it could be at its peak.

Mark had called. Patience had radioed him and said she and Ian were together. They were in Ian's tent to wait out a storm that had taken them by surprise. Of course. It had been a very crowded tent in the night. Why the fuck did they wait to call? Christy asked Mark. Why didn't they stay in contact? Mark paused, perhaps leaning slightly toward the phone and toward Christy whose son he loved, and then he said, " I don't know. I don't think they wanted to be in contact."

Deborah's mother called at six. Maybe she wasn't aware of the time. She woke Christy and Christy told her the puppy made it through the night. Christy told the story about how he was so far up in the bitch he'd have died up there if they hadn't gotten him to a doc in a blizzard.

"Give me the phone," Deborah said.

He said, "No way."

Then he said to Deborah, "She says you need someone for next of kin."

"I know that." Deborah said. "Give it to me."

"I passed that on to my wife," Christy said into the phone. "The dog's breathing," he told Helen, "but the Havalack he's drinking causes cataracts."

Deborah grabbed at the phone. "Don't say anything. Stop talking, Christy."

"Okay, Helen," Christy said. "All right." He hung up.

"Christy. Are you crazy? Why'd she call here?"

He shrugged. "Why's she do anything?"

Deborah stood in the corner, her leggings tatty, her hair flattened on one side. They had been all legs and arms, fending off the wind. She had slept with her leg sprawled over Christy's belly. They didn't fight. They made a lair until the wind stopped banging against the windows and roaring and they waited for the phone and when it rang the message didn't bring relief, it demanded continued endurance.

Christy leaned against the post that held up the kitchen roof, cocked his shaggy head, and merely gazed at Deborah, then looked down, and he knew she would think he was being sarcastic. "Oh," he said, "your mother's coming for Christmas."

"My mother?"

"Helen," he said.

"Christy, my mother has never been up here. She would not come up here for Christmas. She was going on a bus trip to New York."

"She's taking a bus trip here," Christy said.

Christy went out the shed door. She thought he was getting firewood. But he didn't come back. They had made a lair, but then he had to go. It had been Ian who had explained this to her in Patience's hospital room: Sometimes he gets scared and he has to go someplace else. So Deborah was alone to face this, too.

She couldn't stay in the cabin. She left in the early hours. She saw tracks in the snow not far from the road she had meant to keep to. The tracks were two narrow paths side by side that she knew were probably deer tracks and they drew her to them. It would be a deer attracted to the red berries on the thorn bush or the prickly holly bush that Sonia had planted so many years ago in the back of the homestead because she had to have green in the winter.

She followed the deer tracks in her old pair of rubber Mickey Mouse boots and wished she'd put on the snowshoes. Ian would have crampons, snowshoes, skis. Be prepared. Where was Ian now? The moon would have been enormous and yellow and low in the sky, she knew it would have been if the clouds had not been dark curtains and the moon invisible.

She followed the tracks to the homestead. Snow was blown through the decomposing porch and into the front room and kitchen and hall which were as wintry as the woods. The snow lay a foot deep across the porch and angled down so that inside the house a dusting of the hard cornlike snow covered everything. An old car battery lay on its side and over it were the tracks of mice.

She stepped over the sunken porch and frozen and thawed debris of books, magazines, rusted, flattened tools. She went to the back room where wallpaper still clung to the wall and thin organdy curtains hung on rusted and bent curtain rods.

Christy had gone, but he had been with her in the night. Not in the way he had been in their marriages, in a different way. She did not know how, but there had been more substance. She felt it now while she strained for the sound of Ian's truck.

After the overdose, Christy had said, "Courage is a hard thing." Courage was what he had loved her for in the beginning and what he held her to, although she never knew what it was to him. Only that the war must have made him think he didn't have any. She had little faith in war's judgments. She knew that much about war. And she had enough experience with men to believe that they sometimes have women to complete themselves, to bring joy to their sorrow, or imagination to their rigidity, or passion to their reserve, or ambiguity to their hard-and-fastness.

Deborah looked around and thought of the grenade they had found here. She imagined the feel of it in her hand. She became very calm. She sat on the mattress and listened and waited. The children were mountain-wise. And, strangely, Helen would appear with her coiled white hair.

She held on to the idea of the grenade firmly. She never went to the outhouse after that day but she thought about the grenade and the possibility of an explosion. She knew that the longer a grenade was exposed to the elements, the more unstable it became. Even if you didn't pop the pin or even if the fuse had been removed, high explosives remained within. The brittle wax inside melts and the older the grenade, the more sensitive it is to shock. She had learned about weapons. She had learned about soft-head bullets and full metal jackets. Ian was the one who held her grief, and she didn't think she could survive letting him go.

25. Moon Enough

THE beginning of dawn came. Ian was aware of the shape of Patience's thigh. It was tucked into the back of his thigh. Her arms were folded in front of her chest. He felt them rise and fall. The deathly cold had gone away. When Ian opened his eyes again, she was staring at him. Then she got up. She put on whatever she could find dry of Ian's, dry long underwear, a T-shirt, bulky socks. She got water boiling, adding snow as it boiled. She made two cups of tea. He liked to look at her round, pronounced, high cheeks.

Ian started to put on his socks, his pile shirt, his balaclava, all of which Patience had spread around to dry.

She said, "Oh, well."

He glanced up from pulling up the socks against the damp wool. She gave him the tea. She pulled her not-quite-dry shirt over her. She pulled on her boots. He threw her an extra pair of socks. Her ankles were narrow and he was fascinated by the way the socks gapped around her ankles when they had always hugged his own.

"Who were you with?" he said.

She shook her head. "Just some guy who gave me a ride."

"Why didn't you come home?"

"I don't know. I couldn't shake myself out. Ian?"

"What?"

"What if we died?"

"We didn't."

"Ian, if we got married, would we live together?"

"I'd move down to Rindge."

"You'd have to move into my room."

He nodded.

She said, "I'm not going to die."

"No," he said.

"I love so many things. I love this stupid cup."

"You're crazed," he agreed.

"If she'd just have taken one more step," Patience said. "That girl in the paper. She'd have seen the window."

They stepped out into the morning. The morning was still and silent and they could see the outline of the moon. The mountain was pretty much the way it had been all the other times Ian had traversed it. A well-trodden mountain. They could see Cannon to the east.

They broke camp quickly, strapped on the snowshoes, and were on the trail.

"Do you have any pot?" she asked.

"Getting cocky," he said. He packed the trail down in front of her.

"I know you do."

"You probably know everything."

They walked on. The sky was pink on the horizon. The moon hung low and blatantly exposed, without a shred of cloud cover.

They descended, trudging through the snow. The pink gave way to more and more light. The wind subsided. They heard the guttural call of a raven.

"It's the day before Christmas," Patience said.

"I'll take him out," Ian said. "That guy."

"Good," she said. He could imagine her breath and her body that had warmed him.

Ian lumbered down the trail, packing the new snow in front of her. He was slow and easy. Something was lifted from him. He walked down thinking about other things, not all the ways he'd been useless, trudging like he had someplace to go under this pink sky.

The bushes were getting taller where they walked. They were passing through red spruce and black spruce trees, a Christmas landscape.

It was fairly easy walking now. Patience lifted her feet in the snowshoes and sometimes slid down steep descents on her rear end. The fear was gone from their muscles and maybe it had to do also with the fact that it was nearly Christmas. Patience's eyes had become very dark and very pleasing to Ian. He found himself turning back to watch her and sometimes wrestle with her when she toppled over into him. They came down the trail like cubs.

Now they were in the hardwood section of the mountain, passing maples and oaks, trees Ian knew by their shape against the sky. Snow dropped from their branches. Patience took off her hat. Now he could see her brown hair to her shoulders. Something about the way it swung from side to side reminded him of Sonia. In the hardwood forests they followed a path where the branches of the sugar maple and the silver birch were laced over the sky and rays of pale light barely filtered through.

Ian called in at the base. Mark answered at the station. "Hey, we got no problem up here," he told Mark. "Just waited it out."

"What'd he say?" Patience stood on a rock and had her ear up to the radio. Her cheek rested against Ian's stubby beard.

"He's not saying anything. He's yelling out that we stumbled back to the living."

Mark had come back. "Yeah," Ian said to him. "This Patience. Same same."

Patience stepped down from the rock. "I can't keep my eyes open. My body can't even stand." And so she sat in the soft new snow. Ian watched her while he talked. She had a straight nose like an English girl's. He was seeing her, he realized, not for the first time, the way other guys would see her, who had not grown up with her.

"Yeah, sure, I'll come by."

Patience had leaned up against him. Her eyes were closed and he realized she was asleep.

"No, it wasn't that way. Gotta go, Mark."

Patience was leaning back against Ian's shins and he could feel the pressure of her body against him there. Her head dug the zipper of his ski pants into him.

"I gotta crash," he told Mark. "Hey, I'll be in. Just call off the dogs."

He fished in his gear for the keys to his truck, the same truck he had been driving since seventh grade. It was parked over there waiting. But then he heard another vehicle coming up the road into the parking area. He hoped to God it was Jamie and he would beat the crap out of him. If it wasn't Jamie he might beat the crap out of whoever it was. That's how he felt with Patience and her English nose asleep there. But then he listened to the vehicle and knew it was the old Ford before he saw it. Christy pulled into the parking area, the car jerking and puffing smoke, none of which woke up Patience. The Ford stopped short when Christy saw them.

He got out, leaving the engine on, and ran toward them. He didn't ask anything and Ian didn't offer anything, but as Christy got closer, his face changed from terror to something much sadder. By the time he stood in front of them, he would have realized the girl was unhurt. Ian knew he didn't have a look of helplessness in his own eyes. Patience and Ian were together.

Christy was in old work boots, hatless, his curly hair silver gray in the sun. There were his father's eyes on Ian and then the eyes shifted to Patience. Ian and his father had spent a day at a time, a week at a time, in silence in the cabin. And now he seemed too proud to show relief, if that was what he felt.

His father was an intrusion. Ian had never thought that before. He himself had been the intrusion on his father. He didn't want his father in this sunlight. But there was something open about Christy's eyes, something a little strange, a strange light, like he held a question in his eyes.

"Hey, man, we're fine," he said to his father. "How's the puppy?"

"He might make it."

"That's good," Ian said. "Good job."

They were under a white pine, each of them with their hands by their sides, now low below tree line, standing among windfall boughs and pinecones.

"Some women down there are presuming you're dead."

"We just couldn't make it out before this," Ian said.

Christy brought his hand to his mouth, his brow wrinkled, in his pose of academic pensiveness. At first Ian had assumed that Christy had come to see Patience but now there was something in his eagerness with Ian. He seemed on the verge of asking a question. But then Patience, sound asleep, rolled into Ian and wrapped her arms around his leg and held him so tight that the stripe from Ian's ski pants would be imprinted across her well-defined, round cheek. Christy stopped. They were both oddly embarrassed, two men who had had women in and out of their lives and their beds openly all of Ian's life.

Ian picked her up. He carried her to his truck. This was no

easy feat because Patience was a tall, broad-shouldered girl, but he did it while his father watched. If she woke up in the truck, Ian did not tell her that they were pulling away from Christy who had worried for them all night and now wanted something from his son.

IT was Christy who saw the pack and the odd doll with painted lips strapped on to the pack. He bent in the snow to look at it, believing that it belonged to Patience. Inside was a shirt that had been his son's and female things. He tossed the pack on the seat next to him and headed back. The whole story of the night was something he thought he might never hear, though his son would.

26. The Diner

Come on," Sonia said. "Come home. The coffee went off."

"Good," Deborah said. She was huddled on the mattress in the ruined homestead. "It went off." She had curled herself into her pea jacket, and waited for the day to come or the sound of Ian's old truck that wouldn't be cracking ice but flying along the new snow, soundless like it was moving through clouds. She opened her eyes and saw Sonia's pale red hair around her face which was leaning toward her and she saw Sonia's brown eyes. "What do you know?" she asked.

Sonia shook her head. "It's clearing."

"Christ it's cold."

Sonia took her in her arms as if Deborah were the child and roughly rubbed her arms and blew into her neck and on her cheeks and they laughed and looked around them at the pieces of debris — the rusted water heater, the odd enamel saucepan, lit by a streak of light that escaped through slats of wood.

She could smell Sonia's shampoo and something she put on her face. She saw that she hadn't slept.

"What's happening?"

"Stopped snowing," Sonia said.

Deborah looked out the window and imagined Ian in his red snowsuit.

"They called?"

"Not directly."

"Not directly. Sonia." Deborah shook her head.

"I have a sense."

"Of course you do," Deborah said. "Why'd you come here?"

"Tracks. Let's go," Sonia said. She had deep brown eyes that were wise and in the night had accommodated the fear.

Sonia smiled. Deborah said, "What are we going to do now?"

THEY sat in the day-before-Christmas uncommon warmth on Sonia's porch watching globs of snow drop from the white pines around the cabin. Icicles dripped from branches and the porch railing. They kept watch for the truck and drank Sonia's coffee.

Sonia stood up and began pacing. She wore a bulky sweater and her only pair of jeans. She was not steady on her feet. Deborah shut her eyes and pretended they were sitting on the high wooden shelf in the sauna. She could smell the bottle of herbed water they passed from one to the other and sprayed on their hair, and could see the sweat glisten on their breasts and bellies, and she imagined it this warm where Ian and Patience were.

"Could you live anyplace but up here?" Deborah asked Sonia.

"Of course. I always thought I would stay just till I get the garden in. Just till we dig the well. Just till the store breaks even. I never thought I would stay my whole life. I don't think anyone did."

They had Mark's call first.

Second, they heard the muffler. This wasn't the truck. This was Christy's old Ford. They heard it backfire and could probably each imagine the black exhaust belch against the whiteness over the homestead entry, the whiteness that covered the battery and the mouse tracks, now smoky with Christy's exhaust.

Then they heard the truck. Deborah watched her surrogate daughter run, wearing her son's baggy plaid shirt and ragtag jeans, long dark hair down her back. Patience ran to Sonia and Deborah watched her encircle her mother in her much longer arms. Down the trail she saw Ian and raced and threw her arms around him with such force that he ended up holding her in his arms, and Patience shouted, "Ian, you creep, you little creep, what if you made us miss Christmas?" She was kidding and possessive in a new way and it was clear they were different with each other.

Christy ambled up to Sonia's cabin. He had a pack and he dropped it on Sonia's porch.

"I thought you left," Deborah said to Christy.

"I did," he said.

"Defected."

"Just cruising." He shrugged. "They were hiking out."

They sat on the porch step. Deborah had Ian by the arm. Christy looked off into a stand of birches where the weight of wet snow bowed their branches almost to the ground.

HELEN'S plan was to take the Vermont Transit bus up to Littleton. She would call when she got to the Dunkin Donuts, where they would drop her off. She wasn't accustomed to this kind of travel, but there were no flights.

Christy pushed open the door laden with his and Jane's coats hung on wooden dowels on the back side, pushed past his barrels of potatoes, ducked under his hanging onions and dried cultivated roses. He poured himself a cup of black coffee while he let the fire heat up in the old silver van that he'd converted to a sauna. Christy sat at the table surrounded by a flight of stone Buddhas he had picked up for Mackie's shop, but for now they were hanging out with him. After a while Ian came down the stairs bare chested, his jeans slung low on his hips, barefoot, his hair splayed over his face. He sat at the table opposite Christy.

Christy was aware of him. He had watched his descent. Then he got up and checked to see if the puppy's heart still beat, touching his belly with two fingers.

The puppy was stretched out on the hearth. Christy sat back down at the table. They never did this. They kept their distance. Christy was careful because he thought his son took anything he said as an assault, so they talked to each other from such a distance they could barely hear each other's voices.

"He looks about the size of a borrower dog," Ian said. "Did Patience make you read *The Borrowers?*"

"Twice," Christy said.

Christy poured his son a cup of coffee that was remorseless and bitter and not tempered with milk or sweetened.

"I fired up the logs for the sauna," Christy said.

There was a slight questioning in Christy's eyes, as if he might need something from Ian or at least would like to ask him something.

"Sure, I'll sit in the sauna. You want to sit in the sauna?"

Christy sat back, crossed one leg over the other, studying how the snow lay over the garden, thoughtful, attentive. He said, "Close call up there."

"Not really," Ian said. "Just something we had to wait out."

They stayed at the table, waiting to hear what more the other could say.

When the wood burned hot, the men walked out in the buff

through the snow and into the metal sauna. They drank beers and the father and son seemed to sweat the silence out of themselves. They began telling war stories about the mountain, about avalanches and hotel pyrotechnics, everything, at first, except women.

But then Christy asked, "So what's he like, this Vincent?"

Ian looked at him.

"Vincent the fisherman?"

"Yeah."

"Kind of burly dude, big teeth, like it gives him a big grin, a shock of black hair."

"Big teeth?" Christy said. He wasn't drunk and it was already midday. He leaned back on the wood seat, sweat pouring off his chest, and narrowed his eyes and imagined his wife's lover.

"What if we let go a little, Dad? What if we let her marry the guy?" Ian said. "You know, have a regular life. Regular crap. You know, Dad?"

At first Christy was most aware of his son's use of the word, we. Then he got up. He leaned over his son. He put his arms around his son's shoulders. He put his forehead to his son's forehead. He only said, "If I were a larger man." He pulled down the handle on the door which he had jerry-rigged with a rope and went out to kick up the fire. He heard the phone ring and took his time going in, but when he got there it was still ringing. It was Helen on the phone saying she was waiting at the bus stop. Christy called the store to tell Deborah about the relatives having come, but no one answered.

He went to say to Ian, somebody better go in to Littleton, but Ian was in the zone and not moving. Christy wrapped a shirt around the puppy and put him in an old wooden flat used for plants. He couldn't leave the puppy who had died once already this morning and Christy had revived him, massaging his tiny chest with his thumbs until he felt the lungs rise and fall. He put on his clothes, went to the car carrying the dog in the flat, put the flat in the passenger seat, and he and the dog went to the Dunkin Donuts bus drop off.

Helen was sitting on the granite wall above the sidewalk. She wore a long straight linen skirt, and her hair was swept up in a French twist. On her cheeks was a delicate blush over her skin that was loose and creased with age and grace, and her eyes were outlined in blue so subtle she might have been made with that fine color. It wasn't that she didn't look seventy-three, it was that she made seventy-three look quite fun. When Christy pulled up in front of her she worked herself down from the granite wall. She walked toward him, easing the linen down her legs, and he saw again she was almost as tall as Deborah. He leaned over and opened the door.

She just missed sitting on the flat. She picked it up and the little puppy shook with the tremor that he saw controlled Helen's hands. She sat down hard and put the box across her lap. She said, "You never learned to love anything but a dog. What's the matter with you?"

"Merry Christmas, Helen."

"Gawd I'm hungry."

Christy thought about taking her back to the sauna. Then he pulled up in front of the diner there on Main Street. On the radio a woman sang, "I love you, honey, I love your money."

Helen said, "I thought you only listened to revolutionaries."

"Helen, I'm not a revolutionary."

"You always looked like a Bolshevik."

He nodded. They had not seen each other in eight years. He glanced over at Helen. He sighed. He wished he were a better man. He thought about holding his wife around the hips to keep her with him. That was as far as he could get. He had no words he could speak. All the words stuck inside him so that they were never words. There was only a dreamlike image of holding his wife around the hips. He thought about her at the

Three Eves where she would be now, working with the others. He wondered if he would be able to put his hands on each side of her hips and his thumbs on her hipbones. The idea of cutting his wife off, and she him, as his son's suggestion implied, now was making him shake. A long shiver cut through his body. He would not drink today. If he could withstand his family, he could have them.

He said to Helen, "Come on, Helen, let's eat," and he went around the car and opened her door. She walked up the stairs, holding her right hand over her left wrist, and in this way seemed to control the tremor of her hands. They got a booth and ordered pancakes that came with individual bottles of maple syrup. Christy hadn't eaten since the day before, but he only drank coffee now.

Helen was frail under her mountain coat and he was fascinated with the veins in the flesh around her wrists. Her boots looked brand-new, he thought, because they'd never been any place nasty.

A sign for a Red Cross blood drive was posted on a bulletin board by the door, indicating an extra need for blood around the holidays.

"How many gallons are you up to?" Helen asked.

"Gallons of what, Helen?" He leaned forward because her words were a little slurred.

"Blood. I always admired people who gave blood. I never got up the courage."

Christy gulped his coffee.

"I'm too old to give now," she said. "So I can stop feeling ashamed."

"I never gave blood," Christy said.

She said, "Shame. Shame. A healthy young man like you."

Christy got a look at himself in the window — it was overcast again outside and some people had put on their individual table lamps — and Christy saw his face and wondered if it were true, that he had more years to go. He had always thought of himself as old.

Christy lit a cigarette, and Helen was fascinated with the smoke. He told her Bethlehem stores were starting to do a little business around Christmastime.

Helen said, "I'll take one."

"Yeah, sure." Christy gave her a cigarette and lit a match. She leaned forward and inhaled.

"I loved Deborah's father. I miss him now, but he was not a happy man. I lived with him fifty-one years and he never woke up smiling."

Christy wanted to go to his and Mackie's store. It would be three things. It would be cold. It would be empty. It would be collapsed. He was going to have to come up with some cash to jack it up. But he was still selling the little Buddhas, and a sly cat in stone with a twisted face, a burro, a St. Francis, stone birdbaths.

"He wasn't a handsome man. I'd just like to have dinner with him tonight. I miss my family."

Christy tried to catch a waitress. They were very busy. He said, "I guess a lot of people got the day off." He remembered that Deborah had made a basket, a woven one from thick strands of pot-holder cotton. It held a pair of earrings that chimed, which he had bought in Bangkok for somebody but at the time he didn't know who although it was clear when he met the girl in the Portsmouth cemetery, they were for her.

Christy glanced over to the counter and saw among the crowd, Patience. He was surprised. He thought she would have needed sleep, but then he remembered the diner was one of her places. She would come and drink coffee at the counter where she was now. Her brown hair was shiny and brushed and she was wearing jeans and a blue sweatshirt. He was going to go down to her but first he turned back to tell Helen and Helen had disappeared. He stood up. There were no empty tables for her to sit at. Was she sitting with some other people? Had she gone to the ladies?

He glanced at Patience. Looking at her now, he knew something was wrong. What had his son said? There had been a man she'd hitched with. But he had to find Helen. He looked at each table one by one, searching for the coiled white hair, searching until he came to the chalkboard at the far end that listed the specials, the Belgian waffles with strawberries and whipped cream, the omelet with American cheese.

He glanced at Patience, who had seen him and who threw no glib remark across the room. Her face was tight and unsmiling.

He found Helen behind the counter. She had wanted more coffee and when the waitress didn't come, she had gone to get the pot. Customers had then signaled to her for refills. She was working up the length of the counter, topping off, her lips taut and concentrated.

He waylaid Helen near where Patience sat, her cup and saucer surrounded by empty white half-and-half containers.

A young man had just taken the seat beside her. He wore a greatcoat, like an officer's coat with a wide belt. The belt hung down on either side of the round stool. He didn't look at Patience. He watched the waitress, his arms crossed over each other on the counter. "I'll take one of those," he told the waitress, who had brought oatmeal to a customer near Patience.

Christy was standing, trying to retrieve the pot from Helen. Patience had not looked at him, pointedly.

He was aware of the man in the coat. He'd seen kids dress that way. Christy sat down on the stool at Patience's right but took her lead and did not address her.

Helen looked at the girl's dark eyes. She put down the coffeepot. Patience placed her hand across the ridges of the cuff of her sweatshirt. Christy looked at the guy to her left, a young man about twenty-one, twenty-two, with a finely shaped face.

Above his head was a sign that said the diner could no longer accept Canadian currency.

"Come and sit here," Christy said to Helen. He got up and stood over to the left to make room for her. The booths were full and there were people besides Christy who had stepped back for somebody else to have one of the stools at the counter. The background hum of voices was music with laughter like bells. The bells blasted through his head. He would like to escape the bells.

"How does it feel to be so good-looking?" the man leaned over and said to Patience.

"Look," she said, "I don't have to talk to you."

"I think you owe me something. I got you up here."

Christy had heard the discordant note. It was not admiration in the voice. It was assault. It took hold of his stomach. The man was close to Patience. She sat quietly on the stool. "I just want to wish you Merry Christmas." Helen seemed to have an instant comprehension of the tension. She would have known who the girl was by her resemblance to her mother. Helen kept her eyes on the miniature boxes of corn flakes and Sugar Pops under the mirror and the Christmas balls strung above. Patience slopped coffee on the cuff of her blue sweatshirt and Christy was aware of the wet stain spreading and darkening the blue to black.

"Sweetheart, it's Christmas." The young man made to reach his hand to touch Patience's sleeve. Christy had come behind. He caught the hand and pressed it into the counter. The man was taken by surprise and cried out in pain at the same moment that somebody started Jimmy Hendrix on the jukebox. The man and Christy briefly exchanged looks. Helen was a statue. Christy pressed down on the man's hand. It was easy to do. The man tried to ignore Christy and jerk his hand away while he was still surly. "Hey, Patience," he leaned into her. "You have a perfect name." Christy would break his hand. He realized he would do this. While he was thinking this, he remembered Jane's students and the little girl who had tied his bootlace and asked him how he got around in Vietnam. They did not know about helicopters. They listened about them as if to a fantasy. He was a storyteller. They had loved him. He had loved them. He had told them and stopped and looked into their innocence with affection. He was a kind man. He taught history with kindness and a psychic disassociation that enabled him to be unkind. Was that yesterday? And then he cracked the man's hand.

When he broke the man's hand, he could feel the bones shatter. His own hand was very wide, the same hand that had felt the diameter of Sonia's cervix and then held the baby's black, mucous head and the gush of blood before he saw the living eyes. He had pressed the man's wrist up hard on the paper placemat with the face of the Old Man whom people had come to associate with Live Free or Die. As he had pressed the heel of his hand, he had jerked his fingers and the hand cracked sharply and all the small bones were crushed and the man's face had gone white.

When he cried out, Christy lifted his hand. He stood back. He was unaware of the crowd. Helen did not move. He became aware that Patience was not on her stool where she had come to drink coffee. The guy in the greatcoat was not there.

Helen got up and went back to the booth with their own lamp. Christy followed her. Helen pulled the string of the lamp. Its shade had yellow cut-out shapes of stars and moons. Helen's hand shook with her fork, making her hand do things of its own will. They could smell fresh, homemade doughnuts someone had brought in from the kitchen to sell at the counter. The cook used to make doughnuts in Vietnam that Christy would never forget the sweet smell of, and the sweet smell of new doughnuts now made him sick to his stomach.

He looked and Patience had come to sit across from him beside Helen. He inhaled. Slow down. Talk to the girl. She was home. She was sitting across from him. He would like her to describe a place to him where she spent her time.

He glanced at Helen as the one who could explain his wandering mind to him, but then he simply accepted it as he accepted the women who were not his wife who came in and out of his house over the times of his life. Four dark eyes looked across the table at him.

He shoved his plate away. He said, "I'll tell Emile to watch out for him."

Patience shook her head.

"I don't know what that was about," Christy said. "You want to tell me?"

She shook her head and couldn't seem to turn her eyes away from Christy's hands which lay motionless, the fingers open, on the table.

Christy scowled with irritation.

"He was just gonna take a price for my ride last night," Patience said.

"You hitched with him?"

She nodded.

Helen drank her cold coffee in silence. The lipstick was worn from her lips and on to the cup. She put her hand with the sea blue veins over the girl's hand.

PATIENCE took Helen with her. She was driving Sonia's truck. Christy drove back to Bethlehem on his own. He drove slowly. The mountains around him were magnificent. They were the result of 400 million years of ancient seas and ice and rock continually shifting. The notch below, his notch, was a U-shaped valley made by two million years of ice coming through. The ice followed the curve of the earth. It made the rivers and the springs. He drove down snow-packed Mount Cleveland Road, dazzled by the sun which shone through the bare branches of trees, and he craved to stop the roller coaster of emotion she brought him. He craved this to cease. The sun blinded him. To let her go was to abandon himself. He stopped, frozen to the sun.

27. Gentlemen's Night

Ma," Ian called from the door.

"What are you doing in there?"

"Just looking," Deborah called back.

"Looking for what?"

It was dark. Deborah stood in the middle of the homestead, in what might have been the dining room.

"Where are you, Ma?"

"Over here." She was wearing a parka and an evening gown, holding a kerosene lantern. The metal handle cut into her cold fingers. She was getting ready to leave for the Christmas Eve shopping night at the store, which they had used to do up in a big way, and Val kept the tradition. She had brushed her hair and shaken out the evening gown, which was off-white and had an overlay of a speckled, gauzy fabric, long sleeves, fitted at the waist, something that a visitor to Bethlehem might have worn at one of the hotel dances in the hotel days, only with speckled slippers and not work boots.

Ian thundered in through the entryway and into the kitchen.

"Hey, Sweetie," she said. She kissed his cheek.

He picked at a strand of her hair that usually stood up. He surveyed her. He turned her around. "Looking good," he said. "So what'd you lose?"

Deborah held out her hands, palm up, as if to say, Who knows? You tell me. She paced the length of the room.

"Dad had some war stuff here. Did he ever show you?" As she asked this, she felt a devotion toward the war stuff, toward Vietnam itself, toward the Vietnamese who didn't talk too much about the war, but because of it they came to America and opened up businesses and thrived. They made her heart race, maybe it was the adrenaline rush of war. All her senses were at their peak during the time with Christy and she had never had that rush again. The war stuff was Phuong. He had said something to her, one day, a Valentine's Day, when he brought in gold rings or some such, he was always selling things. She asked him, What do you call someone you love? "The most loved?" he said. "You say to them — you call them, myself. How is myself?"

Ian wore an orange stocking cap pulled low over his ears and his slight smile on his lips as if nothing bothered him, Hey no way man, nothin', and looked around the place. "Sure, there was stuff," he said.

But he wanted to talk about that afternoon. "Dad broke the guy's hand. He's lucky it wasn't me at the diner. I'd of punctured his lungs or his eyeball. The guy got off. But Patience said Christy was funny. His eyes were funny."

This would be the Jamie. Deborah wanted to know this story, but she had to know about the grenade. She said, "When you were a little kid, Sonia and I found a grenade. I tossed it down into the woods."

"Yeah," he said. "I know. But I wanted to tell you about Dad."

She paused. "You know about the grenade."

"We found it."

"Who?"

"Patience. She was a pest. She kept bringing me things just like Dennis did."

"You two found it?"

"I don't know. Her or Dennis. And I don't know if it was the same grenade."

Deborah thought of Patience in the corn and she and Ian could hear frogs at night, and in the dawn deer would be near, and also they'd hear the cry of the coyote. She imagined the children. Five-year-old Patience sitting cross-legged in the garden, the grenade in front of her in the sun, and Dennis barking, and her calling *Ian, Ian, Ian, look what we found.*

What did I find, Ian?

It's like a bomb.

Patience's eyes would have been banjo wide.

They would look at it as if it would explain Christy, who went five days and more without talking to them. Would it explain how his mother could leave all the vegetables growing and the pond and the pond's frogs and go away to the city?

"I buried it," Ian said.

The grenade excited Deborah. She thought of all the winters that had passed and with each winter the ground froze and thawed and vegetation would grow into it and give the dirt oxygen and gradually the cycle would push the grenade to the surface.

"Where?" she said.

"Off in the woods," he said. "Below the spring. Ma, I came to tell you, you want to just hang out with Dad for a while?"

She had been walking and walking, scuffing the leaves, and stopped at a window with the lantern, looking around the fallen homestead, the kitchen with the broken-down appliances, the sink on its side, the fallen floors, the remnants of clothes, the scattering of leaves and animal droppings and birds themselves who had built nests in the john.

Ian shoved his hands in his pockets and leaned up against the exposed lathes of the wall. She glanced at him and the light of the lantern caught the glint of his eyes below the orange cap.

THE Three Eves had the same faint smell, of mothballs, marijuana, slightly sweet, the smell of the rooms, of the vintage apparel, of the women, of the clientele. The smell was immediate to Deborah and also so long ago that the women who ran the place could have been pictured in one of the black-and-white stereoscopic pictures she used to take Ian to look at in the back-room cupboards with glass doors at the Littleton Public Library.

Walking in to the Three Eves on Christmas Eve, it was the smell that got her. The clothes smelled like her young womanhood. She was a mommy with a baby. She could feel the weight of his sleeping body in her arms and there were flashes of moments — between daily things like filling the water jugs or hauling wood — when all of life made sense. It was such a relief to find the sense. Flashes of moments knowing the feel of her baby's weight when everything wasn't shaded with if onlys, or, I'll do this one last time and then I'll leave, seeing everything as finite and requiring transformation of oneself or somebody else, or at least a geographic move, something, always agitation, but the weight of the baby was the smell of baby powder and sweet new child's skin and breath and serenity.

Valerie was by the front window, her hands on her waist, which hiked up the man's shirt she wore over her broad hips. Her hair was straight and had barely known the touch of scissors. She was making a small adjustment to the mannequin in the window. The mannequin was in a red gown, slit to her thigh, and through the slit showed a bare toe, shin, knee, thigh.

They had picked that outfit for her that afternoon. "Not your basic midnight hippie girl," Deborah said.

"Merry Christmas." She hugged Valerie. Her hair was turning dusty and she smelled sweet like ripe peaches the way she always did.

Deborah took her parka off and puffed out the layers of her gauzy, browning, off-white gown.

"Who's here?"

"Fran's here."

"Frannie!" She could smell Aqua Net in hot August air— the cat's brushed tail the night she met Frannie. The buttered corn they all ate.

Valerie smiled her wry and dry smile. "Did I tell you she's an economist? Economist," she repeated thickly. "Oh well, I'll get her to look at the books."

"Good," Deborah said. "Val, my mother's coming."

"I know. Your mother's here. Come downstairs. We ordered Chinese."

Deborah could not imagine her mother downstairs.

"Don't worry about it. Come downstairs."

They went downstairs to the little room by the furnace compartment that they used as a dressing room, and where they used to eat grapefruit and read. Sonia and Patience were setting out wooden bowls that had to be left over from the restaurant, and white cardboard boxes of pad thai, fried rice, cashew chicken. The light was soft and warm and the small room was packed with a number of models, many ages and shapes. Patience put a bowl of pad thai in her hands. Deborah found Helen on the couch, looking quite elegant in a chocolate brown skirt and matching tights. They weren't sure how to greet each other and ended up touching cheeks. They had never been a physical family. To kiss her would have been almost intrusive, certainly too intimate to know the feel of her skin against Deborah's lips. Deborah sat on the worn and flattened pillow cushions on the floor. Then she got up and sat beside her mother.

They ate hungrily. They drank plum wine Valerie saved up every year for the women on Shopping Night.

"'Stop searching forever. Happiness is just next to you,'" Sonia read from her fortune cookie.

"Christy got me," Helen said to Deborah.

"Where you staying, Mom?"

"At the Baker Brook."

"Ah, with the Hasids."

They drank more of the rich, sweet wine that burned just a bit. The world became clearer or less clear.

They were a little relaxed, and leaned in as if in collusion, over the pineapple on toothpicks, the fortune cookies, the soy sauce they had poured into antique shot glasses, the wine.

"'You will soon be crossing the great waters,'" Helen read, not looking at Deborah. Deborah thought she was meant to think of Helen's own great age, Helen's own great waters. Helen, the queen of innuendo, and Deborah, nurtured to grasp her remarks with acuity. She and Patience opened up all the extra cookies for the fortunes.

Sonia went upstairs and began playing on the old clunky piano they had kept in the corner of the store with the shelf of books for kids and men who were waiting and anybody who needed to play from *Thompson's First Piano Book*, which lay on the music holder, or to read *The Story of Ferdinand*.

Deborah was left with her mother. Finally she said, "So how come you didn't go to New York?"

Helen shrugged.

"What'd you come for, Mom?"

Helen said, "Patience and Ian came to see me. I have a little cabin. It's very rustic, but they have toilets, so I know you'd find them fancy."

Deborah sighed and looked over at two girls who were

painting their faces. They painted eyes and holly berries on their cheeks.

"You never came before. All these years."

Helen said, "They told me about the whiteout."

"Yes, and you disliked them still."

"I liked them."

Deborah nodded. She was becoming aware that Helen's spoon was tapping against her bowl. She glanced at her mother's hands. They were shaking. Helen put down the bowl and made a fist with her left hand over her right hand and held it in her lap.

"I have to go, Mom. We're going to open." But the tapping began again. "Well, so you came up. Why'd you come up?"

"No reason, Deborah. Barbara and I decided to go for New Year's Eve instead."

Deborah knew that Barbara was a poet, about eighty-three years old, a retired professor. Helen got together with her on Thursday mornings and they sat formally in a Falmouth McDonald's.

"Okay, Ma."

"Don't okay-ma me."

"I have to go up."

Helen's fingers beat the spoon. Deborah reached over. She held the back of Helen's hand and the fingers relaxed slightly on the spoon.

"So I'll be talking to you," Deborah said.

"Deborah, Christy and you. You might as well get back together."

"You're a little late, Ma. Why don't you come upstairs."

Deborah followed the girls up.

"Here, put this on." Deborah had gone to Sonia. She was wearing her brown cords and a black sweater buttoned down the back and her hair fell just to her chin and her black shoulders. Her face was bright and smiling and hugely freckled, and still, even in wintertime, her freckles overflowed on her lips.

Deborah gave her a cropped velvet jacket that she put on, tied loosely at the neck. She shoved over on the bench and Deborah sat beside her. Deborah put her head on Sonia's shoulder and they were schoolgirls.

Valerie was handing out beers to the shoppers. "Remember, in the old days, Christy had a way of bringing everybody in here," Valerie said. "He was the only hippie that got along with the locals. He hung out with them and learned plumbing and he got them pot."

"Yup. He's an operator," Deborah said.

Valerie had gotten some people to wear the cocktail dresses, and the long chemises that were turn of the century, and navy coats, and to drape themselves in beads and lace and then just hang around and help the men figure out their wife's size when they said, Oh, about Leslie's size, Oh, about like Valerie, give or take . . . and then they held their hands out trying to be precise.

Deborah was struck by how beautiful the store was, how beautiful the women were, how beautiful the men in the road crew were. She and Valerie and Sonia had strung garlands around the door and lit the store with candlelight. But Deborah felt uneasy until she saw her mother's chocolate skirt amid a group peering into the glass-covered cases at silver hairpins and shoe buckles and hotel artifacts.

Ian and Patience came in.

"We came to make some cash," Ian said. Patience held out her tarot cards. "Ten bucks a reading. What d'ya think?" She laughed. Her eyes were luminous. She said. "I told him if he wanted to really make money we should go to the airport and I could sing and Ian could play his guitar."

"She's a loser," Ian said. "They'd be tearing off to board their planes."

"He's just afraid I'll get arrested," Patience explained to Deborah. "He can't live without me. Where's Helen?"

Where was Helen now?

"I met her with Christy," Patience said. "Then she invited us over, Ian and me. You know Christy? Tall dude? Intellectual type? Yeah, they're together."

"Still open." That was Christy talking to Val. "Good for you." It was like he was saying, Still alive, are you, well, good for you.

He looked around and Deborah knew he was looking for her. He had called her so many times from the pay phone outside and from nearly every pay phone he passed: Hey, Deborah, it's four degrees. Don't you want to come up for a while? Or when he hooked up the woodstove to the abandoned van and turned it into a sauna: It's a regular resort, Deborah. Now's your chance.

"Have a beer," Valerie said. She reached back to the ice chest they'd set up by the cash register and pulled out a brown bottle. She studied Christy briefly, as if she were saying, Look you jerk, get a life. But she went on talking small talk while men came in stomping snow off their boots.

Christy was looking at Deborah with boyish eyes. He had showered and looked like he was going someplace — clean jeans, clean shaven, hair wetted down, if a little slick from the oil they kept in the sauna, nothing in his teeth, in baggy trousers like he was from out of town, and the same aged leather jacket Deborah had gotten him used, seventeen years ago.

He stood, taking everything in, maybe her outfit, maybe behind her where print skirts hung, like the ones she used to wear that smelled like wood smoke the way all their stuff used to.

Deborah couldn't move further away from him than the top of the stairs. They had made love in most of these rooms, especially the furnace room downstairs. She had curled into his body beside the furnace.

Deborah listened to Sonia's piano, standing there, the refugee, looking at these people she knew through to her bones.

Sonia played the piano with Henry on the cello, sweet, sad Christmas songs. Henry told her once that when he tucked the cello up under his heart he could feel the vibration. It was sensual, and his playing made them cry. On one of those Christmas Eves, Patience had said to Sonia, You can't die, can you? So she said, Let's do everything together, and she had taken her mother's arm and not let go of her all the evening.

Her heart raced and she yelled cavalierly to Christy, "Hey, you, what's all this hoopla in a tourist town?"

He walked over to the stairs and to her.

"You're done up," he said, his hands deep in his pockets, standing almost sideways as if he were, in his imagination, some other place.

"Have you seen Helen?" she said.

He said, "Yeah, she and I were on the porch having a smoke."

He was sober. He had that forlorn turn of his shoulders that would lift when he settled into a few drinks.

They snaked through the crowd to take a look at Helen on the porch, having a smoke next to a guy in a brushed black coat who was waiting to use the pay phone.

"I should go help Valerie," Deborah said. But she didn't go. It was an interesting sensation standing in a public place next to Christy. They watched the children. She said, "How do you think Patience is?"

He was edgy and said glibly, "She's planning a trip to Mexico to live on peyote." He gave her his sly grin. "She and your son."

Deborah hardened there by him. That had come with the years, that ability to harden. It would have felt okay to stand by the door with her hand on the knob, the exit preplanned. She remembered a time in the furnace room. They had been kids and he had touched her body and said, Tell me this is only for me. There had to be something else besides learning to stand by a door and learning to do this gracefully.

She walked away from Christy.

Deborah sat with Sonia while she played. Sonia began to shiver because the door was opening and closing all the time and Deborah sat closer. They had both spent a lot of time alone and now that was a very seductive thing, especially here in a crowd.

Deborah pretended her fingers were on Sonia's tough, working fingers and together they could feel the solitude come in to them through their hands. Deborah pretended she was someplace warm and found herself in the cabin where she had slept with the professor the first winter. She was in his sleeping bag on the mattress and they held each other all night.

The old Mr. Hudon, Emile's father, came into the store in his red and black plaid hunting jacket and a shotgun that Valerie made him leave out front against the wall. They kidded that she might as well have put up a gun rack out on the porch. Patience put a flannel shirt around her mother's shoulders and stood beside her and Henry. "Your lips are blue," she said. She played the intro and they sang in their sweet harmony, "Babe, I'm gonna leave you. Tell you when I'm gonna leave you." Henry played a long, quivering stroke that was something the people in the room could feel more than hear. "Leave you when ol' summertime summertime summertime comes a'rollin'."

Patience stood, her hands on her hips. "Mommy, you're insane," she said.

"I know, " Sonia said, smiling up at her.

Helen had come in and watched the family and Deborah watched her. It was like having a fantasy and a reality slam up against each other, her mother's long and still-elegant legs in brown tights crossed as she sat on a kid's chair with a beer in her hand with the old hippies and the natives who'd found some like paths.

Sonia's next song was like cold rain. It was sweet and erotic and amazingly painful, sharp as metal.

Deborah went down the narrow stairs. In the room by the

furnace now, girls were changing outfits. They smeared a sweet-smelling, flesh-colored cream on each other's cheekbones, highlighting their jawlines. She studied each girl's face. She had been an awkward, large-limbed, silent girl whose eyes followed Christy through lectures and later through black, insomniac nights. In a certain light her eyes were lilac, he had said, looking at her blue eyes, the way somebody had said Elizabeth Taylor's were, somebody who had seen Elizabeth Taylor in a café in Jamaica — where the winds would keep you safe. What a storyteller.

In the mountains they taught her to drive around with a bag of cat litter in her trunk to use to disarm ice, because this is New Hampshire where it ices over everything just as smooth as icing on a sheet cake. Except when you are skating and then there are open spaces of water far from the banks.

She watched the girls and her mind wandered to a daffodil, separate from anything else. For a second it was spring and daffodils had come up all around the cabin and she was twenty-one. The daffodils had been planted by Christy's last lover before she had left in the fall. They smelled like Deborah and Christy's quilted, nylon comforter, the one they slept under, and jealousy, and the shock of spring after being bears under the slippery nylon and their slow, addictive sex.

"You look very good in this." Christy had followed her downstairs to this room that he'd have remembered, too. His shoulders were stronger and not so forlorn. He put his arm around Deborah at her hip.

She placed her hands on Christy's shoulders, first one, then the other.

They stood at the bottom of the stairs in the doorway.

The music built. Sonia and Henry were playing something familiar, maybe Vivaldi's Solstice music. Deborah raised her hand to Christy's face and touched it lightly but then withdrew.

Christy shut his eyes. She made small talk. She told him about things she had to do to her house. She told him some boys had smashed a cellar window. Christy didn't know the people she lived by or worked with. He didn't know Phuong.

The piano got very loud.

"You've been running a long time," Deborah said.

He put an arm around her waist and they danced across the hallway. Deborah thought she laughed, but didn't think she had been able to bring the lightness from the back of her throat. She felt the pressure of his hand on the small of her back, and he took her in the ballroom position, and at that moment she did not know how she could have lived away from him. Sonia had begun something in slow four-four time and Henry's strokes made the store into velvet and tapestry.

"Sometimes I am strangling," he whispered. "Sometimes the truth is such a shadow, the way it moves and grows and shrinks."

He held Deborah tightly and she felt the sinews in the back of his neck.

They did a clumsy, close-quartered waltz step and Christy hummed the tune to the sentimental song about a second marriage and a man in a suit and a woman in her off-white dress, almost hokey, something Christy never could be.

Sometimes when Ian was in Portsmouth, Christy would visit him and then sleep in the car. Deborah would come and unfold him from the cold. She brought the old thermos and they'd drink coffee as if, if you do it in the dark in the car, you're not really doing it. You're just drinking coffee in the dark, having a conversation and watching your own breath as you exhale and later, when you woke up in the light, the world was safer and you could breathe deeply enough to fill your lungs, because he was still charming and could still make you laugh and he loved you.

It compressed her chest, with each step she took in his arms, so that soon she knew she would succumb. The off-white dress was just the moth's paper wings. But for the moment they danced and the girls changing costumes stood in the doorway and watched them.

THE customers were gone. Just the three Eves were left. Valerie poured into their cups the last of the hoarded plum wine. They sat side by side on the deacon's bench in the children's corner, listening to a tape of the Burns Sisters singing Christmas songs.

Deborah pulled her feet up and sat with her arms wrapped around her knees. It was ten degrees outside and the wind had picked up through the evening.

"Do you remember when we worked here," Val said, "when it was the Milk and Honey? I remember Christy making the rounds. You know how it was when a new girl walked in. I can see him going to get his coffee and standing with his left hand in his pocket getting ready."

They started laughing.

"He was always a son of a bitch." Deborah cried, she was laughing that hard, probably with plum-colored tears.

"'Good fortune comes to people with good judgment,'" she said.

They could not stop laughing.

The room had gone midnight, as Deborah had read that the military described Iraq when the stealth bombers shelled it.

Sonia lit a candle.

"So who've you been bartering with," Deborah asked her.

"Emile." She shrugged.

"They've only been on and off for something like seventeen years," Valerie said.

Deborah leaned back against the wall, exhaled a large breath.

"I wasn't very good at the homesteading. I was like Patience. I kept going to town."

"You used to hang out at that café in town, reading," Val laughed. "There we were working our butts off making our own food."

"But I remember everything," Deborah said. "I just saw a picture of us. Christy had saved it like he saves everything. We were so young. We wore old work clothes with holes in the ass, yeah? and our skin was smooth and we had secondhand boots from the thrift store in Littleton. We were babies. We giggled over professors and it was nothing to carry jug after jug of water from God knows where, wherever there was any."

"Smoked so much pot," Sonia said. "Slept with any guy who brought some."

They listened to the wind.

"I bet it's twenty miles an hour on Cannon," Sonia said. "I heard Emile talking on the radio."

They stood now at the front window facing across the way to the men's antique store. Mackie and Christy had pulled the bottles and glassware in for winter, but heavy stoneware stood on the sunken porch as well as a wooden-armed overstuffed chair, concave with snow, and the round EX-LAX sign and DRINK COCA-COLA sign hanging from the wall, outlined in red and green lights.

"Sometimes I'm weary," Sonia said.

"Weary of the mountains?"

"No. Weary of sorrow. Sometimes I can live with it. It just walks with me, and I think, Oh, there you are. And sometimes it stops me." Sonia smiled her beautiful smile. "It says, Hey woman, where do you think you're going?"

They sat in silence for a long time, finishing off the wine, which the Premies wouldn't have done if somebody'd left some wine in the early morning when the bands had gone and the Milk and Honey was wrapping up for the night.

28. The Prevailing Moon

I т was a cold, glorious night. The temperature rose slightly, the moon was whole, the sky was bigger than Deborah remembered it. It was clear and not blocked by the summer canopy of the trees and now at midnight there were no town lights, so there was nothing for the moon and stars to do but expose themselves. This was the moon Christy had made Deborah aware of.

Deborah walked up to her old cabin, just to see if Christy wanted to get married again. The storm had left a soft extra ten or twelve inches over the last snow.

Christy was sleeping on the couch, one leg sprawled on a wooden bench, his mouth open, his navy sweater rising and falling over his chest and belly, his hair was ruffled and spiked, and he looked sturdy and he was holding the puppy, the tiny rat who had not died because Christy had a will to keep things alive that were determined to die if left to themselves. Neither of them was looking good. The puppy's skin was cracked. Deborah sneaked nearer and could see small lesions on the puppy's body and his feet swollen up. Looking at Christy, she didn't think he looked that much better.

She remembered Christy saying that pain was on the heels of joy, as this moon might have been his pleasure and then his sorrow. But she thought not this time. Now they were philosophical with age. They were deliberate and measured. What had their waltz been to him? Was this finally contentment? Deborah wanted the joy to overcome them and the doubt she felt inside her to fade.

Christy opened his eyes. He saw her and tried to shake himself awake.

He pulled off his sweater. He still wore the baggy trousers and shirt he'd worn to the store. He had rolled up the rumpled cuffs to his elbows and he had over his arm his holey plaid flannel which the dog must have slept in. He said, "You want to hold him?"

"What do I do if he stops breathing?"

"Massage him, like I did."

Christy handed her the puppy.

"Where are you going?"

"To bring Dennis in."

She had the puppy in her hands and when Christy was out the door, she stared at the poor thing that looked like it was never meant to live and no wonder it was with Christy. She went to the cupboard in the bathroom and found some baby oil and sat by the woodstove in the rocker and rubbed baby oil into the tiny puppy's skin. She held him in her lap and waited. She waited for the puppy's next breath and she waited for Christy to come back. Dennis came in looking more than inconvenienced. She went immediately to her spot under the table and would not eat the food Christy put down. Christy put the puppy on Dennis but she bared her teeth at it.

Deborah paid closer attention to the walls, now, at this time of night, the walls done in maps. Many were small black-and-white newspaper maps from the *Boston Globe* of areas in strife. The former Yugoslavia, the nation-state breakdown of the Balkans. Cambodia where Pol Pot and been found hiding in the jungle. They were neat compact graphics of war, with arrows and stripes showing movement of people.

"I haven't had a haircut since you left," he said, which was an exaggeration, but Deborah put her hand on his neck, under his coarse curls. His neck was broad and muscled. She put both hands there. She dug her thumbs into his flesh and pressed with her palm. She put her hands down his shirt and pressed hard on the flesh of his shoulders and then around to his clavicle. She shut her eyes and smelled the smoke and the evergreen on Christy's clothes. Her thumbs and palms worked down his skin. He put his hand over hers and over her arm.

She thought of the people she had seen in the South Street cemetery where she and Christy had met. It was six in the morning, this particular time. The cemetery was acres of stones and trees and plastic mementos people had left for the ones ripped away from them. That morning people were walking across the way from Deborah, beyond a pond where she and Ian and Patience used to ice skate. When Deborah looked again, the people, in all the expanse of the cemetery, had laid out their blanket and were sitting in a row. With all the space of the world and souls, Deborah could see them in the distance among the stones, sitting shoulder to shoulder on their small blanket. And of all the space in the world and all the stones, that's how she felt about Christy, shoulder to shoulder on a blanket watching a row of middle-sized ducks, teenage ducks, walk in a column into that pond.

"We'll get a license in the morning," he said.

"Where do you want to live?" she said.

"I don't care. I want to live with you."

"Ian says we're losers," she said.

"No, you're a loser. I sell antiques."

"You only sell stone statues. Your store fell down. What are we going to do?"

"I don't know. Open a hotel."

She put her arms around him and they seemed inevitable and sad. She loved to touch his hair. He said he'd make them some tea and he made it and brought a cup to Deborah who had gone up the stairs and now was sitting in their bed in her bride dress, though she'd taken off the boots. Their maroon blanket with knotted tassels was wrapped around her and she was warmed by the air rising from the stove. With her eyes shut it could have been December, or it could have been August.

Christy pulled Deborah to him, as if they were in the pond and she were sitting with her back to him. She sat with her back up against his stomach. Had there been a photograph of them in this position? drinking tea out of thickly curved lopsided cups that Swede had thrown in Jamaica and when he came back he had told them how he did it, how he sat around with the old women on Nevis, the old potters, and they gave him some clay and they laughed at him. They said, Look at the way they do it in America.

Look at the way they do it in America, Deborah thought. The tea was fine. The cups were large and sea green. Christy laid his cup down and stroked Deborah's shoulders, down her ribs and her hipbones. Everything seemed eternal. His hand on her hipbones. The pressure of his belly against her back and her ass. His mouth. He was unlacing the laces of the dress.

She stroked his hair. "I'll give you a haircut," she said. "Do you remember when Sonia and I plastered the outside wall of the living room of our cabin? We were smoking and creating designs in the plaster."

"Yes, I do."

"Ever since we did that, I've thought about plastering over these two-by-fours and tar paper up here."

"I think we should do that." He looked around. "I think that needs to be done." Maybe they believed they must do this because it seemed like they were preparing for forever.

Deborah, still in the evening gown, though it was unlaced, went in search of chicken wire. She went to the shed off the kitchen and found a roll of it that she managed to get upstairs, rolling it head over toe, so that she arrived breathless and some buttons ripped off and her face was bright and smiling. Christy was not there. He had gone for the plaster. She went to Christy's old deacon's bench, preparing to angle it so that they could work into the corner. On it were things Christy must have emptied from his pockets. Nothing of consequence. She could shove it all in a drawer. Christy's pocket change, plant seed, penny nails, jackknife, crumpled business cards, dog biscuits, and then beyond them, a grenade. Her eyes shifted from the dog biscuit to the grenade, back and forth.

A dog biscuit becomes a high explosive beside a grenade. She touched the grenade. It was not a toy. It was cold metal. Her first reaction was of wonder. She put her hands by her side and watched it. Her heart raced, but she could not hold in a slow, very long exhalation. She felt an odd sense of decompression. She held the chicken wire by her side. She felt enormous relief. Here it was. The shoulder of her dress had slipped and she lifted it up. Then she picked up the grenade. It was a heavy slug of metal made of scored cast iron, the scoring to assist with the fragmentation. She had been reading about grenades. She knew that real ones have yellow stripes around their circumference, inert ones have blue stripes. This one had neither. Any paint had worn away.

She held it in her left hand very firmly like an enormous egg and, lifting her dress to keep from tripping, she got back into bed.

Christy came in. "I've been wanting to do this," he said.

He saw her in the bed with the chicken wire. He came and kissed her, a long kiss that ended with his getting in bed beside

her and he shoved her dress up above her thigh. She didn't stop
him. He smelled like the spruce tree. But she said, "Why do you
have it?"

He saw the grenade in her hand.

He tried to take it, but she moved her hand.

He said, "It's an old friend."

"Can I have it?" Their voices were hushed.

"No."

"It's a relief for me to be so close to it. It's finally concrete. It's
much better than imagining it."

"What do you mean?"

"You died over and over and over."

"It's not armed," he said.

"How do you know?"

He kept one hand on Deborah's thigh. "I disarmed it. You
unscrew the top, pull out the fuse, let the thing fire and burn
away. Then you get rid of the explosive."

She nodded. "So you can arm one."

"There's easier ways," he said.

She nodded again. She felt physically drained. She leaned
against him. The grenade was too heavy. She lowered it and
held it with both arms to her stomach.

"What do you want, Christy?" she whispered.

"I want to make love to you."

"I want to make love to you, too."

He took the grenade from her and placed it on the deacon's
bench. He lowered her sleeves. He ran his hand through her
hair, the same hand that had broken the kid's hand in the diner.
He had loosened the laces so that the dress was no longer fitted.
He touched the outline of her nipples. Then he slowly pulled
her sleeves down over her fingertips and when he exposed her
breasts he held them again with both of his hands and took the
nipples into his mouth, against his tongue and teeth and cheeks.

"It's all right," she whispered, when he looked up at her. He exhaled and watched her and he eased the crinkley fabric of the dress up her legs. She sat up, giving herself to him, and when he had taken off his jeans, she took him with both hands and her tongue and mouth, slow and steady. He took the dress off of her and took off his shirt and they made love very slowly, watching each other until they both gave over to it. And it was in the bed that had always been their bed that they had the last time.

She didn't want him to move his weight from her and she smelled the spruce scent on his skin and her sex on his breath.

"Where are you?" she said.

"I'm with you," he said.

He absolutely was.

"You know I would never hurt you," he said. "You don't have to be so sad."

"Yes, I know."

Christy took care of her body. Christy brought her coffee. He took her splinters out. He took her to the ocean to watch the sunset. He brought her eyes beauty. He loved the moon. With Christy she was aware of its waxing and waning, its robust sideways leanings, its disappearance.

THEY crushed sections of the chicken wire and fitted it in between the two-by-fours. They began to spread the plaster with something like large putty knives. Deborah looked at the white plaster in awe. It was the most beautiful, most timeless curve of white. She made long swooping curves of plaster, over and over and over in sections of wire and wood.

An early morning light came in the windows, making a pale white arc of light so there was a contrast of light and shadows across the new plaster walls. Christy and Deborah molded wire and plastered the whole side and made rounded ascents up to the ceiling.

Then they went crazy. The plaster had eight hours to dry so

they decided to make use of that knowledge of time. They imprinted one corner with small branches from the Christmas tree. They got a white rose Christy had dried. They pressed it into the plaster and it was the end of the rose, but its imprint would last forever in the plaster wall. They drew a dragon with the tip of a screwdriver. They pressed in one of Deborah's burgundy earrings for his eye. Then they decided the dragon was not nearly big enough. They kept making the dragon bigger and bigger. Finally it covered the entire wall facing the mountain. In addition to the Buddhas downstairs, Christy was holding a stash of junk shop jewelry, fake jade rings, skull and crossbones pins, pearls and diamonds, and these they pressed in for the dragon's tail. They pressed in tinsel for fire.

"What about the grenade?" Deborah said.

They agreed he needed the grenade and finally they pressed the grenade into the dragon's fiery mouth.

CHRISTY sorted through the mushrooms on the wooden counter with quick movements, tossing a mushroom to Deborah from behind his back. Christy didn't think about cooking, he did it by instinct. She watched him chop stuff up. He never felt like he'd eaten unless he chopped things. He chopped peppers, red onion, garlic. Somewhere in the bookcases was a paperback on properties of mushrooms and they had collected them. That was when he used to photograph her, in the early mushroom days. He stood at the stove, turning eggs into the black skillet, then the vegetables.

When the food was nearly ready and it was just full light, they heard footsteps crunching through the snow. Patience and Ian came in.

"Good," Christy said. "We were about to send the dog."

They were groggy looking and Patience stood with her head on Ian's shoulder. They had stayed at the craft cabin. Ian said they had gotten a good fire going (but it wasn't that warm,

Patience said) and there had been some propane left in the tank. Not much. They had slept in the loft, but there wasn't any food and now they were famished.

"Don't you sleep?" Patience said to them.

"No, we don't sleep."

"You already saw this," Patience said. "So it's no surprise." She pulled the very weathered-looking doll she had made out of her pack and shoved it toward Christy. "It's from the story I made you read to me that summer."

Christy took it, in its two-year-old's clothes. He set it in a kitchen chair and it sat there, one green leg slumped over the other, its face weathered but still slightly awed. Christy sat down with it. He regarded it for some time, leaning over his long thighs.

"It's supposed to be a china doll," Patience said.

He looked up at the girl and something lifted from his eyes. He looked exhausted and pulled back from somewhere, as if the green doll kept him from falling.

Maybe he was thinking the child loved him. He had a family. His son had picked up the puppy and it was drinking the formula from the little bottle and his son was a man.

Patience went on to talk about the doll while he looked at it. It was certainly one of the more odd-looking creatures they had had in the house. Maybe it made Christy think of when Patience and Ian were little kids who distracted him from his work with mundane things like socks and peanut butter and honey sandwiches and ponytail rubberbands. Maybe he allowed the doll to suck him into the past where it was always clearer.

He looked at Deborah and shook his head. He began to laugh. He laughed until tears ran down. They all watched him, but then smiles started stealing, against their will, across their lips. Against their will, because they might have been laughing with a crazy guy sitting across the table from a funny green doll.

Christy looked up at Deborah, wiping laugh tears off his face. "We did all right," she thought he said, or "We are all right." He kept looking at her and they both understood each other quite well. It was more complicated than they had thought. He had been so smooth. She did not forgive him, but they understood each other, all their deceits, and vanities, and manipulations they would never say in words, because what could they do but deny everything. They would say, It was only because I loved you. But all the deceits were laid bare.

And the final manipulation of the grenade was laid bare. She almost taunted him with her eyes. So are you going to do it?

Still she laughed with him and was in love with all the details of his body, his manner, his intellect, his voice.

Do it if you have to.

He didn't do it.

Do it in front of the children for proper effect.

She still loved his hands, open on the table.

Do it quickly, so we can get on with our lives.

It was anger mixed with acceptance that she could grant him always, but she wouldn't try to stop him anymore. She wouldn't try to make him happy anymore because she could not. She thought of the old woman who had been at the Frost house all those years ago, dreaming about her lover. She had shrugged and said, "She didn't want what I want." That's all.

Deborah started to cry.

Patience said, "Molly helped with the mouth, which is supposed to be the clue that she is a china doll, even though she's stuffed."

"I see that," Christy said.

"Mom," Ian said, because Deborah had begun an explosion of sobs and tears.

She was loud and shaking.

Ian looked at her. He looked at his father. "What's going

on?" he said. He was asking his father.

"We're tired," Christy said.

"It's the doll," Patience said. "She loves the doll."

Deborah nodded her head, but she couldn't stop crying. Christy let her hold the doll. Mostly she cried because she was okay. The way Ian looked at her, she thought he knew this.

"Mom," Ian said. "We can't talk. You're making it hard for us to talk." He put his hand on her back, the way he had when he was four years old.

Christy shook his head. "Maybe we have to let her out with Dennis."

Deborah convulsed with sobs. She put her head in her hands. She pulled Jane's shawl off the back of the couch and put her face in it and wiped her tears and blew her nose, but she couldn't stop.

"Oh, well, let's eat," said Patience, who had noticed there was food, "and maybe she'll stop." They pulled the table away from the wall to seat all of them, including the china doll who maintained her nonchalance in her own chair. A symbol of one way a family might be, whose dismantling, like the wooden boards of the college, were their mythology and their endurance.

Deborah would go home, and when the snow thawed and the swans went inland, she'd begin scraping her house. She was ready to make her own life. However, sometimes Christy would leave the mountains. She supposed some people's families met in cars. He'd pull up in front and she'd put on several layers and come out, still smelling like paint and with paint chips in her hair and she'd bring a picnic. Or maybe roll sleeping bags onto the beach if the cops didn't catch them, start a fire, invite Phuong and Helen, Sonia, Emile, and Emil, and the kids. The family. A family in collusion, still trying to come out the other end larger.

◆ ◆ ◆

DEBORAH pulled in at the Baker Brook, a large ring of brown cottages on the outskirts of Bethlehem, about a mile past the Arlington and the Alpine with golf, perhaps gold, out the back door. The letters were very weathered and it could have been either. Only two of the cottages at Baker Brook had been dug out from the last snow. Her mother had let drop the number of her own cottage so that when Deborah pulled in she knew it was the first cottage she came to. She knocked on the door. Her mother came in her nylon pajamas and nylon bathrobe.

"Merry Christmas."

Inside she saw her mother had a stone fireplace and a view of the frozen pond, a little kitchenette.

"There's a bus at two," Helen said.

"That's fine," Deborah said. "And Barbara will be home?"

"Yes."

"I want to show you something. Do you remember when you were with Grandpa at the inn in Vermont and the man with the white hair came in. And the waitress leaned down to tell you that was Robert Frost?"

"Oh, yes," she said, "He was an eccentric. He had a grimy hat."

"He lived in Franconia, too. Would you go for a ride with me? I want to show you his place."

Helen got dressed while Deborah made some coffee in her little commuter pot that brewed two cups.

They drove into Franconia and up Ridge Road with an endless view of Mount Lafayette and the valley below. Deborah stopped in front of the old Frost farm. The last time she had been there it was summer and the stone wall was buried under wild roses and buttercups and lupines. If anyone wintered there now, they left no sign in the unshoveled drive, no footsteps to the door.

Deborah and Helen got out. Deborah walked in the new snow and made long deep footprints down to the crusty, icy snow below. She made a path for them and they stopped at the waterwell, a few yards from the front porch, where pennies would cover the bottom under the snow.

They watched streaks of light come through the sky. Already the days were getting longer. Deborah cleared off the top step of the porch stairs and they sat on Frost's front porch, sharing the mug of coffee. Deborah's leg grazed her mother's leg. She imagined the texture of her cheek, what the flesh felt like in all its wrinkles. Helen had taken the time to highlight her cheeks with blush though her hand was very bad with tremors this morning.

When they looked down they were looking into the belly of Lafayette. They watched for some time and didn't talk but watched the sun with the old man who had wild white hair and it was in his house Deborah had made for them a home, where her mother had tucked her in the coarse sheets, upstairs, in the steel frame bed, and she could begin to fill in the missing parts with imaginings and nasturtiums and the poet's clean, simple sorrow.

IT was night. Deborah and Christy were at his place. Deborah still had her coat on and had that wispy scarf wrapped around her neck. They were sitting on the bottom step of the stairs, side by side.

He knelt and put his head in her lap, which he had never done. She stroked his hair. She told him about the woman next door who was round and female and she'd given herself over to nature and now had a generous body and Deborah told about the man who went to her.

"Why don't you eat?" he said.

"I eat," she said. Then she asked, "Who do you think of yourself as?"

"What do you mean?"

"Just somebody you identify with."

"Sisyphus, of course," he said. "And you think of yourself as a fat lady with lovers."

"No, I think of myself as Harvey Keitel. I just imagine being tough in the world in Harvey Keitel's body."

"Keep your own body."

"I'm not going to come anymore," she said.

"No, don't."

She had on her layers of sweater, vest, and jacket over her turtleneck and jeans. "So good night."

He stood up. "Good night. Take some coffee, Deborah. It's a long, dark drive."

"Only if it's hazelnut."

"Take the goddamn coffee in this goddamned mug I made for you."

"Good night."

"Good night, Deborah."

"It's okay."

"Yeah."

"Just let me go," she said.

"Yup." He walked her out the door and to her car.

"Don't be telling me any garbage. It's manipulation," she said. "How many women do you need? Don't tell me any more about your dreams about me."

"I don't have them anymore."

"Shut up, Christy. Good night," she said. They hugged. She got in the car and he walked back, head down.

"Only on Tuesdays," he yelled from the woodpile.

Acknowledgments

THANK you Robin Dutcher, my editor, for cherishing and nurturing this story. Thank you to my friends in the mountains, most importantly Alan Strell. And thank you to the Ragdale Foundation, which provided time and shelter to work on parts of this book.